Desert Haven

PENELOPE STARR

Rattling Good Yarns Press
33490 Date Palm Drive 3065
Cathedral City CA 92235
USA
www.rattlinggoodyarns.com

Cover Design: Rattling Good Yarns Press

Library of Congress Control Number: 2024930038
ISBN: 978-1-955826-55-6

First Edition

"Each of us has that right, that possibility, to invent ourselves daily. If a person does not invent herself, she will be invented. So, to be bodacious enough to invent ourselves is wise."

—Maya Angelou

Contents

Introduction

The second wave of feminism, the civil rights movement, and gay liberation converged in the back-to-the-land movement to form the perfect conditions for utopian women-only communities.

As a young woman, I was enthralled by the freedom the counterculture promised me—the sexual revolution was gaining steam, and feminism was kicking ass. The 1960s were a time of change and experimentation. The absolute control of old white men was challenged on the streets, and more quietly and importantly, by people just dropping out, going underground to live unconventional lifestyles. Radical young people were eager to be part of the solution, not the problem.

The values that propelled the women's land movement are still essential and applicable today, but history shows us the execution had varying results. Although the future is uncertain, many women's lands survive, and some thrive. This social experiment is mostly hidden from mainstream media, probably ignored as fringe. The radical aspects are frightening and unsettling. And they should be, because it is radical to upend the status quo and live life on your own terms.

I feel lucky to have lived through such a dynamic part of history. Through storytelling, my intention with this novel was to combine my love of women's history with my real and imagined experiences to shine a light on possibilities and inspire discussions about what it means for women to create a new culture.

~Penelope Starr, 2024

Dee 1977

After the pregnancy scare and the nasty breakup, and after getting fired from her job at Woolworth's lunch counter because she couldn't cook a hamburger to order, Deirdre figured the time had come to move on.

Pulling out the nightstand drawer where she stashed her tip money, she dumped the cash on her desk, catching a whiff of bacon grease, or was that just her imagination. Stacking the bills in the same direction as she saw Jilly do when closing out the register, she sorted them by value. Mostly ones, a few fives, and that one twenty left behind by a nattily dressed grey-haired gentleman, along with his phone number and a note that said, "yore cute, call me." She piled the quarters into five-dollar towers and didn't bother counting the small stuff. Two hundred and seventy-three dollars plus change. That, plus the hundred and seventy-five in her savings, was all she needed.

She went to the kitchen, dialed a number on the wall phone, and took the receiver into the hall, around the corner, into the bathroom, barely closing the door and stretching the spiral cord as far as it would go. She worried that one of these days, the cord would snap or the phone would be pulled off the wall.

"Marcie, I did it. I saved enough money to leave," she said, grinning into the phone when her best friend, her only friend, answered the phone.

"No, you can't go yet," Marcie said. "You told me you weren't leaving until after the New Year. I'm not ready to lose my best friend yet."

"You could always come with me," Deirdre said, knowing what Marcie's answer would be.

"Oh, DeeDee, we've been over this a million times. I can't leave my job at the bank, and my parents would kill me if I broke up with Bill. I think they love him more than they do me. And besides, I'm not like you. I don't want to go off into the unknown; I like my life in Long Island."

"Okay, keep your boring safe life, just promise me you'll be happy," Deirdre said and laughed lightly to soften her tone.

"I'll try," Marcie said, with a sigh of resignation and a tinge of sadness in her voice. "It will be hard without you. Send me picture postcards for my collection, so I know where you are."

"I will. Bye, Marcie, say goodbye to Bill for me," Deirdre said, walking into the kitchen to hang up. Staring at the telephone, almost not believing that she was really going to leave, she was lost in her thoughts and was startled when she heard her mother's voice from behind the refrigerator door.

"You want some ice cream?" Her mother asked, holding the door as an invitation.

"No thanks," Deirdre said, reaching around her mother and grabbing a Coke, ignoring the whiff of something rotting in the bowels of the fridge. She hesitated, not sure how her mother would react, and added, "I've got enough money saved up to go on my road trip,"

"That's great, honey. Would you help me open this pill bottle? I don't know why they put the lids on so tight."

Deirdre twisted the top off the bottle and read the label before she handed it back to her mother. "What's this for?"

"Oh, that's for the pain in my ovaries. The doctor said that I should take it with food."

"But I thought you weren't supposed to have ice cream because of the gout," Deirdre said, trying to keep a patient tone in her voice, but it was hard. Her mother had so many things wrong Deirdre needed a dictionary to keep up. And she was tired of being the one to remind her mother of things she couldn't keep track of.

A quick twinge of guilt took over. It wasn't her mother's fault. She just had bad luck. What would her mother do when Deirdre was gone? Daddy would have to do it all.

"Oh, just a little won't hurt," her mother said with a weak apologetic smile. "How soon are you leaving?"

"If I can get everything packed today, I'll leave in the morning," Deirdre said, watching her mother try to scoop the ice cream unsuccessfully. "You want some help with that, Mother?"

"Thanks, that would be nice," her mother said, shuffling over to sit at the table. "I'll miss you. You are such a big help to me. But I know you've dreamed about a bigger life than caring for a sickly mother. Your music is important, and you've got talent. Honey, I don't blame you for wanting to see the world. I felt the same way when I was your age. Remember, your Daddy and I eloped when I was your age. That was pretty adventurous for a nineteen-year-old."

Deirdre watched her mother relax into a chair, eyes unfocused like she was viewing a replay of her youth. The stories of her parents' cross-country trips in beat-up jalopies, camping under the stars, and taking odd jobs until they got pregnant with her and had to settle down were family lore. They always chose time to pursue their interests over money. Mother did photo retouching on the dining room table when there was work, and Daddy was a part-time car mechanic. They got by.

"When is Daddy coming home?" Deirdre asked. "He said he'd show me how to check the oil in the Nova." Suddenly feeling antsy, she added, "I've got to finish packing," and put the bowl of ice cream in front of her mother. Returning her focus to her trip made Deirdre giddy, and she gently shook herself back into her body.

Her room, the one she had lived in most of her life, reflected her interests in different ages and stages. Her collection of international dolls lined the window seat, dolls her grandmother sent her every year instead of visiting. High School graduation photos of her classmates crammed together on the bulletin board, people she hardly saw anymore because most of them went off to college, some to Vietnam, and she didn't really care to socialize with the eternal townies who stayed. Marcie was really her only friend. The collage she made with pictures from teen magazines of her idols, Joan Baez, Tina Turner, Janis Joplin, Stevie Nicks, and Mama Cass, covered the mirror she didn't want staring at her.

Deirdre put a Joan Baez record on the turntable and gently set the needle in the groove. She sang along to the sweet sounds of *Diamonds and Rust* as she surveyed the mound of clothing piled on her bed with a bit of disdain; they were the old Deirdre's. She had already decided to take only the items she felt most comfortable in that expressed the new Dee. That's what she was going to call herself from now on. No more

Deirdre, the name no one could spell, and definitely not DeeDee. She was too old for that nickname.

Bell bottom, low-riding dungarees, concert t-shirts, sneakers, sandals, and one wrap-around skirt just in case she had to dress up for something. A couple of soft flannel shirts and a down vest. These clothes defined her look, her image of herself, down to its basics. The real Dee.

Respectfully peeling scotch tape from the mirror and flattening the photos, she placed her women-in-music crew into the bottom of a box containing other necessities for her new life. The mirror was bare for the first time in many years. She stared at her image and became curious. Nervously dropping her clothing to the floor, one piece at a time, she saw her entire figure displayed. She fought the impulse to close her eyes but forced herself to inspect her naked body. Hair, a mousy shade of brown, but that could be fixed. Eyes, also brown, but deep and soulful. Her best feature was her smile. She knew that because everyone told her so.

Her legs weren't bad, other than the saddlebags. Tits too big for going braless like those skinny hippie girls. Or maybe she would. Who knew where she would end up. She pivoted to see her butt, a little large but cute. Maybe that was what the dirty old man at the lunch counter was commenting on. Not an ideal body, but not so bad. Why had she been avoiding it? Those extra pounds she put on made her feel like a stranger to herself, and she hated the muffin top over her jeans. Solution? Wear bigger jeans. Problem solved. All the skinny jeans went into a pile for Goodwill, along with the frilly blouses her mom got her. Wishful thinking. Deirdre was never a girly girl.

"Hi, Sweetheart," her father said, pushing the kitchen door shut with his knee, balancing three large paper bags in his hands. "Guess what I've got," he said, swooping a bag under Deirdre's nose.

The sharp smell of sweet and sour, the grease from the egg foo young, a little whiff of spilled soy sauce, and the accompanying stain on the bag all said that he had stopped at Mee Hong on his way home.

"Pizza?" Deirdre said, grinning like a mischievous five-year-old even though she was grown up. She couldn't help but fall into her kid role with her Daddy; he was a big kid himself.

"All right, smarty pants, now please set the table so we can get down to this feast. Where's your mother?"

"She might be sleeping. It's almost seven o'clock."

"Then it's just you and me and enough food to feed a Chinese army," her father said, reaching for the container of wonton soup.

"Daddy, I'm leaving tomorrow."

"So soon? I thought you were waiting until January, DeeDee."

"I'm ready to go now," Deirdre said, stabbing at a piece of shrimp swimming in an unnatural orange bath. "But are you and Mother going to be okay?"

"Don't you worry; I can take care of her. It's time for you to fly, my little songbird. Here, have some chicken."

The next morning, after her father showed her where to find the dipstick and helped load the car with her two suitcases, guitar, a box of important things, her old Campfire Girl sleeping bag, and a Tupperware container with a mishmash of last night's leftovers, they said their goodbyes at the curb.

"You be careful on the road. Don't pick up hitchhikers, and call us every Sunday at noon, so your mom is sure to be awake."

"Give Mother a goodbye kiss from me when she gets up. I love you, Daddy." Deirdre said, her eyes tearing up with the realness of what she was about to do. Her father gave her a big hug and opened the car door. The March morning was crispy-cool. Dee pulled her ski hat down to her eyebrows. Turning on the engine, she cranked up the heat and drove down the tree-lined street, past the elementary school and baseball field, past the strip mall and the fast-food restaurants on her way to the bank.

Withdrawing all her savings, she closed the account and told the teller she didn't think she'd be using it anymore. Dee kept forty dollars in cash and bought traveler's checks in twenty-dollar denominations so they would be easy to cash, just like Daddy had advised.

Once she was on the road, her whole body buzzed with excitement. Her fingers tingled, and she thought she must be radiating glitter. Stopping at a gas station, she got a map of the United States to figure out where she was headed. She drew an arrow from New York going straight south and figured that was a start. Getting back in the car, she inhaled a lungful of freedom.

Dee took her time, driving on country roads instead of highways, excited by the new sights, regional food, and local accents. Most of the music she heard in bars was either country or old-timey folk music, but she was looking for the new folk-rock scene. Her guitar playing was simple, but her voice was strong. A few times, a band had asked the girl in the front row with a guitar on her back to sit in for a song or two, which was a thrill. If she got into a new town early enough, she would set up on a street corner in the afternoon sun, guitar case open, busking, hoping to meet like-minded musicians. She didn't suffer from the lack of companionship; she was used to being her own company and certainly didn't want to get in a sticky situation with a guy. Watching Three's Company or The Love Boat at night on the motel TV was plenty of excitement for her.

Everyone she met was talking about the music scene in Austin, so she turned west in South Carolina. When the weather was fine, she rolled down all the windows, and the wind in her hair felt like it was blowing her to her fate.

It was in a bar in Austin that she hooked up with a girl for the first time. The skinny blond, Zena, asked Dee to dance, but it was too awkward with her guitar on her back, and she was afraid if she left it on her chair, someone would steal it. So, she bought Zena drinks, and when they were very drunk, they walked to Dee's motel room.

"I've never done this before," Dee said as she shut the door and flipped the lock.

"What? You look like such a dyke," Zena said, and when Dee raised her eyebrows, she quickly added, "It's a good thing, don't worry."

Dee felt her familiar resistance when Zena tried to pull her t-shirt off.

"I always leave my shirt on," she said, sounding like it was a done deed, expecting compliance.

"Why?" Zena asked, dropping the shirt and pulling back.

"Because I don't let anyone see me naked."

"You want to have sex with me with your clothes on. And hide that sexy, curvy female body from me. No way," Zena said, pulling at the hem of the shirt.

"You think I look good?" Dee said, leaning forward, hoping what she heard was true.

"I think you are beautiful. I don't know where you got the idea that you aren't," Zena said and kissed Dee. And kissed her again, softly, gently, pausing, waiting for permission.

Dee pulled back slightly and looked into Zena's eyes. This was very different from the hurried sex she had with her boyfriend, the unwanted grabbing, and the sandpapery cheeks. It felt foreign and very familiar at the same time. She wanted more.

"Okay then, tell me what to do," she said, suppressing the heat of shame, transforming it into desire.

Zena ran her hand down Dee's arm and said, "Follow me," taking the responsibility of instructor to heart. They spent an acrobatic night of research, finally falling asleep towards dawn.

In the morning, while pulling on her clothes, looking shyly at her new lover, Dee asked, "Last night, you said I looked like a dyke. Does this mean I am one now?"

"Sure, if you want to be," Zena said.

"All I know is that I liked being with you last night. So maybe I won't take on a label and just do what feels right."

Zena nodded, and Dee took that to mean the conversation was over. A cool rush of relief replaced the tightness creeping into her solar plexus. Dee understood that Zena wasn't going to put any pressure on her. There would be plenty of time to see where her sexuality landed.

Dee had been in Austin for a week and hadn't found her people. She didn't know who her people were, but she trusted that she would recognize them. Meeting Zena was a good start, but she was ready to hit the road again. On Tuesday morning, she went to Zena's apartment to say goodbye, but Zena looked so sad at the news that Dee said, "You want to come along?" She thought it would be polite to offer but didn't expect Zena to accept on such short notice. And besides, they just met.

"Where are you going? I thought you wanted to make music, and this is the right place for it."

"I'm not sure about music anymore," Dee said, embarrassed at her indecision. "And I'm not sure where I'm headed either, maybe to Arizona to see the desert. I hear Tucson is pretty hip."

"I read about some women's land there. I think it's called Desert Haven or something like that," Zena said, looking a little too excited about it for Dee's taste. Maybe she shouldn't have been so hasty to invite Zena. But then again, it might be fun to have a traveling companion.

"You know how to get there?" Dee asked.

"No, but it shouldn't be too hard to find. We'll just hook into the lesbian underground hotline, and we'll be set."

"Is that a thing, a lesbian hotline?" Dee asked, worried that she might be entering a cult or something. Maybe take it slow.

"No, silly," Zena said, kissing her cheek. "I'm just teasing you. Give me an hour to pack and let my roommates know I'm leaving."

"We're not girlfriends or anything, are we? Dee stammered. "I just want to know because, like, I'm not really into relationships and all," Dee said, feeling sorry that she had to say all that but knew it best to put it all out there.

"That's fine. I totally get it. We are just travel friends who have sex with each other. No strings. But I have to tell you something. I don't have any money. So, if we go together, it's on your dime. I don't eat much, and I can exchange entertainment for my contribution if that's cool with you."

"I'm good with that. I've got enough to carry us for a while. Now go get packing, and bring a sleeping bag if you have one."

Forty-five minutes later, they were at the curb. Dee tossed Zena's small duffle and sleeping bag into the back seat of the Nova and climbed behind the wheel.

"Cute car," Zena said, rubbing her hand over the shimmering finish. "I like the color, kind of a lavender-flecked thing,"

"Yeah, thanks. It was a graduation present from my folks," Dee said, and immediately knew from the look of mistrust on Zena's face that she would be keeping that information to herself from now on. Even though it was a used car and her father fixed it up for her, it sounded like she was bragging.

Leaving before noon, they got partway across Texas before the sun blinded them. They stopped in a small, forgettable town for the night. After dinner in the town's one diner and buying a postcard for Marcie of oil pumps that looked like pecking chickens, they found a cheap, dingy motel and slept in their sleeping bags instead of in the stained sheets.

Turns out Zena was a good driver who loved having the radio blasting with the top down, and Dee started to think it was a pretty good idea to have her along.

Zena gave a rundown on what she knew about women's communities.

"There was this magazine in BookWoman bookstore about women's lands. Mostly what I remember is that men are not allowed. It's like a movement. They want to drop out of this fucked up capitalist society and create a safe place for lesbians.

"You think they are socialists?" Dee asked.

"I don't know," Zena said. She thought about it for a while and then said, "What's so bad about that anyway?"

"I guess we'll see when we get there," Dee said, grinning at the uncertainty and the rush it gave her.

They rolled into Tucson around five in the afternoon. Stopping for coffee at a cafe in the Fourth Avenue arts district, they asked if anyone knew how to get to Desert Haven. The woman behind the counter had a girlfriend who had stayed there for a few months. She drew a map on a napkin.

Dee dropped her postcard to Marcie in a mailbox on the corner after she scribbled Texas! Now Arizona! Love, D on the back, and added a thirteen-cent stamp. The travelers headed out of town, arguing about which direction was west.

The last leg of their journey seemed the most tedious. They were driving on winding roads through a prickly landscape, following a map drawn by a woman who didn't know the names of the streets. Wrong turns and false starts made a forty-five-minute drive last for almost two hours. Finally, turning into the Desert Haven dirt driveway seemed almost anticlimactic.

"We made it!" Dee said, leaning over to hug Zena. Hopping out of the car, she declared to the sky and trees, "We made it!"

She saw a gathering of women sitting around a pile of stones surrounding a pile of scrap lumber and twigs and made a beeline to them, with Zena following close behind.

"Hi, you here for the full moon circle?" asked a tall woman with long grey braids.

"Sure, okay, sounds good," Dee said, surprised that the moon was full, and she didn't know it. "And we are interested in staying here if that's a possibility. Who's in charge?"

"This is JoJo's land. She'll be here soon. Want something to eat?" asked a woman in a plaid flannel shirt, pointing to a sagging wooden table holding the remains of a potluck.

"Thanks, that would be great," said Dee, never one to refuse a meal. "I'm Dee, and this is Zena."

"Welcome. Where are you from?"

"I'm from New York, and Zena is from Texas," Dee said.

"Um, actually, I'm from Detroit," Zena said, looking at Dee and shrugging. Dee realized that she knew nothing about this casual acquaintance other than how she smelled and what she liked in bed. She even wondered if her name was Zena.

"The ritual will start when the sun sets, in around twenty minutes," Flannel Shirt said.

The sun dipped behind the dusky purple mountains, and the sky dazzled the two newcomers with colors they had only seen on postcards. Someone lit the fire. More women arrived, and when they arranged themselves in a circle, they were twenty-strong. Kyra with the grey braids began the ritual by inviting in the four directions and led the women in chants honoring Isis and Hecate. Astarte was invoked to bless the circle.

Everyone except Dee and Zena knew the ritual, and they tried to follow along. They held hands and laughed at their awkwardness. The circle was closed with the women bowing to each other, saying Blessed Be, and moving in for a group hug.

Dee turned to face Zena and said, "Thank you for bringing me here. I had no idea that this existed."

Drums and rattles came out. Someone had a recorder. Dee retrieved her guitar from the car and sang some tunes, feeling embraced by the spirit of the group. A woman named Sage sang harmony on a few songs and told her she should play at the monthly women's coffee house. Someone said she sounded like Mama Cass.

The two women spent the night in the car, sleeping in their clothes, Dee in the front seat fighting with the stick shift all night while Zena got the back.

"I've had sex in a car but never tried to sleep in one. Now I know why," Dee said when the sun came up. They unfolded their limbs and went looking for a place to stay.

JoJo told them they could stay in the empty underground house she had built a few years ago before she got her trailer.

"What an amazing place. A real hobbit hole," Zena said, walking the perimeter of the circular structure. "Did you do it yourself?"

"I designed it but had lots of help digging the hole. We had to go down four feet, and this earth is rock hard," JoJo said. "The dome is made from concrete. I must admit I'm proud of my engineering skills in making it work."

Dee peered in and saw built-in benches with thin sleeping pads on two sides of the small room squeezed around a little potbelly stove and was enchanted. "I love it. How much do I owe you?"

"Pay what you can—that's my policy," JoJo said. "If you can afford four dollars a night, it would be great, but if not, don't worry about it."

Dee dug through her wallet and pulled out a few bills. "Here's enough for a month," she said and saw Zena looking at her with a puzzled expression.

When the transaction was settled, and the women carried their belongings into the cozy den, Zena said, "You want to stay for a month? I thought this was a road trip."

"I like it here," Dee said. "It feels like a good place to hang out while trying to figure out what I want to do with my life. You don't have to stay. I'll buy you a bus ticket back to Austin or wherever if you want to leave."

"I'll check it out for a while, but it's good to know I can escape if I need to."

Desert Haven was a primitive campsite arrangement with a central water source and electricity only in JoJo's trailer. The women adapted to the alien environment, learning to safely shit in the desert after several mishaps with sharp plants or surprise appearances from scary critters. They made a list of what they needed to set up housekeeping in their underground home: sleeping pads and pillows, cooking and eating gear, and groceries. Flannel Shirt, whose name was Bliss, gave them instructions on how to get to Miller's Outpost for gear and the Food Co-op.

There was a gathering every night. Sometimes a ritual circle and music making, sometimes a potluck, sometimes someone put on records, and they danced to Chris Williamson or Jefferson Airplane, or they'd go into town for the Women's Coffeehouse, and Dee would play. And once a week, some women met for a CR group.

"What is CR?" Dee asked when Sage invited her and Zena to join the group.

"Consciousness Raising. It's a safe space to share our stories, good and bad, and to understand what we have in common," Sage said. When Dee still looked a little puzzled, she added, "And to get support."

"I don't need anything like that," Zena said. "I grew up in a house full of crazies, so I don't need to hear a bunch of women whining about their lives."

Dee was one of those people who had one good friend and didn't need to belong to a crowd. Marcie was all she had until Zena, and she thought that was enough. But this was different. This was a group with a purpose. She was intrigued and wanted to learn more.

"Thanks, Sage. I'll be there."

"You're getting on my nerves with all that feminist crap from your CR group," Zena said after a tense dinner in their makeshift kitchen. "We've been here three weeks, and you just learned that sleeping with men is giving aid and comfort to the enemy. I already know that. That's why I'm a lesbian."

"But that's not all it is. I wish you'd come, just once," Dee said, clearing the table and putting the dishes into the plastic bin for washing. "I've learned a lot about how society treats women and how we don't have to be victims anymore.

"You can go if you want, but it's not for me."

"Oh, thanks for giving me permission," Dee said, not trying to keep the sarcasm from her voice. She was tired of how grumpy Zena was all the time. Complaining about the food and the noise. She isolated herself and didn't even come to the nightly gatherings anymore.

"You don't need my fucking permission to do anything. Don't you see?" Zena said, her voice gaining volume and irritation. "You have everything going for you, talent, looks, a nice car, and you act like you're some kind of a hippie chick."

Zena's harsh words felt like a slap. Dee's nose began to run, and she wiped it with the back of her hand. "You don't know anything about me. You never ask me how I feel or what my life has been like."

"Oh, I know you, Miss Convertible for Graduation, but you can't even imagine the violent hellhole I grew up in."

"Well, you are not the only one with violence in your history," Dee yelled and froze, stopping herself from saying more. She couldn't just blurt it out in this horrible way. No, she had held on to this secret for a long time, and if she was going to let go of it, it had to be in a place that was safe.

"What, did your mom not buy you the right color prom dress? I don't want to hear it. It's time for you to buy me that ticket like you promised. I want to go to San Francisco."

"Fine," Dee said, feeling tears about to spill. But she wasn't going to let Zena see her cry. "I'll drive you to the bus station," she said, turning away to get her wallet and car keys.

"You mean she left just like that?" Bliss asked when she noticed that Dee was alone for breakfast the following day.

"This wasn't the right place for her," Dee said, knowing she was telling the truth. "Want some coffee?"

"Nah, I've already had enough to float my kidneys. But thanks." Bliss said and added, "Let me know if you need anything. I've been living on women's land for a long time now, and I might have a trick or two up my sleeve."

"Like what?" Dee asked.

"Like how to live on air. Like how to survive relationships and breakups. Like how the community can heal any hurt."

"Thanks, Bliss," Dee said, blinking wildly. She didn't know if she was about to cry because Zena left or at Bliss's kindness, but she wasn't going to let go of her tears. "I'll see you at the group tonight,"

By the time Dee sat cross-legged on her pillow, joining the circle of six women, everyone knew that Zena was gone. "So sorry, Dee." "I didn't see that coming. I thought you were a long-time couple." "It's hard." "Let me know if you need anything." The women's words of condolence soothed Dee's jagged parts.

Relaxing into the closeness she felt for these women who told their truths, expressed their rage, and strategized new ways of living in a fucked-up world, she took a deep breath and slowly exhaled all the tension from her shoulders and neck. They had been strangers a month ago, and now she felt part of a family of friends. Oh, her parents were great and accepting, and they loved her forever, but there were certain things that she just couldn't tell them. She had one big secret, even from Marcie, and maybe this was the right place to share it. She had never felt this level of acceptance and trust in a group.

"We had a fight, and I realized she wasn't someone I could depend on. We are just so different. I'm glad she's gone; I don't need her negativity in my life," Dee said, no longer holding back her tears, grief tearing at her throat. Someone passed her the tissue box.

"When I met Zena, I felt terrible about myself, and I hated my body." Her voice cracked, and she took time to blow her nose. "The thing is, I had a boyfriend, and he made me have sex with him." Her voice lowered to just above a whisper as she went on. "I let him go all the way because he wanted it so much. I loved him and thought it was something I could give him. But once we did it, I realized it was a big mistake."

Dee looked up at the circle of faces, all intent on her words. Bliss quietly said, "It's okay. You can tell us."

"I told him I didn't want to do it anymore, and he was furious. He said I was playing him and that I would give him what he wanted if I really loved him. He said if I didn't, he would tell everyone I was a cocktease, and he only had sex with me out of pity."

"What a bastard," Bliss said.

"I was paralyzed by shame and fear. I didn't know how to stop him. After the sex, he would be contrite and grateful and tell me he loved me. So, I'd go out with him again, thinking it would be different, but it wasn't. When I said no, he threatened me, saying he would hurt me if I resisted, and I was petrified." Dee's voice broke, and she went quiet. She picked at invisible threads on her sweater, waiting to see if anyone would say anything.

"It's called date rape," Krya said into the silence. "It happened to me many years ago. You are not alone, but that doesn't make it any easier."

A few voices said, "Me too."

Dee daubed her tears with tissue from the box in the center of the circle and waited until she felt she could go on. "I thought I was pregnant, but I was afraid to tell him, so I just cut him off. He threatened me and spread gossip about me at school. I was freaking out and had no one to talk to, especially not my parents, who love me, but we never talked about anything to do with sex or bodies. I couldn't even tell my best friend because I thought it was all my fault, and I didn't want her to think I was stupid."

She began to sob, and Bliss said, "That's okay. You don't have to say anymore."

"I need to finish the story. I need to tell it," Dee said, standing, stretching her arms out and swinging them from side to side. "Thank god I wasn't pregnant. I was able to graduate from high school, but then I kinda dropped out of life. I hated my body because I thought it had gotten me into trouble. I was confused and desperately needed a change. That's why I went on a road trip by myself.

She plopped back down on her pillow and continued, "It wasn't until I met Zena and learned that making love could be mutual and beautiful that I began to enjoy sex. Zena helped me realize that I wasn't responsible for what happened to me." Dee looked up and gazed around the circle. Bliss scooted over and put her arm around Dee's shoulder. Dee leaned into her.

"I had a feeling that if I faced the truth and told my story, it would have less of a hold on me, but I didn't know how to tell it. Being in this group, listening to how honest and accepting you all are gave me the strength to share my secret. I still have the bad memories, but I feel more removed from the story." Dee smiled a tentative, small smile that grew as her confidence rose. "Thank you, every one of you," she made eye contact with each woman, "for listening and for being here for me."

A soft silence blanketed the room, everyone going within to let the moment cover them.

"Thank you for sharing," someone said quietly.

"Is that why you are lesbians?" Dee asked, hugging her arms around her torso. "Because you had horrible experiences with men?"

"No," Sage said. "For me, it's about being in the company of women, having the support from my sisters. It's not about men. It's about women."

"And don't forget, women are softer and smell better," Bliss added to everyone's laughing agreement.

The mood had shifted, and after a respectful pause, someone asked, "What are you going to do now?"

Dee sat with that question for a few minutes, and a surge of relief filled her chest. She was living in a lesbian community in the middle of the desert with no lover and no plans. She silently sent thanks to the Goddess for her good fortune.

"I love it here, and I'm going to stay a while, at least until it gets really hot. The garden could use some attention, and I'm a good weeder. Sage taught me songs she learned at the Michigan Women's Music Festival she went to last year. I'm going to meet her there next summer, so I'll focus on my music."

After the group came to a close with hugs all around. Dee returned to her cozy underground nest, sidestepping barbed desert plants and stinging insects, taking a long moment in the cool, fresh air to enjoy the endless blue sky, figuring she had found her new home.

Martie 1981

"Lola calls herself a sexologist, but if you ask me, she's just a sex-crazed lunatic," Anne said, jabbing her finger at a quarter-page ad in the local alternative newspaper. The color photo featured a partially clad, big-haired woman wielding a fringed leather whip straddling another woman whose naked butt allegedly begged for abuse. "What's up with her name - Juicy Jam? That's disgusting." She shoved the paper across the table to her companion for closer inspection.

Martie took a gander at the ad and chortled. "I don't know what's funnier, your reaction, or how dumb Lola looks in that get-up." She slapped her hand flat on the table and snorted a laugh that got the attention of two women at a nearby table, who glanced over and quickly turned back to their conversation.

"It's not funny!" Anne said. "She is a disgrace to the sisterhood. What does she think she is doing, flaunting her big boobs and grinning like a maniac? She's an embarrassment to all lesbians."

"Oh, come on now," Martie said, a little surprised at Anne's prudish reaction. Her assumption, which got her into trouble more times than not, was that all the women who lived at Desert Haven were of a liberal bent when it came to sex. But Anne was still a bit of a mystery. Since her arrival a few months ago, she always seemed to be on the move, driving to her part-time job at the animal shelter or meeting up with friends. Martie had accepted Anne's invitation to ride into town partly because she wanted to get to know her a little better. After going to the food coop and the women's bookstore on Fourth Avenue, they treated themselves to a coffee at the Café on this hot summer day.

"She's just exercising her right to freedom of expression and probably making good money while she's at it. You just have boob envy."

Anne ignored the comment and unconsciously smoothed her Lavender Menace T-shirt over her chest. "She is humiliating other women for money. What the hell? We live on women's land for

Goddess's sake; we're reinventing society where women can be free, not pawns of the patriarchy. We are better than this."

"Oh, Anne, now calm down. Who are you to judge someone for their sexual proclivities? It's only been a few years since the DSM II deemed that you're no longer a pathological deviant."

"What's the DSM?"

"The Diagnostic and Statistical Manual put out by the American Psychiatric Association. I learned about it in my Psych 101 class. Shrinks said we were nut cases in the DSM I, and then, in 1973, just eight years ago, they changed their minds. We are not crazy anymore. Just kinky,"

Martie repositioned her Yankees baseball cap and leaned across the table, a teacher excited to find a captive student. "Maybe you don't like that she's so public about it. Showing off. Are you going to have a hard time looking Lola in the eye after seeing this?" The thought of the two women sitting next to each other at a moon circle cracked her up and set Martie off on another round of chuckles. More disapproving looks from their table neighbors. Martie turned her body to face them and stared bug-eyed, challenging them to say something.

"Martie, don't be a child. Drink your coffee and leave them alone."

Martie couldn't resist acting the fool because it seemed to annoy Anne. She got a kick out of disrupting normal expectations of behavior. Good girls didn't stare at strangers. Nor did they talk about sex.

"Have some respect for my feelings here," Anne said. "I have a right to think Lola is gross." She slightly puckered her lips and twisted them to one side. Martie didn't know if Anne was annoyed or suppressing a smile and was secretly laughing at her.

"You are so quaint and old school," Martie said, grinning. "I remember reading *The Joy of Lesbian Sex* and being shocked that they thought women didn't like power play in the bedroom. They were pretty limited, don't ya think?"

Anne looked blankly at Martie as if she couldn't believe what she was saying. "It never occurred to me that women would want power over other women. We have enough pain inflicted on us by men; we don't need to do it to ourselves. We should be supportive of each other, not punishing."

"Should!" Martie said. "There are no shoulds when it comes to consenting adults in the bedroom. Or the yurt, or in the camper van, or wherever women are having sex. We are fighting for liberation, and yet we impose these judgments and inhibitions on each other. When are we going to find out what we want, not what we are told we want?" Martie sat back in her chair and took a sip from her now cold cup of coffee. She loved the glow of self-righteousness.

"I know what I want," Anne said, leaning forward, looking directly into Martie's eyes. "I want to make love with a woman who is my peer, not my sex slave. I want to feel safe and respected between the sheets as well as on the streets."

"Now you sound like a flowery poster from the women's bookstore," Martie said. "It seems to me that you don't want to challenge yourself. It sounds like you are okay with accepting men's definition of women's sexuality. The baby maker, the little woman. How fucking boring."

"Who are you to say I'm boring? I heard you haven't had a lover for three years."

"It's only been two years. Don't exaggerate." Martie was a little surprised that Anne turned the conversation personal, and it pissed her off. A lively political discussion, weighing the pros and cons of a point of view, was Martie's comfort zone. Maybe she was pushing too hard, and Anne was trying to get the upper hand by attacking her.

Anne said, "Two or three, who cares. The point is that you, Ms. Women's Lib, are avoiding love because you are scared shitless of getting close to anyone. With or without the whips."

"Hey, I don't need your analysis, Doctor Anne. If you haven't noticed, there are a lot of very needy women out there, and I'm not about to be a caretaker for a basket case who can't come out of the closet or hates her mother. If I could meet a nice, sane woman who's a little adventurous in bed, I'd live happily ever after. And besides, you don't have an exemplary track record yourself."

"I have a whole lot more sex than you do, even if it is what you would call white bread in bed. I don't need to live happily ever after; one night at a time is just fine with me." Anne abruptly got up and went for a refill on her coffee. She looked over the fresh pastries in the brightly lit display case, but she didn't return with one, so Martie figured she thought they were not worth the calories.

They finished their coffee in silence. Martie wasn't sure if Anne was angry at her or if she enjoyed a good disagreement. She was hard to read, hiding behind her thick brown hair and wide-eyed, innocent look.

When the silence began to feel uncomfortable, Martie stood and said, "Let's get going. It would be nice to beat the rush hour traffic." She scooped up the two coffee cups and deposited them in the bussing bin, hoping that Anne appreciated her joke about the nonexistent traffic on the zigzagging country road going over the mountain to their desert home.

Anne sat a moment as if she wasn't done with the conversation. She folded the newspaper slowly, tucked it in her bag, and dug for the car key in her pocket. "Okay, let's go,"

The shock of a sizzling summer afternoon was amplified in Anne's steamy baby blue Falcon. Visible heat waves rolled out when she opened the door. "Damn, this steering wheel is hotter than hell. I forgot to put the towel on it. Guess I can drive with my fingertips."

"I hope our food hasn't cooked in the car while we were indulging in air-conditioning," Martie said, twisting the wing window around to try to catch a breeze. All she got was a blast of hot air as the car pulled away from the curb. "Once we get away from all this pavement, it will be better."

The sky was intensely blue. Arizona summertime blue. As the car pulled onto Speedway Blvd., heading west, they pulled down the small visors and sat a little taller to shade their eyes from the blinding sun. Dots of cotton-ball clouds were collecting over the mountain peaks, suggesting, but not promising, rain.

It was too hot to talk, and the saguaros sported long shadows in the slanted afternoon sun, so the women quietly enjoyed the scenery on their journey back to the land. Martie's thoughts drifted back to their conversation. She knew that it was wise to be cautious. She'd rather have no relationship than put up with anyone's shit again. Samantha, her last girlfriend, seemed perfect at first, but the longer they were together, the clingier she became. It got to the point that Martie couldn't even chat with other women without provoking a scene. Sam had been burned in a previous relationship, and it seemed to scar her psyche in the trust department. She said Martie wasn't intimate enough for her, whatever that meant.

Martie thought if she wanted a girlfriend, she could just sit tight. Her underground house was comfortable, and she had already survived two summers alone there. Lots of women drifted through Desert Haven, although not too many in the summertime. Most of the women who followed the informal circuit of women's lands went to higher climes until the weather cooled off. Anne was the exception when she showed up a few months ago before the heat settled in, saying she wanted to learn the ways of the desert. Trial by fire. Martie appreciated her gutsiness.

The women Martie managed to meet had a lot of baggage, even though they wanted to live with minimal possessions. Some were survivors of abuse, some were stoners, some lived with mental illness and couldn't or wouldn't get help, and some were artists who needed to pile on new experiences. Some were just everyday misfits. But the thing they all had in common was their frustration with the system and a desire to create a new society run by women.

Martie had her own story, having escaped a confining marriage for the open road. She tried not to think too much about leaving her thirteen-year-old kid behind. She was a kid herself when she gave birth at nineteen. Martie believed in her heart of hearts that her daughter was better off in a real house with a father who had a good job, and not with a mother who couldn't handle that kind of pressure and responsibility. Guilt was the cost, a consequence she was learning to accept.

Anne appeared to be somewhat normal, except if you want to count the sleeping around thing. Kind of cute in a wholesome way, a bit uptight, but that could be fixed with a bit of patience. She had a nice athletic body that she was comfortable in. Pretty sexy. Would she be uptight in bed, or was that just an act?

Martie snapped out of her daydreaming when the car turned into Desert Haven's driveway, a little self-conscious that she had been fantasizing about Anne. They were just pals. Landmates. Nothing was going to happen.

They drove past Lola's trailer and noticed her car wasn't there. "She's probably busy enslaving some unsuspecting woman somewhere," Anne said.

"I'm pretty sure it's consensual," Martie replied, assuming that the players were involved because they wanted to be.

Getting out of the car, Anne asked, "You want to keep anything in the refrigerator in my trailer? It will last longer than in your cooler."

"Thanks. Maybe some of the fruit." Other than not having a fridge, Martie didn't miss electricity. She knew she could always get a propane unit from Lehman's catalog that supplied Amish households with all sorts of tempting goodies. But then she'd need a propane tank. And money to fill the tank. And the delivery men wouldn't be welcome on the land. It's complicated. Better to stick with the cooler she half-buried on the north side of her house.

While they were sorting their groceries, Martie said, "How about I make us some dinner?" The two women had never shared a meal other than at group potlucks. The spontaneous invitation could be construed as a possible date, or it could just be a friendly invitation. Not risking too much, not putting herself in a potentially awkward situation, but risky enough to get Martie's heart pumping.

"Thanks, I would like that," Anne said, her face lighting up with the kind of lopsided grin that Martie could not interpret.

Martie felt the first few gigantic drops of rain splat on the brim of her hat. Tightening her grip on the grocery bags, she trotted the last few yards to her house, skipped down three stairs, and pushed open the door to her little underground kingdom. Feeling lucky to beat the downpour, she scrambled to close the western window so rain wouldn't blow in. She didn't want soaked bedding and a muddy dirt floor. That would never do if she had a guest tonight.

The cacophony of a pelting rainstorm on her tin roof was one of the many perks of living in her snuggery. Martie was flooded with gratitude towards her foresisters who mastered the skills of cob building to create this engineering marvel carved out of the desert floor. She had seen old photos of the strong, bare-chested, muddy builders. First, they dug down three feet into the sunbaked soil to create a rectangular eight-by-twelve-foot hole. Straw and sand were added to the removed dirt, and then they held foot-stomping parties to create the right mixture. Lumps of the stuff were kneaded into solid walls nearly as durable as concrete. This house was the last in a series of structures built in the early 70s, so it had the improvement of roof overhangs to prevent the walls from melting in the rain. A few of the original earthships were still standing, but some had been cannibalized to create new structures.

Martie knew her outdoor kitchen would stay mostly dry. Monsoon rains didn't last very long, and she could start cooking soon. Barley and kale stew? Tofu with sweet potatoes and carrots? What was a good seduction menu? Strawberries and honey for dessert. She pictured herself dipping a plump strawberry into a yellow bowl of drippy honey, placing the crimson fruit slowly, intentionally, into Anne's open mouth while staring into her deep brown eye. A perfect moment. She felt hot just thinking about it.

Flashes of lightning illuminated the trees framing the east window. Martie watched rainwater move swiftly down the swale away from her house and out to the community garden behind the ocotillo fence. All that trench digging paid off. The rain was tapering off, and it felt like the temperature had dropped at least thirty degrees in the last half hour. Squinting to read the thermometer on the porch post, she confirmed it was a chilly sixty-eight degrees. Grabbing a flannel shirt from a hook by the door, she stepped outside and was startled by an alarming series of shrieks coming from the direction of Anne's trailer. She sprinted towards the noise and found Anne lying under a mesquite tree, surrounded by seedpods. One leg in the air, her head thrown back, mouth agape, eyes glazed. The leg suddenly thudded to the ground.

"Anne, what happened?" Martie said, rushing to her in a panic.

Anne was beyond the formation of words. Fear and pain flashed from her eyes. She yelped and whimpered; agony made audible. Her hands gestured towards a welt growing on her limp leg.

"Did something bite you? Did you fall? What can I do?" Martie yelled over Anne's cries. She reached out her hand and was violently waved away. Women rushed over to see what happened. Martie circled Anne to see if she could figure it out from a different angle.

"Maybe she got bit by a rattler," Dee said, backing away slightly as if a snake might still be around.

"That's no snakebite. I've been bit, and it's not that kind of pain," JoJo said, reflexively rubbing the scar on her forearm.

Anne moaned. Her red face was wet with tears and snot and sweat. She reached to touch her leg, struggling to form words. "Can't. Move. Leg," she managed to choke out.

Martie felt icy fear creep up the back of her neck. What was going on? She needed to do something. Anne looked exhausted and scared. She moved around to cradle Anne's head and shoulders.

"Holy shit. Ow ow. Fuck fuck fuck."

"What happened?" Martie asked, pulling damp, sweaty hair back from Anne's face.

"Pee. Big wasp. Red shiny. Instant pain." Anne winced, her eyes darting from one woman to another.

It didn't make much sense to Martie, but JoJo interpreted Anne's shorthand. "My guess is that she came out here under the big mesquite to pee and somehow pissed off a tarantula hawk. I heard the sting from those buggers is the second most painful insect bite in the world. Don't remember what's the first." Hugging her arms around her chest, she said, "I feel damn lucky that I've never been stung in the seven years I've been living out here."

Anne stretched her leg and wiggled her foot a little. Her calf was as big as a grapefruit and angry red. "I can move it again. It was paralyzed. I was so fucking scared," she said, leaning back into Martie's arms and surrendering to gasping sobs.

The women sat in silent support, giving Anne space to cry it out. Someone sang quietly, the sound blending with the wind rustling the trees. Someone else placed a handkerchief in Anne's hand. Slowly, her tears subsided, as did the lump on her leg. She wiped her face and looked around at the women, smiling weakly.

"Do you think you can walk?" Martie asked.

Anne inhaled deeply and let out a long, slow sigh. She closed her eyes for a moment and seemed to gather her strength. With help, she was able to stand. Supported on both sides, she was guided to Martie's kitchen and gently lowered into a rattan chair.

One woman brought an ice pack, another had some vinegar to apply after the cold compress. Martie wet a washcloth for Anne's face and hands. JoJo said she had some Benadryl if Anne wanted it.

"Thank you all for coming to my rescue. I think I'll live."

"We didn't do much," JoJo said. "Just gotta ride those damn things out. The worst of it should be over. It may itch as it heals for the next day or so."

"Let us know if you need anything," Dee said.

Martie fetched a five-gallon bucket, placed a pillow on top, and offered a light blanket. Not knowing what else to do, she said, "I'll just fry up some veggies and tofu while you rest."

She measured a cup of brown rice into a cast-iron Dutch oven on the camp stove and added water from a gallon jug. Scraping a kitchen match on the rough plastered wall, she lit the burner. Anne watched silently.

"Would you like some wine? Or, I have a little stash of bourbon if you'd like something stronger."

"Bourbon, please. Take the edge off." Anne looked at her propped-up leg. "It feels like it's a specimen in a museum of natural history, not something that is part of me. Good thing I peed before the sting, or I'd be a smelly mess right now," she said.

"If you can joke about it now, you must be on the mend," Martie said, handing her a small jelly jar half-full of brown liquid. "Sorry, no ice. Want me to get some from your freezer."

"This is fine. But damn, that was crazy." Anne's voice drifted off as if she didn't believe what just happened to her. "That was the worst pain ever. Much worse than breaking my hand last year. Having a tooth pulled is nothing compared to that stupid wasp sting." She took a sip from the glass and her face puckered. She looked at the glass as if it was her salvation and took a greedy gulp.

"Give me a hand with this pillow, please," she said. "I'm afraid to move." She adjusted her leg and lightly touched the red area around the tiny black dot of the sting. "I'm exhausted." She leaned back in the chair, eyes flickering a few times until they slowly closed.

Martie figured Anne was in the letdown stage that comes after a huge adrenaline rush. Pouring herself a glass of wine, she attended to her kitchen chores, washing up with biodegradable soap and recycled hand-crocheted scrubbers, while Anne nodded off. Just thinking about Anne's pain scared the shit out of her. One of Martie's biggest fears of living on the land was the vast array of critters and vegetation that could cause pain.

Cholla buds with hooked barbs that hurt more on the way out than the way in. Mesquite tree thorns the size of large sewing needles that defy you to harvest their beans. Gila monsters whose locked jaws chewed toxins into you. And, of course, the deadly and ubiquitous rattlesnake.

She knew she had been lucky so far, reaching up and reflexively knocking the side of a wooden crate to keep her luck going. She never wanted to go through what Anne just did. But the accidental encounter did seem to have an unexpected consequence, Martie thought with a twinge of guilt. Here was Anne, soft and sweet, allowing herself to be taken care of. She was not her usual efficient, in-charge self. This glimpse into Anne's vulnerability was sexy.

No, those thoughts would have to be filed away until a more appropriate time. Now, it's about nurturing her wounded friend. Later, she can think about seduction.

The cooking activity and tempting aroma brought Anne back to the present. A small folding table was covered with a floral cloth and set with mismatched silverware. She was able to stand so Martie could move her chair up to the table.

"Here you go," Martie said, putting down two plates piled with rice, sautéed zucchini, red pepper, corn, and asparagus.

"Beautiful colors. Thanks. Who knew you were such a good cook?" Anne said.

"Just one of my many talents. Do you want something else to drink? More bourbon? Wine? Water?" Martie wondered if she appeared too eager to please and didn't want to betray her lustful intentions, so she let it drop when her guest shook her head.

"How are you feeling?"

"Other than having a leg that was shot with a poison arrow, I'm fine. No other symptoms, so I feel lucky I didn't have an allergic reaction. Guess I'm not going dancing in town tonight. I told Becka that I would meet her there. If I knew her number, I'd call from JoJo's phone. I guess she'll figure it out when I don't show up."

"Which one is Becka?" Martie asked, running a string of Anne's girlfriends' faces past her internal movie screen, hoping the proper visage would connect to the name.

"She's the artist. Lives at Eagle's house. Red curly hair. Installation art. She did that thing with the mattress at the car wash, remember?"

"How could I forget walking through a car wash with all those giant brushes coming at me. Even without the water, it was still freaky. So, you've been seeing her?" Martie asked. She looked away and tried to keep her voice casual, trying to assess the situation. She knew that she was getting caught up in a fantasy of her own making and wanted some confirmation of mutual interest so she could decide whether to pursue it or not.

"Are you asking if I have been having sex with her? We did at first, but it wasn't a good match, so now we are just dancing buddies." Anne bent her knee and brought the red bump on her calf closer for a new inspection. "Anyway, Becka and I had a sweet thing going for a little while, but then she started saying things like, 'Where are we going with this relationship?' and it turned me off. We weren't going anywhere; we were already there as far as I was concerned."

Martie made a sound indicating she was listening but hoped it didn't convey agreement.

Waving her hand over her plate, Anne said, "This is really good. All these fresh organic veggies are going to fix me right up. And I wouldn't mind another shot of bourbon. That was really good too."

"I didn't know you were such a lush," Martie said, enjoying the opportunity to change the subject and tease Anne a bit. "I might as well join you. I wouldn't want you to get drunk alone."

Liquid confidence—that's what she needed right now. Anne was making it clear that she didn't want a long-term relationship, but that didn't answer the unasked question—was she attracted to Martie at all? First things first.

"Well, hello, Astro," Martie said, smiling at JoJo's unkempt but cute Sheltie peeking around the corner. The dog took that as an invitation and sauntered into the kitchen space, wagging her tail enthusiastically. She pushed her head into Anne's hand, insisting on pats and neck scratches. Then she went over to Martie.

"No need to do dishes," Martie said, putting her plate on the ground for the dog to lick. Anne followed suit, and they sat and watched the dog's tongue go to work.

Now what? Martie thought as she picked up the plates and placed them in a plastic tub. "You up for a little walk?" she asked Anne. "Astro and I usually take a stroll about this time of day to watch the sunset,"

"I'm getting a little stiff sitting here; maybe it would help to move around. Unless I'm too tipsy to walk. That bourbon did the trick." Anne got up tentatively and put weight on her leg. "Seems okay, just itchy."

Astro put her nose down between her front paws, her butt in the air, and whipped her tail back and forth, looking at the women expectantly. As they started to walk, she yipped with excitement, ran a circle around them, and raced ahead to the road. There was hardly any traffic on the dirt road that passed Desert Haven, so Martie knew the dog was safe. And, besides, Astro was a land dog and knew how to take care of herself. Just like the land dykes. Survivors. Adventurers. Independent and strong.

They walked up the driveway and turned right. Unpaved road stretched out before them in a long, straight ribbon, appearing to reach the horizon. That's the thing about the desert, thought Martie, when you carve out a path, it stays carved out. Four-foot-tall cholla cactus edged the lane. Astro expertly ran between the prickly bushes, chasing a whiptail lizard.

They walked in silence for a few minutes, Anne increasing her stride to match her leggier companion. Martie could smell the dust rising from their footsteps and her own nervous sweat. Anne was cute, and Martie felt brave after a glass of wine and a big shot of bourbon. What could she say? Before their conversation at The Café today, the only thing she knew about her was what was displayed on her T-shirts.

Was she willing to risk it? Rejection would be awkward. She'd seen couples break up and try to continue to live in this tiny community, and it was painful for everyone. It must be the booze talking. Or was she just so sex-starved that her brain took a back seat to her hormones?

Anne suddenly stopped walking, turned to the west, and said, "Look at that beautiful sky!" She opened her arms up to the heavens above like she could hug the brilliance. Red, purple, orange, yellow swirling into each other. A Van Gogh sky. She looked so happy and sweet that Martie impetuously reached out and encircled Anne in an embrace. A hug. A friendly hug. A close hug held long enough so she could inhale Anne's unique scent. Anne didn't pull away.

Astro observed them and bounded back from a hundred yards down the road, knowing the walk was over. The dog sat at their feet, waiting, watching for what would happen next.

A kiss. A tentative friendly peck. A pause and then a longer, deeper kiss. A dizzying kiss. Their mouths broke loose. They gasped for air and looked away from each other. They kissed again. Astro was done waiting and barked to go back home.

"How is the sting?"

"It's fine. Let's go back to your house."

Martie surveyed the room when they entered the dugout. She was glad she had made her single bed and tidied her tiny house because anything out of place was obvious. Like the vibrator hanging by its cord from the standing lamp next to the bed. Oh shit, she forgot to put it in the drawer last night. Is Anne going to think it's an invitation?

Well, it is. Since she brought this beautiful, wounded Amazon to her lair, she might as well advertise some of the tricks she had up her sleeve. But she was dealing with a self-declared prude, so she better proceed with caution.

Martie watched her guest inspect the small space, slowly taking it all in. She examined the pencil drawings tacked to the walls, ran her fingers across the handmade quilt, peered out the window. Martie didn't know what Anne was thinking, so she steeled herself for rejection. She seemed willing, but maybe not. Although, those kisses felt real enough.

Turning her back to the window, Anne smiled, lowered her gaze, and seemed to be waiting.

"Take off your shirt. I want to see you," Martie began gently, testing to see if she was reading the situation correctly.

Anne paused, looked up, and locked eyes with Martie. She crossed her arms, taking the hem of her T-shirt, and pulled up very gradually. The shirt rose over her belly, her ribs, then exposed one breast at a time. She stopped and held the pose so Martie had time to appreciate the tease. Heat rose between them.

Martie had an urge to yank the shirt off, but she resisted. Anne freed the shirt from her shoulders and waved it over her head like a flag. A small triumph.

"Now, your pants."

Anne's eyes widened slightly. Martie questioned if this was new territory for her. Giving up control, tacitly acknowledging a power imbalance. Anne could have resisted. But she didn't.

Slowly, the zipper lowered. Even more slowly, Anne's cutoff shorts slid down one hipbone and exposed a few stray pubic hairs. Martie felt a rush when she understood – no underwear. Anne turned away and let her jeans fall to the ground, exposing her rump. She looked over her shoulder, waiting. Smiling.

"Lay down on the bed."

Anne did as she was told. "Be careful of my leg...it's still sensitive."

"I'll take your mind off of it," Martie said and kissed Anne's neck, moving down to her breasts and back up again. "You are so beautiful." She felt the warmth of passion deep in her belly. Fingernails lightly scratching. Gentle caresses, assertive squeezes, insistent rubbing.

Anne fumbled with Martie's clothes, trying to undo buttons. Her hands were brushed away. She whispered, "Take off your clothes."

"Not now." Marty whispered, "This is all about you and your enjoyment. Please let me give this to you," Martie said, caressing the outside and then the inside of Anne's thigh. Anne's body instinctively responded to the touch. She thrust her hips and made little whimpering sounds.

"What about you?" Anne asked between gasps.

"My pleasure is in giving you pleasure. Nobody touches me. Go with it, baby, just lay back and enjoy the ride."

Craving, lust, indulgence. Sucking nipples, tongue in belly button, back up to nibble on earlobe, fingers gliding, grabbing, rubbing. Mouth connecting with vulva, tongue magic. Anne stiffened, scream-laughed, and tipped into an orgasm. Head back, eyes closed, she arched her back and rode the wave.

Anne's orgasm brought on Martie's. She flopped down next to Anne, eyes shut tight, crying, "Wow, oh wow, holy shit," convulsing with pleasure, arms wrapped around her torso. When Anne whispered, "Can I hug you?" it seemed to jerk her back.

"Yes, yes. Please. Yes," and she rolled on her side, facing Anne.

Anne wrapped her arms around and pulled Martie close. Suspended, dangling in pleasure, they nestled on the bed, moon shadows decorating their bodies, blissed out, each adrift in her tangle of thoughts.

32

Teagan 1981

Part 1

Teagan directed Samantha to turn right into the parking lot and pull to the end of the strip mall, where the neon sign in the window flashed Natalie's Café.

"I have to pee so bad my eyeballs are floating. Let's go," she said, opening the door the moment the truck came to a complete stop.

"Go ahead, I'll meet you inside," Sam said, turning off the engine, cutting off Kim Carnes singing about Bette Davis Eyes. She reached to the back seat to retrieve her black and orange Giant's cap and pulled it over her short hair, brim facing backward. Leaning forward, she patted her back pocket to make sure she had her wallet and then exited the vehicle, locking the doors.

Teagan shifted from foot to foot, waiting in the hall outside the lady's room. The door was locked. Why is there always a line? She looked up at the other restroom door where the word Men was crossed out with a red marker, and the word Women was written in bold letters. Of course, she thought, this is a women's coffeehouse, and gratefully closed the door behind her.

Sam stood at the counter holding two grande lattes in paper cups, looking for a place to sit down when Teagan came up to her. A large oval table surrounded by assorted chairs was the centerpiece of the room. There were a few empty seats.

"Let's sit at the communal table with the local ladies and meet some Tucson lesbians before we head out to Desert Haven," Teagan said. Without conferring with Sam, she turned to the seated women and asked if they were interrupting anything and if they could join the table.

"Sure, join us. Everyone is welcome. Just passing through?" asked an older stout woman in a lavender t-shirt.

"Yeah, we've been on the road a few days," Sam said. Teagan wondered why Sam wasn't forthcoming with their destination but decided to help herself to an Oreo from a big plate that said "free," sip her coffee and see what was up.

A woman with a blond mullet haircut looking butch in the front and femme in the back, leaned into the table, continuing a conversation that had been interrupted by the two newcomers. "I know what you mean. Those women roam the desert naked, howling at the moon, living on food stamps, having orgies, and I don't want any part of them. They show up here, smelling to high heaven, and take baths in the lady's room, making a holy mess."

A few of the women nodded in agreement, and someone said, "They eat all the free cookies and don't put any money into the donation can. If they want to live like animals, they should just stay at Desert Haven and not bother us."

Sam and Teagan exchanged looks—a slight widening of the eyes and an imperceptible head tilt meaning, "Let's get out of here."

Sam rose and said, "It's been really nice meeting you all. We have to get back on the road."

"Yeah," Teagan said, "Miles to-go before we sleep and all." Neither of them mentioned their destination.

They picked up their cups, smiled goodbye, and walked quickly out the door.

"I guess we know how townies feel about Desert Haven," Sam said, grinning. "I can't wait to get out there and see all the naked women."

Teagan threw back her head and yowled her best imitation of a coyote on a moonlit night. Her caterwaul morphed into great belly laughs as she climbed into the passenger seat of her twenty-year-old 1961 Chevy Silverado and picked up the scrap of paper with directions to Desert Haven lying on the dashboard.

"According to my calculations, we head north and west for about an hour, and we should bump into a nest of smelly women," she said, still chuckling.

They drove down Oracle Road until the intersection with Speedway. "This is where you turn. Does any of this look familiar to you?"

"I wasn't here for that long, and I didn't have a car, so, honestly, I don't remember much about the roads."

Teagan sank back into the passenger seat, grateful that Sam did all the driving while she navigated. Sam didn't have the patience to look at maps and figure out where they were, but could drive on coffee and cigarettes all night.

"Can you believe those pompous middle-class lesbos?" asked Sam. "A good reminder, if I ever need one, to avoid civilization. After a few weeks on women's land, I will gladly exchange the scent of under-washed lesbians for the freedom to not be a horse's ass."

Teagan felt her heart swell in a surge of affection for her lover. The sensation fortified her trust in their decision to leave the Midwest to find an authentic and meaningful new life on women's land. Sam had been talking about moving since they met two years ago and had finally convinced her to pack up and go. But Teagan did have to admit to herself—never to Sam—that she was a bit apprehensive about camping in the back of a truck in the desert with a bunch of women she didn't know. Could she adjust to permanent vagabond status? Would she go crazy without a proper bathroom?

Teagan knew that Sam loved her and wanted the two of them to live happily ever after as a couple, as a two-headed entity, bonded by their shared desire for personal freedom and justice for all of Earth's beings. Their politics meshed, their desire to drop out and escape patriarchal control was in synch, and they were hot for each other—a perfect blending of their hearts and bodies.

The fact that Sam's ex-lover, Martie, lived at Desert Haven still seemed a bit awkward to Teagan. How was that going to work? It could be uncomfortable for all of them in such close quarters. Sam said she was a "one-woman-woman" and reassured Teagan that it wasn't a problem.

Three years into the experiment, Sam and Teagan were snuggled under a summer quilt in their cozy shed, looking at some photos of themselves on the day they arrived at Desert Haven.

"Your hair was so long," Teagan said, rubbing her hands over the fuzz of her partner's buzz cut.

"And you were still wearing your city clothes," Sam countered.

"I loved that blouse. I got it on half-price Tuesday at the thrift store and wore it to death. Here, look, there's a couple of squares of it in this quilt." She did a quick survey and pointed to a few blocks of floral blue and purple material. "And here's that denim work shirt you blew the elbows out of, and I had to hide it from you so you wouldn't wear it every day."

"What's this from?" Sam asked, pointing to a blue and white striped square.

"That was the hideous uniform I had to wear at the nursing home. It was to show the staff and residents who the aides were so they could shit on us. When I quit, I liberated it as a reminder not to take stupid jobs anymore. I got great pleasure in cutting it up."

"I'm so lucky to have a talented girlfriend like you," Sam said, pulling Teagan closer. Teagan gave her a side glance, and Sam said, "No, really, I mean it. I think you are amazing. You sew something beautiful like this and make the most delicious meals from our meager larder with just a camp stove. You are fucking wonder woman!"

"Good, keep that thought when you are pissed that I won't get up at the crack of dawn and go foraging for lamb's quarters or whatever you go looking for up on the mountain." Then, glancing at the clock, Teagan said, "Tonight's the full moon circle. I've got to get up and soak the beans."

She crawled over Sam to get up. Sam grabbed the end of her t-shirt and teasingly held her back but let go when Teagan tugged it away with a limp smile. It was a repetitive routine she didn't enjoy, Sam wanting to distract her from engaging with other women in the community. A little bit of jealousy, a little bit of wanting to be the center of attention at all times.

The bed was tucked into a corner of the eight-by-eight metal Tuff Shed they called home. Sam had tacked insulation between the studs, and they covered the walls with old sheets to keep it somewhat warm in the winter and not burning hot when summer came. At the turn of seasons, Teagan bought different patterned sheets at Goodwill to change up the decor. A small wooden dresser and a three-legged stool completed the furnishings. Clothing hung from hooks on the walls. A table and four mismatched chairs resided in the kitchen ramada they had built out of salvaged lumber and palm fronds. Live traps were set to rehome packrats and mice.

Sam lingered in bed, watching Teagan get dressed. "I didn't like the last circle. There were too many of those snotty townies there. Day trippers. Come out here for a spiritual fix and go back to their cozy, over-heated, over-air-conditioned homes and talk trash about us the rest of the time."

Teagan thought that was a rather harsh assessment of the visitors, but she didn't comment. Sam could always be counted on to share her opinions liberally. She hated Republicans, hypocrites, homophobes, and a host of other types with a vengeance and would go out of her way to let everyone know. Teagan was more of the live-and-let-live school. If someone didn't actively try to stop her from living her life the way she wanted to, she didn't give a fig about them. It was only when those mean-spirited goons in Congress tried to legislate her life away that she got angry.

Anyway, she kind of liked some of the women from town. Those two who owned the bookstore, Kathy and Anna, were smart and funny. And Eagle, who dressed in colorful prints and smelled like patchouli, was the best drummer. But not having gas money made it tough to be involved in the Tucson community. The only people she saw regularly were her land sisters. And besides, Sam wouldn't like it if she had friends from the "outside." With this thought, Teagan felt a pang in her belly, a constriction of sorts. It sounded like she was in a cult or something.

She thought she would get another job when she quit the nursing home, but everything was at least an hour's drive away. And she didn't have the clothes for a job search. And then there was the matter of personal hygiene. She had never gotten very efficient at taking a shower from a garden hose; it was basically just a rinse. The dirt under her fingernails used to freak her out, but now it just seemed normal. She had slowly adapted to this once-foreign environment, and that wasn't a bad thing. Actually, it was a good thing because she needed to feel okay about her life. It wasn't ideal, but whose life was?

And still. It would be nice to have some other friends. Women who saw movies. Went to concerts and attended classes. Women with ideas and exciting lives. She had Martie just a few hundred feet away, of course. At first, Teagan thought Martie's proximity might be a problem, but it turns out they got along great. Both Cancers, they were crafters and loved sharing recipes. Their running joke was about what good taste Sam had in girlfriends.

But when Martie started complaining about how miserable she was when she lived with Sam, how controlling and possessive Sam could be, Teagan shut the words out. She didn't want to fill her brain with any of those negative thoughts. Yes, Sam could be difficult, but at least she truly loved Teagan. She wouldn't be so jealous if she didn't. Right?

Teagan loved that the full moon rituals brought a different energy to Desert Haven.

◆ ◆ ◆

"Well, here come the bourgeois townies in their Lexus SUVs," Sam announced later that afternoon when she heard the first vehicle turn into their driveway.

"You be nice," Teagan directed. "They are our guests." She couldn't predict how offensive Sam would be but hoped that she would contain herself for a few hours. At previous rituals, she'd been rude and blunt but never really picked a fight. Teagan watched and listened, and she saw Sam's growing disdain. It was troubling.

"I sometimes wish they would just all go away," Sam said. "The suburbs could sink into the river, and the city could implode, and all the men and money-grubbing women would evaporate from the Earth. Leave us alone with the four-leggeds and fish and flying creatures. Begin again."

"You want to go back to Eden?" asked Teagan.

"No, I want to create it here. Now. I don't want to go back to anything."

More cars pulled up, and a dozen women joined the circle of residents, doubling their numbers. Earthenware casserole dishes and roasted chickens still in their plastic domes covered the slightly sagging plywood boards set on sawhorses that served as tables. Marigold saw her lover Cassie pull up and ran to greet her with a prolonged and lingering hug. They were the only couple who spanned the gap between townie and land dyke. Sam knew most of the faces but never remembered their names, so Teagan patiently re-introduced her to their visitors.

When Teagan heard Sam ask the women who brought the chicken, "Why would you give your money to a corporate monopoly that is destroying small farms for a poisoned, tortured animal that died a miserable death?" she decided an intervention was necessary.

"I'm sure she has a job and doesn't have time to cook for a potluck, isn't that right? And anyway, it's time to start the ritual. The sun is just about setting. Look at that glorious sky!"

Animosity temporarily put aside, all eyes turned to the deep colors splashed across the horizon.

"Circle up young and old, get your drums, shed your cares, be in the moment," announced Liz, high priestess and leader of the monthly gatherings, ushering them towards the gathering place. Squatting down, she put a match to the dry twigs crossed with three small logs in the fire pit, carefully holding back her long grey braids to keep them safe from the flames. It's not like they needed the warmth of the fire this evening. It was September, and the daytime temps were still in the nineties.

"Who will call in the east? The south, the west, and the north?" Liz waited while four women took their directions. "Thank you, Goddesses. Please let us bring our attention to Mother Earth, she who supports us, who nurtures us, who loves us. Oh, Mother, help us heal, and we will help heal you!"

The energy of the gathering seemed to relax into the present moment. The tom-tom's heartbeat and Liz's mesmerizing voice were the only sounds. She spoke just above a whisper, so everyone had to lean in to hear. The sky turned dark, stars slowly emerged like pinholes pricked in the cloak of night. After invoking a pantheon of multicultural Goddesses, the celebrants were invited to turn their thoughts inward and meditate on personal messages from Spirit. After five minutes, after Sam quietly left to go to bed, but not so quiet that Teagan didn't notice, Liz said, "May the circle be open but unbroken. May the peace of the Goddess be ever in your heart." The group repeated the closing chant together two more times, and the circle was opened. The ritual was complete.

Teagan turned to the woman on her left and looked into her eyes, saying, "Namaste. The Goddess in me honors the Goddess in you." She hugged her and then turned to the woman on her right and did the same. Then she walked into the group for more hugs, feeling joy rise up within her. It was too bad that Sam wasn't there to experience bliss from these simple community rituals. Sam always said that she didn't need anyone but Teagan, but Teagan needed sisterhood to feel truly connected.

Eagle began an insistent beat on a djembe. Some deer-foot rattles joined in to support the rhythm. Becka, a tall woman with long dreadlocks, strummed a guitar, and Cassie's Native American flute floated an intermittent melody. The mellow mood of the ritual slowly but insistently transformed into pounding, energetic music that encouraged frenetic movements and spontaneous dancing.

Teagan twirled and leaped, her diaphanous skirt flowing around her legs, her purple halter top barely covering her breasts. She felt free and deliriously happy. Spying a woman in bright bird colors snaking in and out of the other dancers, Teagan followed her lead and took up the sinuous path. Teagan was taken with the other woman's grace and presence. She felt a soul connection. The two women locked eyes, and their movements mirrored each other. They became an eight-limbed bifurcated creature. The other dancers melted into the background. There was no leader and no follower. The two women moved as one being. One beating heart, one brain. Teagan didn't know how long they were moving together—the songs tended to go on and on, but finally, the musicians paused, and the energy came down, landing on the two of them.

The spectators wordlessly knew what they had witnessed. A profound connection had just manifested itself in front of observers; there was no denial. Everyone understood. And they all knew that Sam was asleep in the shed while Teagan danced with a townie.

Part 2

Her name was Alice.

She read about the full moon ritual in the local bimonthly lesbian newsletter that she picked up in the women's bookstore. Sitting on her sofa in her fifth-floor apartment in downtown Tucson, she placed her glass of wine on the carved mesquite coffee table and read the headline: "Casting the Circle, an invitation to Desert Haven's monthly moon circle." A blast of nostalgia hit her, a yearning in the pit of her stomach that spread up her front and lodged in her throat. A longing for something she didn't know she even missed.

Her therapist had told her to use her body's reaction as a key to her feelings, so Alice made herself pay attention to the physical sensations she was experiencing to unravel these strong feelings.

Her thoughts focused on the monthly gatherings she went to when she lived upstate in Flagstaff. She never committed to official membership in the Goddess worship group, although she went so often that they invited her to become an initiate. Alice declined, preferring her outsider status, so she participated as a long-term guest. She loved to transform herself with costume, tying her hair back with colorful scarves and donning a spectacular purple velvet thrift-store cape that dragged on the earth behind her. Being out in nature, calling in women's energy, learning herstory—all of these things called to her. She loved the spiritual high.

At first, she didn't know that the group was mainly lesbian. Nobody mentioned it. There was lots of handholding and hugging, but she thought that was part of the camaraderie of the experience. No one asked her if she was straight. It didn't matter.

She was straight, she knew she was, even though she felt a strong attraction to Diana. It was just the circumstances. With the heat and drums and heart rhythms. Alice felt excited and joyful. It wasn't really an attraction; it was more like affection. She liked Diana, and she knew that the feeling was mutual. But she was straight.

She cringed to think back on how damn confusing it was—to the point that she stopped going to the circle. And then she got a job offer in Tucson, so that was that.

Apparently, that was the message from her body. A longing for something that was never meant to be. She had accepted it and moved on, so why the intense feelings now?

Moving to Tucson had been an excellent way to shift that energy. She threw herself into her new job. Being an accountant at the hospital was a demanding position, and she took her responsibilities seriously. Working from seven to seven was not unusual. Her friends were people she knew from work; she didn't have time to go out and meet new people. She could barely make it to the gym three times a week, much less attend to her emotional or spiritual needs for connection and community. She had to laugh at herself for how well she conformed to the stereotype of nerdy left-brained numbers cruncher.

She wondered why she was so drawn to women's rituals. They always seemed to follow a pattern, but the variations were endless. So much depended on the peculiarities of the woman leading the circle and her sensitivity to the group's needs. Sometimes things flowed. Sometimes it was chaos. She liked a little bit of disorder, as long as it was predictable and contained.

Alice quit work early and slipped into the restroom to change into jeans, a bright yellow t-shirt, and orange sneakers. She tied a lime green bandana in her hair. The riot of color lifted her mood from the grey and black theme of her work clothes. She stopped by the grocery store to pick up a couple of roasted chickens for the inevitable potluck. It was risky because she didn't know the level of vegetarian fervor, but in the past, she found that protein was devoured pretty quickly.

She checked in with her body and figured that she was excited and nervous at the same time because her breath was shallow. It was a beautiful fall evening, so she put the Saab's top down, popped a Lisa Theil CD into the player, and cruised twenty-five miles over the mountain to the hippy commune, mulling over the unknowns. Was this group going to be all lesbians too? Would they kick her out if they found out she was straight? Would they scorn her for not bringing a homemade offering for the potluck?

According to the sketchy directions, she thought she was to turn right into a dirt driveway. It didn't look like anything but a bunch of broken-down trailers and lots of desert with junk all around. With trepidation, she pulled into a spot next to a rust-colored truck. Or was it a grey-colored truck that was rusted out? She thought maybe this wasn't such a good idea after all, but a dozen pairs of eyes watched her arrive, so turning around was no longer an option. She took a deep breath and grabbed the plastic bag with her potluck offering, putting on a brave face she wanted to look friendly.

"Hi, I'm Alice. I hope this is the place for the full moon circle. I have some food to share," she said as she crossed to the laden table. Then, noticing the women were already eating, she looked around for a plate for her meal.

"I don't see any plates," she said quietly to a woman wearing a cowboy hat and vest with no shirt.

"You are supposed to bring your own. And silverware too. I've got some extra you can use." She handed over a scratched brown and orange Melamine plate and a bent fork.

Alice thanked her and helped herself to beans, salad, and tore off a chicken leg with her hands because she didn't see any knives at the table. Nor napkins. She found an upended log to perch on, balanced her plate precariously on her knees, and looked around. No one looked familiar. But the food was good, especially the beans.

Listening to the conversation, she silently ate her dinner.

"Did you hear that Sky and Marlin are coming soon?"

"I thought they were still in Arkansas."

"They still making that goat soap?"

"Guess we'll hear all about it when they get here."

"Are we out of toilet paper?"

"It's your turn to buy some."

"I can't get a ride to the store to buy any. And besides, my check didn't come yet."

After she finished eating, Alice mimicked what her neighbors did, washing her plate in a tub of soapy water, rinsing it in a tub with watered-down bleach, and placing it in a rack perched on two sawhorses to dry.

The food table was cleared, and the leftover chicken was whisked away. Alice asked a young woman with multicolor chevrons painted on her cheeks for directions to the bathroom and was directed to a wooden structure with a peeling red door. Inside, she was happy to find a flushable toilet and running water at the turn of a faucet. Only cold water, but it would do. No towel, so while drip-drying, she perused the faded photos of naked women and slogans from the second wave of feminism that covered the unpainted walls.

She held the door open for the next occupant and felt drumbeats vibrating the earth before she heard them. Back at the fire she joined the circle of women walking in a clockwise direction to mimic the rotation of the sun. The familiar chants helped ease her into a soothing attitude of surrender and expectancy. They were similar to what she had learned in Flagstaff and close enough to trigger a feeling of intimacy and spiritual connection she felt with Mother Earth. Alice was filled with a surge of affection for the women around her, and her heart chakra throbbed.

Thank you, Artemis, Goddess of nature, Goddess of birth

Thank you, Selu, ancient corn mother

Thank you, Kali, Goddess of destruction and rebirth

Thank you, Inari, for guiding and protecting the spirits of the dead

Alice was swept away by the energy rising from the group. When the ritual ended, and the circle was open, the drumbeats quickened. Alice felt a trance dance brewing. Her foot tapped to the insistent thump of the big drum as musicians gained confidence and added to the song. The thought of dancing with abandon was wildly exciting, but her default of reserve had kicked in. Standing near the drummers, not yet in the circle, she swayed to the perfect rhythm and waited for the music to melt her shyness.

Women leaped and twirled. Feet stomped, and hips shook. Heads bobbed. Alice relaxed in stages, like descending flights of stairs from a high tower. The music swept her into a sense of comfort and rightness as the rest of her life slipped away, and she started to dance. There was nothing but the cooling evening breeze, the feel of her hair whipping against her cheeks, and joy. Just joy. Building, swelling, filling her with bliss and goodwill.

Alice joined the flow guided by a supernatural language that only she could interpret. A winding path, sinuous motion. Her vision blurred, and she saw an exquisite creature moving with such grace it looked like she emerged from the dust that arose from her sandals. The woman locked eyes with her and commanded her to move her body this and thus. No words.

Part 3

Damn it, why did the full moon have to come on a Tuesday, Alice thought, sitting at her desk in her office on Wednesday morning at seven-thirty. Her head was tipping off her neck and jerking back up again, teardrops leaking out from half-mast eyelids. Were they tears of exhaustion or from joy and disorientation? She closed the folders on her desk, realizing that she had not read any of the papers she had just shuffled through. All those columns of numbers were making her dizzy. She grabbed her wallet out of her purse and stood, thinking a triple espresso with two sugars would make it all better. A freezing blast of air hit her when she opened the door to the corridor. For the umpteenth time, she got angry at the waste of electricity. Why is it always so fucking cold in hospitals? Maybe so that the patients get numbed out and don't have any nerve endings left for fear, especially when they see their bill.

Looking over the food offerings in the cafeteria didn't do her shaky stomach much good. She hadn't tried to function on two hours of sleep since grad school. Thinking protein might wake her up, she chose a cheese omelet to go with her large cup of caffeine.

Returning to her office, she balanced the tray and shut the door with her foot. Alice always ate at her desk because the sterile atmosphere of the cafeteria turned her off, and besides, she might meet someone she knew. That was not how she wanted to spend her breaks. They were her quiet time. She always had a book in the bottom drawer of her desk, along with a black sweater, extra sugar packets, some candy bars, aspirin, and Tampax. Everything a working girl would need.

Stirring carefully, she waited until the sugar completely dissolved in the steaming paper cup before taking the first cautious sip. Slow, deliberate movements kept her grounded. The omelet tasted salty, like

Teagan's sweaty dancing skin. The coffee tasted sweet, like Teagan's lips. She felt a twinge of desire, an aching in her gut. Her cheeks flushed as she remembered the sweetness of the natural progression of their flirtation from the dancing circle to the passionate kisses in her car. They had decided to go for a desert drive in the brightness of the moon. And then they ended up in Alice's apartment. And bed. They talked and cuddled and laughed, procrastinating, putting off the inevitable. Then, finally, when the sun was just brightening the sky, they made love.

When the alarm rang at six-thirty, Teagan didn't stir. Alice slipped soundlessly from between the sheets, eased open her underwear drawer, and stealthily pulled out what she needed. She lifted up on the closet door handle so the hinges wouldn't squeak and grabbed her clothes, dressing in the living room to not disturb her... What? Lover? Girlfriend? Her lesbian girlfriend. She had no words. All she knew was it was Wednesday, and she was due at work in a half-hour. The drive to work was automatic.

Her life was automatic. But now, this thing had happened. She had a beautiful woman in her bed, and here she was in her office, sipping coffee to jolt her back to her life. Her real life. The life where she was a straight, respected, and responsible professional woman.

She knew that Teagan would be there when she got home because she didn't have any transportation back to Desert Haven. Warmth radiated from her solar plexus to her heart and down to her nether regions. Thinking about Teagan thrilled her. But that didn't mean she was a lesbian.

Did it? She closed her eyes, and steamy scenes from last night replayed for her. Jerking back to the present situation, she felt her cheeks glow warmly. She embarrassed herself with such thoughts, especially at work. But most of all, she was terribly sleepy and just wanted to take a nap—with Teagan.

Her omelet was getting cold, and globules of fat congealed in the bottom of the Styrofoam box. Her stomach flipped and she knew she had to go home. Maybe she was getting a bug? Grabbing her coffee cup, she rushed past her secretary saying she wasn't feeling well, shouldn't have come in, and to please cancel her appointments for the day. Hurrying to the garage, she felt like she was getting away with something.

The convertible was still topless, and the wind revived her on her short ride home. Not waiting for the elevator, she climbed the stairs to her apartment, each step elevating her mood. No signs of life in the living room, so she went straight to the bedroom. Teagan was sprawled across the queen bed, arms spread like angel wings, her torso and legs demurely covered with a white damask sheet. Her auburn hair fanned across the pile of pillows. Alice's heart pushed out against her ribs, expanding to a size she didn't recognize.

Teagan must have sensed she was being watched because her eyes fluttered and opened after a few seconds. Alice held her breath as her lover returned to consciousness.

"Good morning."

"What time is it?" asked a confused Teagan.

"Eight-thirty. I've already been to work and came home again."

"Is it eight at night?"

Alice laughed at the logical but wrong conclusion. "No, I was just there for an hour, and I left because I am bone tired. You kept me up all night, remember."

Teagan grinned. She was about to speak, but quickly her expression turned from smiles to confusion and then fear. She jerked up to sitting, brows knit, eyes wide open, letting the sheet fall to her lap. Alice took a moment to appreciate the lovely breasts in front of her before the next sentence that she knew would ruin the moment.

"Oh fuck, what about Sam? I'm in deep shit," Teagan said.

"You don't happen to have an open relationship, do you?"

"Hell no! She going to be pisssssssed," Teagan hissed, drawing out the "s," illustrating the extent of the anger that she was going to face when she went home. She curled herself into a ball, tipped over on her side, and pulled the covers over her head.

Alice thought it was so darn cute, but she didn't think it was the appropriate moment to say so. Instead, she said, "I need to get you home, but, honestly, I'm way too tired to drive right now. How about I get some sleep for an hour or two, and then we can head out?"

A hand snaked out from under the covers, searching blindly for something to grab. It landed on Alice's side and began to tug at her shirt.

A muffled, "Come here." Alice cautiously peeked under the covers, and a face greeted her with a kiss.

They woke at one-thirty and were starving. After quick showers, they went to the café across the street for tofu scramble with multigrain biscuits.

"What the hell are we doing?"

"What will we say to Sam?"

"We are rotten for hurting her."

"Are we assuming too much? Do you want to be with me? Are we a couple now? Where are we going to live?" Alice's heart was beating, boom boom in her throat. She couldn't catch her breath. Anxiety attack or love? The intensity of her feelings closed down avenues to her brain. Her fine mind was on vacation, letting other parts of her anatomy have their way with her. She wasn't afraid; she was numbly above it all.

Teagan said, "You did nothing wrong. I'm the one who betrayed Sam." Tears dribbled down her chin, where they hung like melted icicles.

They watched each other's expressions carefully for clues. They knew they were deeply in limerence, that state of irrational bliss that comes before reality sets in, and they didn't want anything to disrupt it. Alice wanted to say the right things to make Teagan stay with her. They danced around each other's feelings and their own, not delving too deeply, just in case there was nothing underneath it all. No foundation. Just the scaffolding of a new precarious structure responding to the swirl of their emotions. Teetering but not falling. But maybe falling in love.

"Sam's going to be so pissed off at me. She has a nasty temper, so it's going to be a scene, but I need to tell her. I need to let her know that things have changed," Teagan said, slipping her hand into Alice's, staring into her eyes, asking for it to be okay.

Fortified by the hearty meal, they decided to drive out to Desert Haven and face the music. Alice took the scenic route through the mountains, dragging it out even longer. They pretended to enjoy the scenery, each lost in her thoughts.

Just before reaching the dirt lane that led to Desert Haven's driveway, Alice pulled over to the side of the road.

"What are we going to say?" She rested her head on the steering wheel momentarily and then looked up, as if surprised where she was. "All of this is so freaky, so new, so unexpected. I don't have my bearings."

"Would you just like to leave me here and go?" Teagan asked softly.

Alice felt a surge of guilt mixed with lust. "Oh, no! I thought we were in this together."

"That's just what I wanted you to say," Teagan said and leaned over for a long, lingering kiss. "I guess we just tell Sam the truth. We fell in love. It was magic. I'm sorry to hurt her, but not sorry. I'm thrilled. But I won't tell her that part."

"Okay, we got a plan. I'm behind you, babe." Alice said, shocked at her own words, especially the babe part. Where did that come from?

The Saab crept down the lane, Alice slowly navigating the ruts and dust. She turned into the driveway like last night. Just last night! She parked the car in the same space. Not even twenty-four hours! They got out of the vehicle, and Teagan led the way to the shed. Were eyes following their journey? Were the women going to hate Alice, the outsider, for stealing away one of them?

The door was hanging open. Teagan stepped up to the threshold, looking at a whirlwind of clothing strewn across the bed.

"What's going on here?" she said, picking up a few garments, holding them up to Alice. "My clothes. They are torn and cut, like with a knife." She looked confused. Alice stepped closer, trying to grasp the situation, putting her arm around Teagan's waist.

Two pillows laid naked, feathers leaking from ripped cloth. The quilt was torn apart, and the mattress was slashed. Alice held Teagan tighter as they moved to the kitchen ramada, surveying smashed jars and dented pots tossed to the ground. The hotplate cord was severed and hung ominously from a broken ocotillo rib.

Alice kept silent, watching, waiting, ready to offer solace. Teagan slowly walked around the perimeter of the kitchen space. She stopped in front of Alice, a small, uncertain smile playing across her face. Her shoulders rose to her ears and then fell in a gesture of surrender. "I guess I don't have to explain anything."

Thea 1989

Thea and Ana had worked hard over the three years of their open relationship, and the fact that Ana had been dating Peggy for about a year wasn't the issue. When Ana suggested that they invite Peggy to move in with them, Thea realized adjustments would be necessary and called for a family meeting.

The kitchen table was set with mugs of steaming tea, a lined notepad, and colored pens when Ana sat down across from Thea. Their hands reached across the table for a reassuring touch.

"Where shall we begin?" Thea asked. "First, I want to say that I trust your honesty."

"And I trust yours."

They smiled at each other, not quite knowing how to start the conversation. Finally, Ana jumped in.

"Peggy has such a long commute from Littleton," Ana said. "It would be much more efficient if she shared our Capitol Hill apartment. It's easy to get anywhere in Denver from here." She drew a line down the center of the pad, put a plus on one side with the green pen, and wrote 'commute' under it.

"I don't know," Thea said. "I like that you spend a day there, and she spends a day with us. It seems like it works. Why change it?" She turned the pad towards her and wrote 'part-time' in the other column in red ink.

"I think that you and Peggy need to get to know each other better," Ana countered. "It's great when we are all in bed together, and I want more of that. More of us time." She entered 'us time' on the line under commute.

"What I hear you say is that you want a triad instead of a primary plus secondary relationship like we've had," Thea said and reached for their copy of *The Ethical Slut: A Practical Guide to Polyamory, Open*

Relationships & Other Adventures, not opening the book but holding it as a talisman.

"I know you will love her as much as I do," Ana said, smiling as if to encourage the love.

"I think she's a very kind person," Thea said, twirling a random bit of string around two fingers. "She's easy to get along with, and I like our lovemaking."

Ana wrote 'sex' in the positive column.

Thea turned the pad toward herself and wrote 'lack of alone time.' She knew a lot depended on her response, and the pressure was beginning to feel overwhelming. "A triad. I've got to think this out. How about we reschedule. Say five o'clock? Okay?"

"Sounds fair," Ana said. "I love that you are willing to grow and change with me. You are the best." She got up and kissed the top of Thea's head, saying, "See you back at the table at five."

Thea leaned back, sipping her tea, placing the balled-up string in her pocket. This wasn't the first time Ana brought up the subject of Peggy moving in, and Thea understood that it was a turning point. She had to figure out what she wanted.

She liked Peggy. Peggy was a calming influence on fiery Ana. The two of them were athletic and outdoorsy, so Ana would have a real hiking buddy. Thea could never keep up with her jock girlfriend, and now she wouldn't have to try.

It would be good to have someone else to help with the rent and household chores. Thea knew something weird was going on with her physically, but she couldn't put her finger on it. She had trouble keeping up with her share of simple tasks and tired easily. Even vacuuming was enough to prompt a nap. She didn't want to be a complainer, and if Peggy lived with them, there would be enough going on that she could get by without calling attention to herself.

She'd been to Peggy's apartment and approved of her tidy, minimalist style, something definitely in her favor. If two people valued an orderly environment, Ana would be more likely to pick up after herself.

The more Thea thought about it, the more she liked the idea.

She knew that living together successfully as a triad was going to involve lots of negotiating and compromises. She and Ana would no longer be the primary couple, they would morph into a relationship with all three women having equal rights and responsibilities. A Triad. They were already challenging societal norms and expectations by being out-lesbians in an open relationship. Was this the logical conclusion? Was it the right thing for all of them?

At five o'clock, they faced each other across the table. Ana looked tense with uncertainty. Thea fingered the string in her pocket, calming herself.

"Well, what do you think?" Ana asked, nodding her head as if to lead Thea's consent.

Thea smiled and nodded. "I think it's a great idea. If Peggy will have us, let's become a Triad."

Ana whooped and rushed over to hug Thea, almost toppling the table. They held each other close, acknowledging the end of what they had built together and the beginning of a fresh future. Kissing Thea's ear and then the tip of her nose, Ana said, "I love you. You won't regret this," and turned to the wall phone to dial Peggy's number.

Peggy moved in the following weekend, and that night, they had an intimate candlelit dinner of take-out Indian food to celebrate.

The Ethical Slut became their study guide. They talked schedules, cried about their primitive jealous feelings, and joyfully romped together in bed. When Thea discovered a support group for "Possible Relationships" offered through Denver Free University, they all signed up.

"Now that we've met people in so many different combinations of relationships," Thea said to her girlfriends one evening over Ana's vegetarian spaghetti carbonara dinner, "our lesbian Triad seems simple. Gay men married to lesbians, people transitioning to other genders who have to negotiate with their spouses, cross-continental part-time married people, those are really complicated loving relationships."

The three women were in their thirties, but they each approached physical fitness through different lenses. Ana worked out regularly at the Y and played softball in the lesbian league. Peggy didn't have a car, so she biked all over town. Thea was the slouch. She would rather read a book than take a walk. Ana teased her, cajoled her, bribed her, and sometimes got her to try something new, but it always ended up with Thea in a humiliated funk. The world of sports and activities was dangerous. Roller skating = broken wrist. Frisbee = turned ankle. She was already in enough pain; she didn't want to court more. Thea prided herself on being open and honest, but there was a lot that she didn't tell her girlfriends.

Like shooting lower back pains, aches in her fingers and wrists, swollen ankles. Some weird fungus on two of her toenails, tooth pain caused by long roots that reached into her sinuses. For someone her age, Thea had a passel of unexpressed complaints. Monthly injections helped her deal with allergies to mulberry trees, ragweed, any kind of pollen, cat and dog dander, bed mites, hard cheese, groundnuts, wheat, and oats. Thyroid pills boosted an underactive gland. The list of things that plagued her was ridiculously long, but thankfully, most things came and went. Thea was thirty-four years old with an embarrassing laundry list of ailments that rivaled any old lady.

But she didn't let her significant others know about them. She needed the illusion of keeping up, trying to fit in. Ana got impatient with her, but Peggy was understanding and kind. In this three-legged relationship they were inventing, Thea believed that each leg had to be as strong as the others. She needed to pull her weight and was afraid to wimp out. As an equal partner, she wanted to feel good about her contribution. When she limped off to a hot shower and bed at seven-thirty, it was seen as her quirkiness. She never told them about the exhaustion, and they didn't know the truth hidden behind her fears.

After a year of settling into a routine that suited everyone's style, the itch for creating something new began nagging at them. They had been endlessly discussing alternative home building methods, growing seasons, and supportive communities. They studied compassionate compromise and non-violent communication in preparation for communal living. So, when Peggy announced she thought they should quit their jobs and leave Denver, no one was surprised.

Even though Thea had second thoughts about leaving her position at the university library, the lure of women's land was strong. She took over research and planning. After much casual discussion, they held an official family meeting sitting cross-legged in a circle on the living room floor.

"I think we all agree that the off-grid women's community in Southern Arizona is our best choice," Thea said, shuffling a stack of papers and looking tentatively at her girlfriends. "I, for one, won't miss the snow of another Denver winter."

"Let's leave the capitalist rat race behind and get ourselves to Desert Haven!" Ana said.

"All in favor, say aye," Peggy said, pointing to her eye.

"Our new lives are about to begin. We'll follow the sun," Thea said, and just then, the lyrics of the Madonna tape they had been listening to rang out:

> *Traveling down this road*
> *Watching the signs as I go*
> *I think I'll follow the sun*

Shocked, surprised, joyfully, they leaped up and danced around the small room, sexily bumping into each other, saying, "It's an omen. It is meant to be."

Arms spread wide, Peggy said, "Long live the Triad!" their rallying cry that demanded a group hug.

Later, snuggled in bed, listening to the quiet breathing of her sleeping companions, Thea wondered if her health would be better or worse in the country. How much physical effort would be required of her and could she handle it?

◆ ◆ ◆

The first snowfall caught them at the Colorado/New Mexico border. After the sheer terror of driving over Raton Pass on nearly bald tires, the rest of the trip was smooth sailing. Ana and Peggy took turns driving the Subaru while Thea was the backseat sandwich maker, DJ, and narrator of all she saw and thought.

"That cloud looks like a long train, getting smaller in the distance. There's an eagle, or is it a vulture?" She propped her pillow against the cooler and drifted in and out of sleep. When she awoke, she related every detail of the dream until Ana asked her to play some music. Thea kept a continual stream of upbeat songs coming from their boombox. Except for Sarah McLachlan's "Angel," which just ripped her heart out, and she couldn't get enough of it.

The tape deck's batteries ran down just as they crossed the Arizona border, so for the rest of the trip, they tried to find something other than country music on the radio.

Even though Desert Haven looked like a primitive campsite with few amenities, the place was teeming with residents on its ten acres when the Triad arrived. It seemed that lots of lesbians wanted to get out of the cold. Looking around, they saw some trailers, occupied vans, and even a few cars that looked like they could be sleeping quarters. A few brightly colored tents dotted the landscape.

The Triad emerged from their car, excited by all the activity.

"Let's see what's going on," Ana said and led them to a group of women pouring a concrete slab. "Hi. I'm Ana, and these are my partners, Thea and Peggy. We'd like to stay awhile. Who should we talk to?"

"Just find a space that suits you, and we can settle up later," said a very tanned middle-aged woman, holding a trowel dripping with concrete. "We have to get this done while it's still light. I'm JoJo, and I live in the green trailer."

After a quick survey of available areas, they cleared a flat space by pushing aside cholla buds and other prickly desert debris, laid down a blue tarp, and pitched their three-person tent. After arranging the blow-up mattresses and tossing their sleeping bags into the tent, Ana set up their camp table and three identical sunshine-yellow folding chairs. Thea brought out a box of Cheerios and three bananas, Peggy came up with the milk carton, and they ate their dinner next to a tree with bright green bark.

Dinner finished, they took a quick stroll around the compound before it got too dark, meeting other residents, and introducing themselves as a bonded Triad. Everyone they met seemed quite accepting – to their faces, of course. Who knew what was said behind closed doors? Or tent flaps.

"You were middle last night, so you are over on this side tonight," Peggy said, sorting out where she belonged, pulling her pillow behind her.

Their arrangement of rotating bed positions had the center woman move to the right, and whoever had been on the left moved to the center. Sometimes Thea forgot where to go, and she appreciated Peggy keeping track for her.

It turns out it's cold in the desert at night in the winter. They were a puppy pile of shivering and icy toes. Their thin summer-weight sleeping bags were not going to make it. The following day, Peggy went looking for a solution, and she came back from the lost and found with three puffy mummy bags, abandoned by former residents. The only problem was now they were separated by down. Or synthetic down. Their lovemaking became a ballet of covered and uncovered skin, putting on and taking off strategic pieces of wool clothing, and getting tangled in the long extension cord of the vibrator. They decided the next purchase would be a battery-run model.

At the first community meeting three days after their arrival, Thea counted thirteen faces. The topic at hand was what to do about the male child who was living in Martie's trailer. Her four-year-old grandson had come for a visit, but then the poor boy's mother went off on a binge with her no-good father, and the two of them ended up in jail for six months after a ruckus in a liquor store.

Could the community abide a penis, no matter how small, living amongst them for the next five and a half months? Everyone knew he was a nice boy who didn't cause any trouble.

"But he still has male energy," said a woman with a long grey braid, 'and it's interfering with Desert Haven's female vibration."

Martie, having lived in the community for eight years, was a veteran of negotiation. She offered to pay the water bill for the whole time he was there as a payment for the disruption. That seemed to appease everyone as a fair compromise. She just had to promise she would not let him pee outside in sight of any lesbian eyes.

Just as the meeting seemed to be coming to an end, a thin woman with wispy brown hair said she'd like to have a minute to discuss something that affected her and possibly other women as well. She stammered and looked very uncomfortable to be in the spotlight.

"I have fibromyalgia," she said quietly, almost in a whisper. "There are many things that make my condition worse."

She paused and gazed around the room. A few women nodded their heads and Martie said, "It's okay. Go on."

"Like scents from strong cooking odors or perfumes and shampoos. They set me off. I know I can't tell people what to cook, and I can just stay away from your kitchens, but I would like to request that people not use scented products in public spaces like the bathhouse and community house. If you want to know about alternative products to use, I can help." She looked exhausted and ended with, "If you don't know me, my name is Juniper."

Thea was stunned. She had no idea that her objection to scents was something shared by other people. She thought it was just one of her annoying sensitivities. Holy shit, maybe it's part of a syndrome or something. Talking with Juniper was number one on her to-do list (there was no number two.)

It wasn't hard to find Juniper in her station wagon outfitted with some of the comforts of home. Thea saw bedding and a jumble of cardboard boxes piled in the back as they sat on two milk crates by the open tailgate.

"All these weird and seemingly unrelated symptoms have been plaguing me for years," Juniper said. "I had a job with insurance, so I went to a bunch of doctors, but no one could figure it out. They finally sent me to a psychologist because they thought it was all in my head. I lost the insurance when I couldn't work anymore. I came here to try to heal in the company of women. And, frankly, because it's all I can afford."

Juniper paused to catch her breath. "Sorry, I don't usually do so much talking; I pretty much keep to myself. But I've done all sorts of research, and I'm happy to answer any questions."

"This is a little personal, but maybe you can tell me," Thea said, "Since coming to Desert Haven, I've been constipated, and I thought it might be because of the toilet situation not being very private. But now I wonder, is that part of the syndrome?"

"It could be. It's different for everyone. Are you cold all the time? I am. Do you get heavy periods?"

"Oh boy, do I. All three of us are pretty much on the same cycle, but mine lasts longer, and I can be a real bitch. Just ask my girlfriends," Thea said with a laugh. "This is fascinating. What else?"

"Do you have specific tender points all over your body? Here, can I try a few? I won't push hard." With Thea's permission, Juniper leaned over and gingerly tapped two spots on the tops of her shoulders.

"Ouch."

Juniper touched Thea's upper chest and the outside of her elbows, eliciting the same response. "Sorry. I was touching you lightly. You are very sensitive."

"Damn, don't I know it. I always felt pain more than anyone else and thought I was just being a baby. But knowing there can be a reason is very reassuring. Now, what do I do about it? How can I get well?"

"That's the bad part," Juniper said, and looked up as if trying to find the answer in the sky. "There is no cure, just symptom management. Don't bother going to the doctor. They don't believe that FM is real, and they will come up with a bunch of expensive tests to try to find another cause. I'm sorry."

"At least there are two of us trying to figure this out now," Thea said, trying to reassure Juniper because she looked so down.

Thea returned to the Triad space, where she found Ana and Peggy passing a beer bottle back and forth. "Hey Thea, this is the last beer," Peggy said, "It's kind of warm. Want a sip?"

"Naw, go ahead. How was your hike?"

"Great," Ana said, peeling off her daypack and setting it on the ground. "We found a trail up to a peak with amazing views. It is so beautiful here."

Peggy took the last sip from the bottle and placed it in the recycling can. "And Ana saved my life."

"What!" Thea said, looking from one to the other to decide if they were kidding her.

"We were at the very top of the mountain. It was a steep climb, so I must have been a little tired. I was leaning over to take a picture when I felt myself losing balance," Peggy said. "I yelled and almost tipped over the cliff. Lucky for me, Ana has great reflexes. She grabbed my arm and pulled me back. It was scary."

"Thank the Goddess I was in the right place at the right time, or you'd be pretty banged up," Ana added.

The intimacy the two of them shared from a near-death experience made Thea feel left out and sad. She'd never get to have that kind of thrilling adventure. She didn't really care to but she wanted to be part of the group experience. She needed a way in—a connection that all of them could share.

"How about a group nap and snuggle after lunch?" she proposed.

"Maybe after a group shower," Peggy said, "If there is enough water in the tank for three, that is."

The following afternoon, Thea called a family meeting. The women gathered around their table in the warm sunshine with cups of steaming dandelion tea. Now that she had Juniper as an ally, Thea felt strong enough to confess that she had been suffering from pain and fatigue for several years.

"I just thought you were a couch potato bookworm and left it at that," Ana said. I didn't know you had a disease." She tipped back on her lawn chair as if trying to distance herself.

"It's not catching, you know," Thea told her.

"Well, I don't know. After all these years, you are telling me now. How could you keep such a thing from me?" Ana replied.

"Oh, Thea, I'm so sorry you felt you had to keep it a secret," Peggy said.

"I just didn't want to dwell on it," Thea said. "But, you know, you are what you think, that sort of thing. I thought if I ignored it, it would go away. So, excuse me if I want to maintain a positive attitude."

"A lot of good that did. You are still sick. You haven't been out of that chair all day," Ana said. Then her tone softened, and she added, "I'm worried about you, girlfriend. You need to let me help you."

"I can help too," Peggy said. "We are all in this together, right Triad? But please, don't hide from us anymore, okay?"

Thea felt tears sliding down her cheeks and a hollow emptiness in her chest. By shedding her secrets, she had made room for more feelings, and as they tumbled in, she felt a sting of pain and joy. Her Triad was there for her. She knew it before, but now she felt it.

While Ana and Peggy organized tag football games or went for long runs down deserted dusty roads, Thea reached out to others in the community in her own way. She and Juniper met with JoJo to talk about safety for those women who had chemical sensitivities. JoJo didn't use weed killers or synthetic fertilizers in the garden, so she was on the same wavelength, agreeing it would be good to avoid scents and other toxic chemicals. The three of them made a list of suspect products and possible alternatives. They posted the list in the bathhouse and the community room.

When Thea read the list at the next community meeting, the women agreed in principle but grumbled about having to buy more expensive products. Someone said she had read an article in Mother Earth News about making soap and lotions from natural ingredients. A lengthy discussion ensued, and the idea was abandoned when it was discovered that they needed rendered fat and lye. Two items that were in short supply at the Haven.

Thea found the library in the community room and began reading her way through it. The move had finally caught up with her, and she was bone-achingly fatigued. It was about all she could do to drag her butt out of bed into a camp chair every day.

On good days, she carried a low stool into the garden and pulled weeds. She loved the healing of hands in the dirt. The slow and quiet rhythm of her days was becoming her new normal. But something had to happen. The Triad was running out of money. Their small stash from selling their belongings in Denver was dwindling. Luckily, their expenses were ridiculously low— rent, a share of the utilities (minus the water bill until Martie's grandson moved), and food. Mostly, they ate beans and rice with fresh vegetables. Ana made salsa with tomatoes and chili peppers from the garden for the entire community. It was their fix of vitamin C, and they swore it would ward off any germ that happened to be around. But beans and rice weren't free at the co-op.

Ana called a family meeting. Huddled together in the corner of the community room, snuggled into an orange vinyl booth pulled out of a diner, warmed by the potbelly stove, Thea knew that this conversation was important for determining their future. They needed to generate some income. Thea had the skills for a better-paying job, but physically, she couldn't imagine being able to work. Peggy had been a nurse's aide and a waitress, but mostly she was a dancer. Ana's past careers included apprentice bricklayer, temporary letter carrier, sports gear salesclerk, and DJ.

"How do the other women survive out here?" Peggy asked.

"I'll do a little research," Thea offered.

She did an informal poll. Two women were teachers, and one was a plumber. Others lived on savings and did odd jobs. One woman lived on inherited money, Juniper was on disability, and JoJo had a retirement pension.

That night, over dinner, Thea presented her findings. Ana said, "How about you go on disability, Thea?"

"Oh, sure, fibromyalgia, the disease that doctors think is fake or doesn't exist,"

"Juniper gets a check. You should ask her who her doctor is."

"Jeez, this is embarrassing, Thea said, covering her face with her hands. She peeked out. "Do you really want me to ask for money for being sick?"

"Yes."

Thea felt ganged up on, but she had to admit it might be a good idea. She seemed to be more nervous and anxious lately. Maybe it was hypoglycemia. She got lightheaded walking up even the slightest incline. Pretending to be checking out the vista, she slowed her inhalations to catch her breath. Every morning, her left hip hurt so bad she had to do a series of exercises inside her sleeping bag before she could even get up. Mostly, she just watched when the Triad had sex. It was too much work to participate.

"Maybe I will. But I still want you both to make an effort to bring in some money. We might have to move, you know."

Heads slowly bobbed in agreement.

"Okay. Let's go into town tomorrow and check it out. I'll go to welfare or whichever place handles disability checks and find out what I need. I should borrow Juniper's cane to look more convincing." Thea got up and pantomimed walking with a limp, leaning on an invisible stick.

"You've been so good at hiding your ailments I wonder what you would look like if you let it all hang out," Ana said.

"Is that a dig?" Thea asked, feeling a little defensive.

"No, not at all," Ana said, raising her hands as if to show she had no weapons. "I just can't imagine how you covered up for so long. Didn't you trust me? We've been together for four years, and I had no idea."

"I didn't want you to think I couldn't keep up with you. Of course, I couldn't anyway. Once Peggy came along, I thought, great, now Ana has someone to play with, and the pressure is off me. But I have to admit, sometimes I am envious of all the time you two spend together."

She had their full attention. This was the kind of straight talk that they prided themselves on.

"Maybe a better way to think about it," Peggy said, reaching out and taking Thea's hand in hers, "is that you have two people who love you that you can count on instead of just one," Both women blinked back tears and looked toward Ana.

"Now, let's not get all weepy," Ana said, her gaze embracing Thea and then Peggy. She reached out her arms for a hug and said, "We are family, and we'll always be here for each other. Long live the Triad."

Marga (and Sparrow) 1995

The ad said: Grow food year-round. 10 acres of beautiful Sonoran Desert. Looking for adventurous women to join us on established women's land. Pets welcome. Write JoJo, P.O. Box 212, Tucson, AZ for more info.

"Holy shit, take a look at this," Sparrow said, waving the San Diego Gay Times in front of her girlfriend's face. "This is exactly what we are looking for. A community of women who share our values, respect Mother Earth, and want to create an organic farm together."

Marga snatched the paper from her lover's hand and held it close to her nearsighted eyes. Her head moved side to side as she read the words. Sparrow leaned back on the blanket, burying her feet in the sand, arching her back so her exposed midriff would get maximum sun.

"Where is this Sonoran Desert, and wouldn't it be hot there?" Marga asked, eyes squinting, bushy eyebrows scrunched.

"It says here it's in Arizona." Sparrow hadn't traveled out of California in her twenty-five years, unlike Marga, who left her home in Germany seven years ago and traveled all over before landing in Southern California. "Have you been there?"

"I think the bus went through it. Lots of nothing, as I recall. But not as barren as North Africa."

"Well, this place must be an oasis in the desert," Sparrow said. When her girlfriend looked puzzled, she said, "Oasis, a place with water and palm trees."

Marga gestured to the row of trees lining the boardwalk and then to the ocean fifteen yards away. "Is this an oasis?"

"No silly, it's just the beach," Sparrow said, brushing her hand across Marga's crew cut.

Sparrow had been thinking that she needed to get the hell out of the city. After high school, she saw no reason to move away like many of her friends did, so for the past few years, she got along on odd jobs, still living with her parents, but San Diego had just gotten too big and too crazy for her. When she was growing up, everyone knew everyone, and it was an easy place to live. Her parents, Amy and Len, migrated west in 1970 to escape Montana winters and find the hippie culture they read about in Life Magazine. They settled in Ocean Beach, where Sparrow and her younger brother, Digger, were born. Her dad occasionally worked as a house painter, and sometimes her mom put on a ruffled apron and hairnet for a double shift at the Fish Shack, just enough for them to get by. Mostly, it was about surfing, beachcombing for lost trinkets and spare change, and growing food in their tiny backyard two blocks from the beach. But the neighborhood had gentrified, and it didn't feel cozy to her anymore.

Jumping up, Sparrow proclaimed, "Let's get wet," and ran into the water, looking back over her shoulder. Margo lagged behind, dodging the splashes of cold water Sparrow stirred up, lingering at the water's edge. Sparrow came back and grabbed her hand.

"Come on, girlfriend, let's play," Sparrow said, pulling Marga seaward. "How come you won't come in with me?"

"I told you I don't like waves. They are too powerful. I'm fine right here. You go, and I'll watch."

"You told me the name Marga means 'pearl.' And pearls come from the ocean, don't they?"

Marga shook off Sparrow's hand as she stood solid, gazing at her toes in the lapping tide.

"Did you ever drown or something?"

"Not in this lifetime," Marga said, turning her palms to Sparrow and shooing her away. "Go ahead, have fun, Honey. I'll be right here."

Sparrow tucked her windblown hair behind her ears, and, shrugging her shoulders, she turned and ran back to the waves.

The day they met, three months ago, they literally bumped into each other at the corner of Robinson and Sixth at the Pride Parade. Marga was in the street trying to get a better view when a security guard told her to get on the sidewalk, and she backed up right into the arms of her future girlfriend.

"Sorry, I should have looked where I was going," Marga said, checking out the cute blond she had almost run over.

"No damage done," Sparrow graciously offered.

"I just got into town, and the first thing I do is bump into a beautiful lady. Lucky me. Do you mind if I hang out here with you?"

Sparrow's wide grin indicated her agreement.

Together, they cheered parade marshal Greg Louganis, drank beer, whistled at seven-foot-tall drag queens, and danced furiously to the pounding DJ sounds of Sister Sledge and Donna Summer.

By two a.m., they were no longer drunk, and exhaustion was setting in, but they didn't want to part. Sparrow lived with her parents and brother in a three-room house, so they decided to drive to Marga's motel.

"I parked my car in an alley." Marga whispered loudly, "But which one? I'm so embarrassed to lead you on this wild animal chase."

Sparrow smiled in the dark and said, "I think you mean wild goose chase." Holding hands, giggling, they finally found Marga's Mercedes after a circuitous search. A parking ticket waited under the windshield wiper.

It was close to four o'clock when they got to the Mission Bay Motel. Sparrow fell onto the bed, pulled a pillow under her head, and was asleep almost instantly. Marga carefully curled up near Sparrow, close but not too close, and drifted off.

At eleven o'clock, a sharp knock on the door and a man's voice woke them. "It's check-out time unless you want to pay for another day."

"You have any money?" Sparrow asked, sitting up in bed. "I spent all of mine on beer last night."

"Guess we'll just have to leave," Marga said with a sly grin, getting up and peeking out the window between a gap in the blackout curtains.

"Wait a minute. I just spent my first night with a girl, and I didn't even get to kiss her," Sparrow put on a pouty face and tried to make it sound like a joke to hide her disappointment. She wondered if she had violated some lesbian code or ritual in her ignorance.

Marga came over and sat on the edge of the bed. "Really? I didn't know. Let's fix that right now, she said, leaning in for a kiss. "We can stay another day if you like." Sparrow slowly sank back to horizontal with the gentle pressure of Marga's body.

Around three in the afternoon, they went across the street for tacos and beer for breakfast. Staring into each other's eyes, holding hands under the table, grinning, Sparrow said, "I guess I'm a lesbian now."

Sparrow never liked the idea of being pigeonholed into defining her sexuality. When pushed, she would claim bisexual for lack of a better term. Her relationships were casual and brief, so she never felt the need to commit to a label. But this. This was special. Marga, with her pale sky-blue eyes and gorgeous muscles. Her adorable German accent. This was love. And if she loved a woman, then it followed that she must be a lesbian.

After breakfast, they bought a six-pack of Dos Equis Amber and brought it back to bed with them. By the time they vacated the room the following morning at ten-forty-five, they had a plan. Marga had a two-person backpacking tent they could pitch in Sparrow's parent's backyard, over in the corner, near the alley. Sparrow said she sometimes slept in the garden anyway—it was better than sharing a room with her brother.

"Won't your parents think it's weird or wrong or something to bring home a girl?"

"Nah, they're cool. They have always let me and my brother do our own thing. They won't judge you if that's what you are afraid of. My brother is a stoner, and they don't care."

They parked in front of a small cottage on a side street near the ocean. Amy was sitting in a yellow Adirondack chair on the tiny front porch, mostly covered by the zigzag patterned orange and green afghan she was crocheting.

"Hi, Mom. Looks like you're almost done with it," Sparrow said, leaning down to plant a kiss on her mother's cheek.

"It's for Emily's daughter's wedding next week," Amy said, turning to Marga, "Hi. You like the colors?"

"Nice and bright."

"Mom, this is my new friend Marga. We met at Gay Pride. I guess I could say she's my new girlfriend."

"Nice to meet you, Marga," Amy said, looking up and smiling while keeping her crochet rhythm.

Sparrow said they were going to pitch a tent in the backyard, and Amy nodded.

Marga joined the little family smoothly, taking her turn washing up after family dinners or pulling weeds and tending plants in the garden. Some evenings, they sat on the tiny front porch, having a beer with Amy and Len. If Digger was there, he would pass a joint or two. Marga didn't say much, but she seemed to enjoy the chatter.

When asked about her knowledge of plants, Marga said her father taught her about growing medicinal plants like arnica, *Johanniskraut*, and chamomile.

"What is that word, something kraut?" Sparrow asked.

"You call it St. John's wort. It's useful for depression."

Every night, they held each other in the coziness of their nest. Some nights, Marga cried out or whimpered from a bad dream, but Sparrow held her, soothing her back to sleep. Marga never talked about her dreams, and Sparrow never asked.

Sparrow wanted to contribute to the family, so she took some babysitting and dog walking jobs. Marga always had cash to pitch in. They hung out at the beach, meeting up with Sparrow's high school friends who hadn't moved away for college. While the old friends gabbed about people she didn't know, complaining about the rich kids and their snobbery, Marga read books about writing. Hunching over a small spiral-bound notebook, she took notes with a stubby pencil that she sharpened with her ever-present Swiss army knife.

"I think you should have your eyes tested," Sparrow said. She was worried that Marga couldn't see and wondered if she was too vain to wear glasses.

"Will you come with me? I've never had my eyes tested before, so I don't know what to expect."

Leaving the optometrist with a prescription, Sparrow drove them to pick out glasses because Marga's eyes were dilated. They both tried on dozens of frames, entertaining themselves with the most outrageous of choices. After waving off the salesclerks for almost an hour, Marga finally settled on large, bright red frames.

"You look very sexy in them," Sparrow said, evoking a grateful smile.

Sparrow was never much of a reader, and she felt slightly inadequate around her literary girlfriend. She took to toting gardening catalogs around and studied them like they were religious tomes. Her interest in growing vegetables and herbs became an obsession, and she talked about her desire to have a garden of her own to everyone. When the ad in the Gay Times caught her eye, it seemed like it was written just for her and Marga.

They began to plan their move.

"This old junker isn't going to make the drive to Arizona," Marga said, frustrated at having to pull over and open the hood to let the engine cool down. "It's fifteen years old, and I don't trust it anymore."

When it died on the Pacific Coast Highway, she had it towed to Import Car Repair, where they learned it was a blown head gasket and cracked engine block. The car needed a new engine, and it would cost four thousand dollars.

Sparrow said, "Jesus, that's a lot of money!"

"I don't want to drive something dangerous, and I don't want to put any more money into this old car," Marga said. "How much will you give me for it."

The mechanic said it wasn't worth shit in this condition, and he'd give her $200. She signed it over. It was enough money for two bus tickets to Tucson.

Len dropped them off at the San Diego Transit Center to catch the 6:45 a.m. bus.

"Since this is your first big trip out of Southern California, you get the window seat," Marga said, swinging her backpack into the overhead shelf. "Get comfortable; it will be a long ride."

They traveled through El Centro and Calexico. By nine a.m., they were ready for a breakfast of banana and honey sandwiches that Amy had packed for them. In Yuma, they bought a tube of Pringles and a Pepsi to share.

The highway became flat and straight, and Marga's head bobbed against the seatback, slumping over onto Sparrow's shoulder. She wasn't snoring, but her breathing was audible, something that Sparrow found adorable. Sparrow was too excited to sleep. Looking out the window at the miles of desert, she wondered about the women she would meet and if she could grow things in a place with no water. The land grew browner with each passing mile, through Gila Bend and Phoenix, to their final destination.

At the Tucson bus station, Marga held the letter they had received from JoJo up to the light so she could see it better. The instructions said to call a woman named Eagle when they got to town. She dug a quarter out of her pocket and dialed the payphone.

"Hello. This is Marga. Is this Eagle? JoJo told us that you can help us get out to Desert Haven."

"Sure, where are you?"

"The Greyhound bus station."

"Downtown. It's too late to go out to the land tonight, so I'll come and get you, and you can spend the night at my house. I'm not too far from where you are."

"That's very nice of you. We will have to get something to eat first, I'm afraid."

"No problem, I have a pot of beans going. Happy to share. I'll pick you up outside the bus depot."

After a short drive, Eagle parked in front of a large three-story brick structure with a deep porch facing the street.

"Wow, is that your house?" Sparrow said. "It's huge."

"It's six different apartments. My name is on the lease for the whole building, but we run it as a collective."

"What does that mean?" Marga asked.

"Everyone who lives here is committed to a list of organizing principles that we have developed through consensus. Things like recycling, no men, and regular community meetings. If a living space becomes available, everyone must agree on who can move in. That sort of stuff."

Four women sitting on an assortment of chairs greeted them as they climbed the porch stairs.

"You can meet a few of my housemates. Thea, Ana, Peggy, Becka, meet Sparrow and Marga. They just got in from San Diego and are headed to Desert Haven tomorrow."

"San Diego, cool. I've always wanted to go there. Right by the ocean," said a woman whose t-shirt spelled out BECKA in child's building blocks. "So, what brings you to the desert?"

Marga sat on the top step in the shadows, but Sparrow stood, prancing in place. "We want to farm the land," she said. "We want to be with other lesbians. Not that there aren't plenty in San Diego, but you know, live with them and be part of a commune."

"We lived at the Haven for a while," Ana offered. "Had to move to town for jobs. There's no way to make a living out there."

"And if you don't have a car, you are kinda stuck out in the middle of nowhere," said Peggy.

Sparrow looked over at Marga to see how this information was received. She was afraid negative reports could unsettle Marga, but she took it as a reassuring sign when Marga smiled back at her.

"Now, don't you scare them," Eagle said. "These two young lovelies have all the enthusiasm they need to keep them on the land. I loved it out there and made a lot of friends." Then, changing the subject, she turned to Marga and said, "Say, where are you from? I hear an accent."

"Germany."

"I was there in the sixties. Hitchhiking around Europe."

The women swapped stories of their travels while the air turned cool, and the moon lit up the mountains in the west.

The next day, Eagle drove them out to the land. Pulling into the driveway and parking in a cleared area, she spied JoJo on a ladder, hammering wooden slats onto a shade structure. The three women got out of the car and stood together in front of the car. "Hey, JoJo, I've got some city slickers here for you," Eagle yelled.

JoJo backed down the ladder and walked over to the car. "So, my ad worked," she said, her bright blue eyes peering out from a large-brimmed hat, squinting at the two newcomers. Her slim frame and sun-wrinkled skin contradicted her strong, muscular arms and wiry sandaled feet. "Welcome to Desert Haven." Two dogs of indeterminate breed, one petite and brown and the other shaggy, black, and gigantic, accompanied her with enthusiastic tail waggings.

"It's great to be here," Sparrow said, giving the big dog a few head pats. "Wow, just look at the view." One hand shading her eyes, she gazed at the wavy lines of blue and grey mountains on the horizon. They reminded her, just a little, of ocean waves.

"Are there snakes here?" Marga asked, scanning the surroundings of strange spiky bushes and clumps of dried weeds. She faced her girlfriend with a what-have-you-gotten-us-into look. "I hate snakes," she said, pushing her glasses up her nose to get a better view of the landscape.

"Oh yeah, but if you don't bother them, they won't bother you." She turned to Eagle, "Thanks for bringing them out."

"No problem. I enjoy the drive, but I've got to get back now."

JoJo shifted her attention to the newcomers, "Let me show you around," she said, taking off at a brisk pace, dogs at her heels.

"This is the bathhouse and the outdoor solar shower. That's my green trailer over there next to the garden. Molly, the goat, lives in that pen. She's real sweet. Many of the women have already left for the summer, so there are just a few here right now. I'll be leaving for Oregon in a few weeks."

Striding past a palm frond roofed structure with a doorway leading underground, JoJo said, "Fran and Georgie live in the dugout. That's Marigold's bus, and the lean-to is where Jolie is staying. Marcie and Wolfie are in the shed, but they are moving over to Santa Fe in a few days, so you can have it if you want. You will meet them at the potluck tonight."

JoJo turned to make sure they were still following and wiped a red bandana across her brow. "It's getting warm already. Pitch a tent anywhere you like. There are some cleared areas, but if I were you, I would rake up any debris because you don't want pack rats that will attract the snakes."

Marga stopped walking. "Rats!"

"Oh, better safe than sorry. They really aren't much of a problem.

"I'm not sleeping on the ground with snakes and rats," Marga said. Sparrow moved over and took her hand.

"Well, you could put your sleeping bags over there on that bed platform," JoJo said, pointing to a two-by-four and plywood structure about two feet off the ground tucked under a palo verde tree. "Harmony didn't like snakes either, so she built the bed. It must have been five or six years ago. Be careful. It's a little splintery."

"That'll do just fine," Sparrow said quickly. Then, changing the subject, she said, "I'd like to see your garden."

The large round space was enclosed by a three-foot-high adobe wall fortified with green and clear glass bottles that sparkled in the sun. A ring of upright bottles formed the topmost layer, making it difficult for most critters to jump over it. The repurposed wrought iron gate looked like it came from a much more formal environment. Planted vegetable beds spoked out in wedges, and a green metal chair sat in the center, like the terminus of a labyrinth.

"That's my throne," JoJo said. "After watering in the morning, I watch the desert to see what changed while I was sleeping. Sometimes, I see a parade of javelinas on their way to breakfast or hawks cruising the cloudless sky." She pointed to two fifteen-foot-tall saguaro cactuses, one plump and green, the other a skeleton of sticks and rubble. "The cycle of growth and decline progresses with us—and without us."

In contrast to the desert landscape, the garden was a riot of green with foot-high kale and collard leaves forming a foliage blanket. Peas hung from a scaffold of wooden rods and twine, and tomato plants were protected from the midday sun by tan shade cloth. Flowers dotted the plot willy-nilly, bursts of hot pink and egg-yolk yellow. Marga smiled for the first time since they got out of the car on this warm, dusty day in this isolated patch of dilapidated huts.

"Looks good. What is that plant?" she said, plucking a leaf, crushing it between forefinger and thumb, smelling it, and chewing for a moment.

"It's cilantro. When it goes to seed, it's coriander."

"*Ach, Korianderblattern*. Are there any other herbs? Any herbs you use for medicine?"

"I don't know much about that, do you? I think that's chamomile over there," JoJo said and led Marga off to a flowering plant.

Sparrow quietly exhaled a long, slow breath of relief. She knew that Marga thought it was a crazy idea to move to a commune or whatever this was. Maybe it was. But here they were, and she wanted to make the most of it. And she wanted to hold on tight to the relationship.

That evening, they gathered under the Grandmother Tree with the other land dwellers.

"You can put your food on the picnic table," a woman who introduced herself as Marigold said. Their potluck offering, a bag of organic corn chips joined the pots of beans and rice and a huge bowl of garden-fresh salad.

Before beginning the meal, the women gathered in a circle, held hands, and expressed gratitude for the abundance of Mother Nature. Marigold started up a simple chant, and a few women joined in the chorus. The simple ceremony ended with "Namaste" and "Blessed Be," and they proceeded to the table with their plates and silverware.

"Not to worry, we always have extra if you don't have your own. My name is Fran. Georgie and I live in the underground house over there," she said, waving an arm behind her.

"Thanks," said Sparrow. "I'm Sparrow, and this is Marga. We came by bus, so we don't have a lot of belongings."

"Check in the lean-to behind the bathhouse for anything you need. Women leave stuff behind all the time. A lot of us will be leaving soon, so keep checking back. Too hot for me in the summer."

"Where are you going?"

"We're heading up to Michigan for the Music Festival. After that, I'm not sure. Maybe down to Fayetteville. We'll see how much money we make at the festival." Fran said, twirling the wiry hairs sprouting from her chin. "Our business is Tie Up and Dye. You know, tie-dye t-shirts and socks."

Marga's eyes began to wander, and Sparrow knew she'd had enough of that conversation. "Let's go get some food," she said steering them to the table. They sat on a blanket with a couple of women who had driven out from town for the potluck. Chatting was easy for Sparrow, so she soon learned their life histories. Marga kept watch for scorpions.

When Marga and Sparrow went to bed that night, they held hands and whispered into the black sky dotted with points of light. Sparrow said she was happy to be on the land. Marga said she was happy that Sparrow was happy.

After three nights in the open under the dark night sky, both women understood what it was to love the desert. They stared into the heavens as layers of stars revealed themselves, a gift for their persistence. At dawn, they woke to a shockingly blue sky and the smell of cactus flowers. Days were hot, but it cooled off the instant the sun dipped beyond the horizon. Everything seemed new and fresh.

Sleeping outside was glorious, but whenever a creepy crawly brushed Marga's ear or crept across her toe, she shrieked, batted at it, and drew up into a ball. Sparrow was amused at first but then realized how stressful it was for her girlfriend. When the shed became available, they moved right in.

The Tuff Shed was intended to store garden tools or bikes in someone's backyard, but it worked well as a shelter. Plastic textured to look like wood, rainproof, sealed to keep out bugs. It even had a window. Marcie and Wolfie had left a mattress, box spring, a metal table, and three folding chairs.

"It's even furnished!" Sparrow said. She thought it was grand. But then she was used to sharing small quarters.

Amenities were few but much appreciated. Having a flush toilet and sink with running water in the bathhouse seemed like a luxury. Over the sink, in place of a mirror, a fading poster chipped around the edges, stated *You make your own path with every step you take. That's why it's your path.* Sparrow couldn't decide if it was profound or inane.

The bath house's unfinished wooden walls were decorated with picture postcards of Eleanor Roosevelt, Frida Kahlo, Angela Davis, Vita Sackville-West, and Marie Curie. It was the communication hub. Recent and yellowing envelopes addressed to former residents were piled on a metal shelf unit near the door, waiting for the women to return. Below was a stack of seed catalogs and a Tucson phone book.

After talking it over with JoJo, the two women began work on an addition to the garden just for medicinal herbs. It was a second circle but smaller. Since the design resembled an infinity sign, they would emphasize it by putting up an identical wall. JoJo showed them how to make adobe mud and insert wine bottles gleaned from a pile of discards behind her trailer, to strengthen and add color and flashes of light to the enclosure. It was slow, hot work.

"This is taking forever. Do we really need this wall? How about we start working on the soil and finish this another time?" Sparrow said, throwing down her gloves and wiping her brow with the cuff of her shirt.

"I guess we could do that. Whatever you say, it's your garden," Marga said.

"What? It's our garden, not just mine."

"I'm starting to think it doesn't make much sense to put our energies into building something on a property we don't own. Maybe it would be better to look for something just for us," Marga said. She put her hands on Sparrow's shoulders and said, "Just think about it."

"No, I don't want to think about it. I want to live here and make it work for us. I don't understand why you think I would want to leave. We just got here."

"Okay, you are right. Let's give it a go. I know it's your dream, and I'll just adjust to being around all these people. I'll think of it as being in a foreign land. The Land of the Amazons."

Sparrow stared at her girlfriend, feeling a sudden chill in the air despite the fact that it was the heat of the day. To reassure herself that everything was still okay, she said, "Thanks, Honey. I love you," touching her girlfriend's shoulder. Marga pushed her glasses up her nose and turned back to focus on the chores at hand, but to Sparrow, it was like a balloon popped. No, not popped. Just a slow leak of air and possibly all her dreams escaping. She looked at Marga, who was intent on her digging, and thought she needed to keep up the positive energy for both of them.

They each had their areas of expertise. Sparrow took the lead in planning what to grow and where to plant it. Marga supplied the muscle power. She turned the rock-hard dirt and patiently busted through cement-like caliche. Borrowing a truck, she hauled forty-pound sacks of composted horse manure they got from a neighbor and dug it into the garden beds of loosened soil.

After a few weeks of prep, it was time for the planting to begin. Sparrow chose herbs advertised to survive the Arizona summer and circled low-water usage plants in the seed catalog. Marga called in the order using a debit card.

"It's a lot of money," Sparrow said.

"Don't worry, Honey, there's enough money in there to cover it."

4:30 a.m. Sparrow peered sleepily at the clock when the alarm went off, but if she wanted to get some work done in the garden, she had to get up and beat the heat. She couldn't believe it was still hot at the end of September. Stepping into her Indian print cotton pants, knowing she would be on her knees pulling weeds today, she grabbed a white long-sleeved shirt for protection after the sun rose above the mesquite tree. Her shoulders were still peeling from the stupid sunburn she got last week.

Marga hadn't stirred. Even Sparrow's whispered "Good morning, morning glory" didn't make an impression. Sparrow smelled sleep and knew it was going to be a while before she saw her girlfriend upright. It all evened out. Sparrow wouldn't last much past ten, while Marga was a warmth-loving lizard and would sweat it out until the sun was high in the sky.

Sparrow loved the morning coolness. Bright green leaves of parsley complimented the dusty furriness of sage. She thought it was funny to be growing sage in sagebrush country. But each of her herbs had been selected for their ability to endure the climate and their medicinal value. The rosemary looked brittle. What did it need? More water, less sun? Everyone said it would grow like a weed, but it didn't look happy. Maybe it was the wrong variety. Everything else looked pretty good except the basil. An alarming number of leaves had been chewed off. Sparrow picked up the mason jar and hunted for the hungry and ever-present grasshoppers. Methodically searching among leaves and stems, she plucked off the offenders and locked them away in glass to drown them later. She felt guilty killing sentient beings, but they would destroy her garden if she didn't. Then she turned her attention to pulling weeds. She loved the process of clearing competing greens to give the herbs growing room.

By the time Marga wandered over, Sparrow had dirt under her nails and a pile of weeds a foot tall.

"If you didn't water them, they wouldn't grow," Marga said, nodding her head towards the debris. Sparrow smiled at the joke, the same one Marga made every morning, and accepted the cup of mint tea from her girlfriend. It was part of their ritual. They sipped, squatting in the dirt, and discussed plans for the day.

"Marcie is going to town around four, and she said we can go to the co-op with her," Sparrow said.

"I'll clean out the cooler and bundle up some herbs to sell. And I could use some more arnica. My elbow is still sore from moving that rock."

"You wouldn't listen to me. I told you to ask for help."

"Now, how would that look if your Sherpa couldn't move a little rock?"

"It was a boulder!" Sparrow leaned in for a quick hug. The animal scent of hard work arose from their bodies, and she felt grounded and good. Then she remembered her trip to town and said, "Is there still money on your debit card? Can I still use it?"

"Oh, sure. It's the beginning of the month, so there should be plenty on it."

"I love that magic card," Sparrow said. Marga was never very clear about where the money came from, even when Sparrow asked her directly, but she was generous, and their needs were modest, so Sparrow tucked it away in the things-she-did-not-need-to-know file.

After a summer with just a few hearty, heat-tolerant landmates, Sparrow was happy to see JoJo return in October and take over care of her goat, Molly. As the weather cooled, a new band of women showed up. They all seemed to know each other from other women's lands and had their ways of doing things. There weren't many rules at Desert Haven, so there were no policies to break, but Sparrow thought there was an implicit baseline of trust and respect that she felt change with the new energies.

The loose system began to break down. This new group didn't take care of things the way Sparrow thought they should. The bathhouse was filthy. Someone left a hose on overnight and flooded the shower, causing a mud and mosquito problem. Occasionally, the septic tank bubbled up, and the odor of sewage competed with the distinct smell of creosote, not a happy combination. Dishes were left to mold in the community house.

JoJo mentioned to Marga that she wasn't getting regular rent payments anymore, but she didn't want to "get into it with anyone." JoJo avoided hassles by staying inside. The pile of wine bottles behind her trailer grew.

The shift of energy on the land was relentless. Sparrow tried not to notice the chaos and kept to her gardening goals. Marga became agitated by the disruption. She didn't say much about it, but Sparrow noticed she was taking long walks out to the desert.

One early morning, JoJo and Sparrow stood by the wall, surveying the two gardens.

"Have you noticed plants disappearing?" JoJo asked.

"Yeah. At first, I thought an animal had gotten in, and I blamed it on rabbits," Sparrow said. "I even thought it could be the goat. But then I noticed that plants were being systematically harvested. So, someone is helping themselves to our garden."

After a lengthy discussion on how to word it, firm yet without hostility, they erected a cardboard sign that said *Please ask JoJo, Sparrow, or Marga before you pick anything from the garden.*

Sparrow called a community meeting, and no one came.

"What the hell? What kind of community is this anyway?" she said that night as she pulled the blanket up to her chin and snuggled next to Marga to share some of her warmth.

"I think we need to move," Marga said, sitting up and closing her book. "Pretty soon, it's going to get cold at night, and this shed won't be sufficient. I love the heat but can't take cold. I had enough of it when I was a little girl."

Sparrow stiffened and stayed silent as Marga went on.

"Let's move closer to town. See if we can find a little house with a big yard for just the two of us. The hell with trying to get along with all these crazy women."

"Into town? I can't leave my garden."

"I know, Honey, and you will have a new one. We'll build it from the ground up. I've been thinking about it, and I have a plan. First of all, we get a car so we can explore. Maybe Eagle has a room that we can rent while we look for a house. Our own house where you can do anything you want."

Sparrow turned to face her girlfriend, tucking stray hairs behind her ears. "What are you talking about? How can we get a car? A house? With what? Is money going to fall out of the sky?"

Marga sat up, took a deep breath, exhaled audibly, and paused, looking like she was trying to find the right words. "I've got a story to tell you."

Sparrow felt a cloud of seriousness descend on them. Watching Marga closely, observing a series of nervous tics – glasses adjusted, left arm flexed repeatably, ceiling inspecting. What could Marga have to tell her? Sparrow plumped up her pillow and leaned it against the shed wall, nodded, and waited.

Marga slowly, almost mechanically, began by saying when she was seventeen, her mother, an American, abandoned her and her father in Berlin and ran off with another man. A Canadian. Her father was grief-stricken. To divert his sorrow, he planned a two-month trip to the Greek Islands for the two of them.

While traveling from one island to another, they were standing on the forward deck of a Greek Hellas express ferry when a cruise liner came too close and bashed into their ship. Marga was at the railing, and as her father watched in horror, she was thrown overboard into the water.

"Oh my god! How awful," Sparrow cried.

Marga went on talking. Crew members were alerted and threw her a life preserver as they lowered a rescue raft. She was a strong swimmer, but the fall broke her left elbow, and she nearly drowned. Neither boat sustained serious damage. The other passengers had only suffered a few scrapes and bruises; Marga was the only one seriously injured.

She closed her eyes as if she was scanning for words. "The memories are painful, and I just don't like talking about it. I'm sorry I didn't tell you before."

Sparrow sat silently, searching Marga's face for something familiar. Feeling lost, she rested her head on her knees.

"Say something, darling. Please." Marga said, "Do you forgive me for not telling you?"

Sparrow crawled over for a long hug. "Oh, Marga, I love you. I just wish that you had told me before. It explains so many mysteries, like why you wouldn't go swimming with me in the ocean and where your nightmares come from." She held out her hand and placed it on Marga's heart, picked up Marga's hand, and placed it on her heart. "You can tell me anything. We are a team." She paused, peering into Marga's frozen face. "You look like there is more to tell me. Is there more?"

Marga peered out the dark window as if looking for something and then back at Sparrow. "After the accident, I became nervous and fearful of everything. I finished school and entered Universitat zu Koln as a creative writing student. I took to going to clubs and came out as a lesbian. I partied a lot, and my studies suffered, so I decided to take a year off and travel. I was on the go for almost four years. Most of the time, I was fine, but I'd have panic attacks or a flashback from the accident every so often. I thought it would help to settle down for a while, so I moved to New York. I found a little studio apartment where I could write, and I began therapy. That's where I met Trudy."

"Your ex?

"Yes. Trudy was a German ex-pat and my therapist." She paused, knowing that Sparrow would have a reaction to this new information.

"Wait a minute. Trudy was your therapist?"

"I know. But the relationship was quite mutual. We lived together for a year until Trudy ran off with another patient."

"Oh, Honey, I'm so sorry. How could she do that to you? She certainly had some issues."

"I was utterly heartbroken. I felt untethered—is that how you say it? Like I could just float away. I sat and stared at the walls for a few months, resisting friends' attempts to bring me back down to earth. Finally, I just got tired of myself. When a friend insisted I go to the Gay Pride Parade,

I allowed her to take me. I had no idea what to expect; I'd never heard of it."

"When was that?"

"June 27, 1993. The twenty-fifth anniversary of Stonewall. It buoyed my spirits and inspired me. On a whim, I wrote an article about it and submitted it to the Village Voice. To my surprise, they accepted it."

"Wow!"

"Wow is right. I'd never been published before. Might as well start at the top, so I pitched them a series of articles about Gay Pride parades around the country, and they said yes. I bought the Mercedes second-hand and took off, following the flow of gay celebrations across the country."

"And then you showed up for San Diego Pride and met me," Sparrow said, thinking that the story ended with her.

"Yes, Darling, I met you, fell in love, called off the magazine assignment, and here we are," Marga said, pushing her glasses up, looking at her girlfriend. "Well, there is one more thing I need to tell you," Marga said, eyebrows raised, lips pursed.

Sparrow sat forward in anticipation, her heart thumping. What else could Marga have kept from her?

Marga told her that her father was terrified when he almost lost his daughter. That fear turned to outrage. He was *ein Anwalt*, a lawyer, and sued both the ferry and the cruise line. Marga got large settlements, and her father set up a trust fund for her. "You should know that the woman you are committed to has a small fortune. It's ours. To share."

"Is that for real?"

"Yes. I didn't want to tell you because things were going so well, and we were getting by so nicely. I was afraid that you would think I was someone else if you knew I had money. I've heard you say things about your wealthier friends. But now things are different, and it's time to make a change."

Sparrow stood up and took a step away from the bed. She faced the wall as the rage growing in her spread from her solar plexus up to her head, bruising her heart on the way. She was stunned to realize that she didn't know Marga at all. Everything felt like a lie. She was living with a stranger. Her head throbbed as she tried to form words to express her outrage.

"How dare you let me love an illusion of you? How could you conceal an essential fact of your life? I feel patronized and dismissed and furious." The words sputtered out in a sloppy stream of anger and hurt and abruptly ran out. Shoulders slumped, sobbing, she turned away from Marga.

Marga stared, frozen. She had never seen Sparrow in a rage, and it immobilized her. "Honey, please, I didn't mean to hurt you. I thought I was protecting you."

"From what, a liar? A fraud? Sparrow faced Marga, her eyes bright with tears. "I thought we were completely honest with each other. Now I learn only one of us was."

"I can't believe that you are furious with me about being rich. Don't you think it's a little ironic?"

"I can't believe that you don't know how you have betrayed me. Our whole relationship is based on deceit. How can I trust you? Who are you? A land-dyke, a rich-bitch? I just don't know anymore." Sparrow grabbed a pair of jeans off a hook and sat on the bed to put them on. Her foot got tangled in the leg, and she flailed around impotently. Collapsing on the bed, her great roar of frustration and confusion filling the tiny space.

Softly, gently, Marga said, "Sparrow, please forgive me. It was never my intention to hurt you. I promise I will never hold anything from you again. You are my love, the center of my universe. I am such a fool. Please, what can I do to make this right?"

Sparrow listened intently to Marga's words, the right ones that calmed her down. She breathed a little deeper, and some of the fog in her head dissipated. Her tears trickled to a stop. She stayed still, curled up, not knowing what to do next. Marga continued to cover her with a warm blanket of reassurances, and Sparrow felt herself coming back to the room. It was as if she had been inhabited by a strange force that was leaving her like exhaled smoke. Had she overreacted? Maybe she should have said something before, asked about the money. She was so naïve. Her pain was real, but there must be a way back.

"Okay, I see that you didn't mean to hurt me, but it does. I love you, and I want us to be a team. When you have hidden parts, I feel excluded.

Is there anything else I should know?" Sparrow sat back and watched Marga's face for clues.

"Nope, that's it. I have a lot of money, and I will share it with you. And we live happily ever after."

"Weird."

"That's what you say when your lover proposes to you?"

"What do you mean, proposes? We can't get married."

"No, but we can have a commitment ceremony. And I can instruct the lawyer to draw up papers giving you equal rights to the accounts. I want us to be partners in all things. Let's work towards our goals, sweetheart. I want to write, and you want to grow a garden. We can find our own place and start a new life together," Marga said and moved in for a hug.

Sparrow held up her hand to push away the advance. "Have you been plotting to move into town all along? I know living on women's land was my dream, not yours. Do you hate it here so much?"

"I can't take the disorder and chaos. It makes me anxious. I want something just for us so we can relax and follow our dreams. I think we are on the same team, Honey." Marga sat back and watched for Sparrow's reaction. "How about a hug?" she said tentatively.

"Well, Desert Haven isn't an easy place to live for someone who likes predictability," Sparrow said, not responding to the invitation. "I'm having a hard time too. I still love the idealism of it. Maybe we could create a space for women to work with us on similar goals."

Marga kept silent and nodded in agreement. Sparrow was on a roll.

"It would be nice to be in a place we could design just for us. Something organized and comfortable. I can visualize you in a cozy writing studio. If we really have the money, I can see how it would work." Sparrow realized she was talking herself into this new vision, and it was pretty exciting. She had never considered owning property. But now that she could afford to, it opened up a bunch of possibilities.

"How much money?" she asked, eyes sparkling from leftover tears and new excitement.

Marga took that as a yes and moved in for a hug.

Sparrow (and Marga) 1996

After viewing dozens of properties, Sparrow and Marga found the perfect place that met all the criteria on their list.

- In town, walkable or bikeable to food shopping, farmer's market, and other local businesses
- More than an acre of land with established trees and room for gardens
- A charming remodelable building with space for Marga's writing studio and Sparrow's craft room
- A safe neighborhood
- Views of the mountains from somewhere on the property
- Away from high voltage powerlines

Since price wasn't a factor, they could focus on their priorities. With the help of a Realtor listed in the local lesbian newsletter, they found a unique place north of central Tucson. The original two-story homestead was almost one hundred years old, built in 1900, and, although charming, it was in pretty rough shape. It came with four adjoining lots totaling one and a fifth acres of land circled by a rickety fence.

Before they moved in, they had the fence replaced with a six-foot block wall. After living at Desert Haven amongst sister landdykes for the last year, they wanted to keep a sense of seclusion even while living in the city.

Sparrow thought buying a house was the most exciting thing she had ever done in her whole life—except for falling in love with Marga, of course. Ever since she learned her girlfriend had a large trust fund, she was determined not to let it freak her out. She was never exactly embarrassed by the rickety little rental house she grew up in, but she did have to admit to a slight measure of envy when visiting her more well-to-do friends' homes. And now, she would have a real home of her own. Their dream house was a bit of a wreck, but they had the resources to turn it into their idea of paradise.

Packrats had moved into two of the house's five rooms, making them uninhabitable. The floor was a foot deep in cholla buds, sticks, and debris. Wearing protective masks and gloves, the women shoveled the mess into a roll-away dumpster, and then sprayed the rooms thoroughly with bleach to protect themselves from hantavirus.

All this space was a luxury after living in a storage shed on women's land for the past year. They could survive the outdated plumbing and electricity while they planned their future urban farm. A bed, kitchen table and chairs, a desk for Marga's typewriter, and some minimalist kitchen gear were enough to set up housekeeping while firming up their plans.

Sitting under an ancient palo verde tree, on rickety wicker chairs they inherited from the previous owner, surrounded by overgrown native vegetation, a pitcher of iced tea, and two glasses on a tree stump, they surveyed their queendom. "I think the best thing to do is to build a new house, maybe straw bale, for our living space and use this house for workspace," Marga said.

The first thing Sparrow thought was, how can we afford that? Pausing, she remembered the trust fund money, and she let her real needs and desires float to the surface.

"Let's figure out where we want the house so I can plan the gardens," Sparrow said. "I want an area for fruit trees and lots of raised beds for herbs and veggies. And chickens. We have to have chickens."

"We'll plan the house with water collection tanks for irrigation. And solar panels, of course."

"Of course," Sparrow said.

Mostly, they agreed on their priorities and how to proceed, but the one area of serious negotiation was the future of the pool. The property came with a sizeable crumbling aqua concrete hole. Sparrow was enchanted by the thought of taking a dip anytime she wanted, and she visualized the rehabilitated swimming pool sparkling in the sun. Marga saw a potential hazard and didn't want any part of it. She was adamant that it must be filled in.

"I don't want to worry about anyone falling in and drowning. No, it has to go," she said, chin jutting forward, arms crossed with hands clutching her shoulders.

"Wait a minute. What about my needs?" Sparrow said. "I think you are being unreasonable."

"Maybe so, but I can't live with it. You can go to the gym and swim where there is a lifeguard."

"Just because you're financing this project doesn't mean that you have a bigger say than me. Or does it?"

"I knew that you had resentment about me having money."

"You know it is hard for me to accept, but I'm getting used to it, so back off," Sparrow said, louder than she had intended.

"I'm going for a walk," Marga announced and left.

Sparrow hated when Marga left in a huff, but she had to acknowledge that they both needed a cooling-off period. After almost two years of living together, she knew that Marga would be back in about twenty minutes with something reasonable to say. But still, it felt awful when communication was abruptly cut off, especially when she was still riled up. The first few times it happened, Sparrow felt bereft, as if the relationship was spiraling down the tubes. After that, she had learned to calm down and use the time to think things through.

Pouring herself a glass of tea, Sparrow sat on the edge of the blue hole, legs dangling, imagining a lovely, shaded patio. They could still have the patio without the pool. Maybe she could negotiate a soaker tub in the master bathroom.

"Okay," Marga said upon her return, wiping sweat from her upper lip. "What do you think is a fair compromise? I honestly don't know if I'll ever get over my water phobia."

"If we fill in the pool," Sparrow said, "we'll have room for a bigger chicken coop."

As part of their move-in packet, the realtor gave them a booklet of local resources distributed by the Gay and Lesbian Chamber of Commerce. Marga did her homework and found a woman-owned design firm that would work with them on building an energy-efficient, passive solar home that was complementary to the old farmhouse. They figured it would take about three months to get the design drawn and permits pulled and another three to six months to build.

Driving home from a meeting with the architects, Sparrow said, "You know, Honey, I love that we are planning our home together. I mean, I think it's wonderful."

Marga watched the road ahead, slowing for a red light. "I'm glad you are happy." After a pause, she added, "Is there more you want to say?"

"You know me so well, don't you," Sparrow said, stretching her seatbelt so she could reach over and squeeze Marga's elbow. "I guess I feel like I don't have much to contribute and that it's your project. Oh, I want some input, of course, and I'm available if you need me, but I think it's important that you take the lead. You've got the house project and your writing. I've got to find my own bliss."

When they lived at Desert Haven, there was always something to do – haul water, build shelter, tend the garden, stay warm in the winter, and cool in the summer. And there was always someone around to talk to, commiserate with, laugh, and celebrate with. Now, it was just the two of them. Sparrow felt at sixes and sevens. Of course, she loved Marga to pieces, but they were so different. Marga needed lots of alone time, and Sparrow needed community.

"I think I'll call Becka and see what she knows about the gardening community here in town," Sparrow said. "She's lived in Tucson a long time."

"That's a great idea. She might introduce you to some kindred souls too. I'm sure you are ready to have a conversation with someone other than me."

Becka told Sparrow about Native Seed Search, a nonprofit seed conservation organization that offered classes on gardening and sustainability. She signed up for all of them. She got a library card and came home with classic tomes on planting and using herbs: Jethro Kloss's *Back to Eden*, Jeanne Rose's *Herbs and Things*, and The *Herb Book* by

John Lust. The women's bookstore regularly called, saying her special orders had arrived. One book led her to another as she learned about low-water gardening methods, vegan cooking, herbal remedies, tie-dying, holistic healing, native plants, natural building methods, and passive solar. She joined a garden club and heard about the Pima County Master Gardeners through the County Extension office. She was elated when her application was accepted for their comprehensive training course.

It was a revelation to Sparrow that she could be a serious student if she was excited about the subject. Social life and friends were her priority in high school, and her grades reflected her lack of interest.

Marga compiled a list of tradeswomen for every aspect of the building project. She determined that straw bale was the way to go and contracted the work to a crew of experienced housebuilders, electricians, plumbers, and laborers, some coming as far as New Mexico, to work on the house. The out-of-towners were invited to stay in the spare rooms. Marga oversaw construction, sometimes working beside the tradeswomen. Sparrow helped provide meals for all the workers in a temporary shaded outdoor kitchen and dining area.

Eight months after they bought the property, when construction was nearing completion, and Marga was consumed with the placement of electrical outlets and what countertop was the most nontoxic, they sat down for a lunch of bitter-greens soup and homemade sourdough bread.

After asking politely about the day's progress on the new house, Sparrow announced, "I'm thinking about volunteering at Wingspan, the LGBT Community Center."

Marga tore off a chunk of bread and dipped it into her soup. "What would you be doing?"

"I'm not sure. I'll find out at orientation. I just think they're doing such important work and I want to help out. I can just sit at the front desk and be the first friendly face someone sees when they walk in," Sparrow said, trying out her most welcoming expression.

"If you can fit it in between your sustainability meetings and sewing classes. You are a busy bee." Marga said, eyes crinkled into a grin. "I'm glad that you've found so much to do."

"Right now, I'm just following my interests, and I have no idea where I'll end up. Sometimes, I feel like I'm all over the place – food, crafts, lesbians, gardening. The only thread I can see is that I love what I'm doing. Guess the bigger picture will be revealed." Picking up their dishes, Sparrow placed a kiss on the top of Marga's head before heading inside to wash up and change for her Reiki class. "And don't forget, I want an outlet at the end of the kitchen island."

Her explorations led her to a community of her own making. She shared at least one interest with each person, often more than that, in overlapping circles. Marga was in some of these circles, but not all. One of Sparrow's fears, when they moved to the city, was that she would feel lonely because Marga was more self-contained than she was. Marga had her writing, a world she occupied in her imagination, where human contact was unnecessary and sometimes annoying. Sparrow's projects were mainly carried out in the company of others.

Marga was the big picture person – she built the wooden frames for the raised beds, while Sparrow was the detail person who meticulously sorted weeds from tender pea sprouts. Both skill sets were necessary to build their homestead, and it brought out the best in both of them. Sometimes, Sparrow felt overwhelmed by gratitude as their relationship grew tighter. When she got weepy and sentimental, Marga held her close and stroked her hair.

"Now that we've moved into the house and filled up the rooms with comforts and pretty things, I think it's time that we figure out what to do with the old house," Marga said. She was lying on the bed, on top of the comforter, enjoying the breeze from the evaporative cooler after a hot June day, watching Sparrow change into an oversized nightshirt.

Sparrow perched on the edge of the bed, pursing her lips and squinting as if she were searching for the right words.

"What is it, Honey? Marga asked.

"I think I want to start a school," Sparrow said carefully. "Well, not really a school, but a center where women can come and learn some of the things I've been teaching myself. The kind of school I want to go to. I discovered that I am pretty good at researching and finding resources, but a lot of women aren't, or they just don't have the time. What if we set up a center where women could learn how to do things for themselves? They could learn from each other—like a guided co-op or something. I don't know. I'm just making this up." She flopped back on the bed, exhausted from birthing her idea out loud.

"Wow, that's a great idea. I love it. I had no idea you were thinking that way."

"Well, it's not a fully formed plan yet, but maybe we could work on it together. I was thinking the old house could have classrooms. And a library."

"Hey, do not forget I claim a sunny room for my writing studio," Marga said, suddenly panicking that her dream was being usurped.

"Of course, that goes without saying. You get the first choice. A room of your own." Sparrow thought a moment and added, "I'll have one too. Something I've never had."

"This is a great idea. Maybe we could even host writing retreats. But what should we call it?"

"I was thinking about something like EcoWomen, or something like that."

A week later, Marga burst into the house and said, "Honey, come on out here and see what I have."

"Can you wait a little while? I'm about to get in the tub."

Marga appeared at the bathroom door, red glasses fogged by the steam, holding out a bathrobe. "Put this on and come with me."

Sparrow forgave her for being bossy because she loved surprises. "Yes, ma'am!"

After descending the stairs, Marga said, "Now, close your eyes. I'll lead you."

Sparrow felt the cool morning air on her face when they stepped outside and the crunchy gravel under her slippers. She could tell she was being led toward the driveway. What crazy thing was Marga doing now? The last surprise was an adorable six-week-old spotted tabby cat.

"You can open your eyes now."

They were standing in the carport, on the driver's side of their green pickup truck. A brand new one-by-two-foot magnetic sign was attached to the door. It was a drawing of a brown tree trunk on a cream background with the words EcoWomen forming green leaves. It took Sparrow a moment to understand.

"Where did this sign come from? Who made the beautiful design?"

"I hope you don't mind. I took the liberty of having a graphic designer make this up for you. If you don't like it, you can change it," Marga said. "Do you like it? Be honest."

Sparrow blinked her eyes rapidly to keep tears from overflowing. "Oh, Honey, I love it. It's fantastic. I couldn't have designed it better."

"You described your concept of the school so well I thought I had a pretty good idea of your vision. So, you want to keep it?"

"Yes, of course. It's perfect."

"In that case," Marga said gently, directing Sparrow to their Prius and then to the utility trailer, all sporting shiny new signs.

"I guess it's real now," Sparrow said and read the sign, "EcoWomen: Sustainability for Women by Women."

One year later, to the day, Sparrow tied a hand-lettered sign to the open gate directing students to the classroom in the newly remodeled original house. The EcoWomen logo on the green door assured the students they were in the right place. The room was freshly painted Classic Sage with environmentally friendly, non-VOC, nontoxic milk paint. A whiteboard on the back wall and padded folding chairs around two sturdy wooden tables gave it a classic classroom look. Blank notebooks, pencils, and xeroxed workbooks titled "My Garden Design" waited for the five women who had signed up and paid their twenty dollars in advance.

Outside, eight chickens and a goat named Nanny roamed the back half of the property. Five-foot-high chicken wire enclosures protected raised garden beds of medicinal herbs. Tabby, the cat, guarded the property against invading packrats. Black tubing snaked through the grounds delivering precious water directly to plants with a series of strategically placed drip irrigation spot emitters. A baker's dozen of trees dotted the property; six deep holes awaited the stone fruit trees on order.

Sparrow wore a special outfit she had tie-dyed for this momentous occasion. A rainbow swirl emanated from her heart chakra across the cotton top and continued onto the matching pants. She felt powerful and vulnerable at the same time.

Stepping out to greet her students, she saw Marga framed in the second-story bay window of the big house, flashing a huge smile, waggling two thumbs-ups. Sparrow beamed back at her and ushered everyone to their seats.

"I want to thank you all for coming today. Some of you know me from when I lived at Desert Haven where I started my desert gardening education. Hi Cassie. Hi Thea. And welcome to those of you I don't know yet. I've done a lot of reading and learning in the past two years, and my wish is to share some of what I've discovered. I bet that some of you have a lot of experience too. So please, let's learn from each other."

That night, Sparrow perched on a stool at the stainless-steel kitchen counter, sipping white wine while she watched Marga prepare a celebratory dinner of free-range turkey with all the fixings. According to Marga, having Thanksgiving dinner tonight rather than on a random Thursday in November was most appropriate.

"So, how did it go? You were brilliant, I assume."

"Thank you, Honey. You are too kind, but, yes, it was pretty fantastic. All that planning paid off, and I felt confident that either I could answer their questions or point them in the right direction. You know the saying: people teach what they have to learn. It was a great group of women, and they said they want to come back for more. So now I have to develop another class, this time on efficient and economical watering. Good thing I have our garden to experiment on. And thanks to your hard work and excellent planning, we will soon have our rainwater tanks in place." Sparrow drank from her glass, placed it carefully on the counter, and leaned back to let herself feel the alcohol's relaxing effect.

"This could be the start of something big, my darling." Marga picked up her glass and toasted, "To the future. Prost!"

Five years later, in 2001, after they survived the nonexistent Y2K crisis and had finally used up all the cans of tuna and gallons of water they had stashed, Sparrow's weekly column in the newspaper, *Sustainability Now!*, was almost a year old. She taught three weekly classes at EcoWomen, and one day a week she drove out to Desert Haven to help with whatever projects JoJo had going on. Sometimes, she gave a workshop. Sometimes, she showed up with a truckload of manure or materials for a shade structure over the tomato patch. Facilitating women working together was her forte. Her favorite activity was being part of a "mud crew," finishing the exterior walls of an adobe structure.

The old house had been enlarged to create a craft studio and guest room for visiting artists, along with two classrooms. An outdoor dye kitchen was against the north wall. Both women had their own offices on the second floor with views of the Catalina Mountains. Sparrow didn't ask about their finances. She left it entirely up to Marga. It was her inherited money, and she could manage it any way she saw fit. Marga told her she had filed the necessary paperwork so that they owned everything equally, but Sparrow wasn't that interested. Now that she had income from her classes and her column, she had her own money to spend.

The property required a lot of work. Gardens and animals, maintenance and improvements, kept both of them active and fit. They hired Becka to help out a few days a week.

Marga usually woke with the sun and spent her mornings sequestered in her writing studio. It was painted periwinkle blue, an intense, happy color. Her large wooden desk sat in front of the window with an ergonomic office chair tucked in neatly. The only other furniture was a black leather Danish modern recliner chair for impromptu naps. A few brushed silver lamps and the decorating was complete. Simple, nothing to distract her.

She was writing a novel loosely based on her life. She told Sparrow that she didn't want to write a memoir because it seemed too personal. By fictionalizing it, she could play around with the timeline and add or subtract characters at will. And it seemed like it would be more fun.

Although she had lived in the States for many years, Marga still found writing in English challenging. Certain words didn't come to her easily. A German-English dictionary sat next to her thesaurus. She had been successful in journalism in the past, but this was completely different.

Sparrow called out from downstairs, "One o'clock, time for lunch." Marga jotted down a few notes and shut her notebook, expecting the invitation. Both women were comforted by their routine. Their simple lunch of sliced tomatoes, goat cheese, and crackers was already laid out on a wrought iron table under a bright blue umbrella. Two glasses of iced ginger lemon tea sat sweating on the placemats.

"Mmm, this cheese is good. Got it from that woman who has goats over in Picture Rocks." Sparrow took a sip of her tea and said, "How's it going today?"

"Not so good. I feel bogged down. Not sure what direction I should be taking. I'm trying to do some of the techniques that I learned in the workshop I took in Phoenix. They are just tricks to keep my writing flowing, but I am kinda stuck."

"I made oatmeal tahini cookies for dessert," Sparrow said, pushing the plate toward Marga. "Would you like one?"

"No thanks," Marga said, patting her tummy to indicate she was full. "I think I might try therapy. I've heard about this thing called EMDR that is supposed to help with writer's block."

"What does it stand for?

"Eye movement desensitization and reprocessing. It's supposed to be a way to quickly and efficiently deal with trauma and stress. I called a therapist that Alice recommended. She told me she had just taken the training and thought it might help me." Marga changed her mind and took a bite out of a cookie. "This is really good."

"Thanks, I made the tahini."

"You are such a kitchen wizard. And garden goddess. You are a successful columnist and workshop genius. I'm kinda jealous of all your talents," Marga said with a wry smile to cover the raw honesty in her declaration.

"Oh, Honey, you are the writer in the family. I just write about my projects as a way to keep up with the latest trends. I don't write for the sake of writing like you do. You are an author. I'm a hack."

"Don't belittle your abilities, my dear," Marga said, taking Sparrow's hands in hers. "I will be an author when my first book is published. Until then, I am a stalled writer waiting for the kick I need to get going. Yes, I think I will go to therapy."

Sparrow ran their conversation around in her head while she cleaned up the dishes. She hadn't mentioned to Marga that the newspaper's editor asked her to compile some of her columns into a book. She didn't say that she was working on an outline because there were some topics she wanted to add. Did that make her a writer? Was she in competition with Marga? No, she didn't think so. Her stuff was practical, not creative. There was no comparison. But maybe she would wait to mention it until Marga felt more confident.

The next few months were pretty uncomfortable. Therapy stirred up a lot of old memories, and Marga was struggling to keep it together.

Sitting at the kitchen table with her journal, a cup of coffee at her elbow, Marga chewed on a pencil and pulled her left ear lobe. Sparrow reached over her for the honey, and Marga said, "Am I in your way?"

"No, I just need the honey."

"Stop crowding me. Give me some space here," Marga said, color moving up her neck into her cheeks and her voice becoming shrill.

"What? What's going on, Marga?" Sparrow said, a bit of panic in her eyes.

"What the fuck!" Marga yelled, face red and hands trembling. "I don't know, I don't know." She dropped her forehead to the table and wept. "I don't know what's going on with me. A bunch of unresolved family issues that flared up in therapy are wringing me out. I feel so stupid and unsteady. Sparrow, I do not want to burden you with this shit."

"But Marga, that's what a loving relationship is. I'm here for you one hundred percent. You can tell me anything."

"This is shit from the long-ago past that I never wanted to see, and honestly, I really don't want to talk about it outside of the therapist's office. Just bear with me. I'll work it out. Just know I love you, and if I withdraw, it's not personal."

But it felt personal to Sparrow. It felt like Marga had a new relationship and was cheating on her. There was someone else who knew more about her than she was willing to share in her primary relationship.

"I see you like a caterpillar wrapped up tight in a cocoon," Sparrow said. "I know this is a process, and I'm trying to be patient, but I'm scared. I don't know who you will be when you finally emerge as a butterfly." Tears blurred her eyes, and she fumbled her way upstairs to the bedroom. Sitting on the edge of the bed, she sobbed.

A minute passed, then two. Then Marga stood in the doorway, saying, "I'm sorry." She looked at Sparrow for a few long moments, her mouth quivering, and sat on the bed beside her. "I'm sorry if I've hurt you. It is not my intention. I'm trying my best to work through this so that we can be more solid, even more of a team. I hope you believe me. Can you trust me, babe?"

Sparrow reached for Marga's hand and gave it a squeeze. "Of course, I believe you. But it's hard. I feel excluded. Just know I'm here for you."

"Honey, that's why I can dig deep and work on healing. Because I know you are there for me. Can I give you a hug?"

The hug turned into a kiss and then a longer kiss, and soon they were under the covers, making love, making up, making do.

When Sparrow looked back at Marga's first year of therapy, a passage of time that that they came to call her "rough period", she realized that it lasted about a year. Once she was able to trust Marga's process and let go of feeling responsible, she got on with her life. She could be supportive and compassionate, but she could not take on her girlfriend's burden.

Marga told Sparrow that the EMDR helped release the residual trauma from her near-drowning incident many years ago, an event that only Sparrow and a few other people knew about. She thought she had gotten triggered when a character in her novel had a similar experience. The character sank into a deep depression, and Marga could feel herself falling too. That's when she decided to seek help.

Marga attended to her daily chores in the garden, doing more cooking than she did before, but she didn't go into her writing studio. She said she wasn't ready yet. She went for long solo walks on the river pathway and even tried jogging but got shin splints, so she quit. Every day, she seemed to be on more solid ground. Her crying jags stopped, and her vibration was lighter, airier, easier for Sparrow to live with.

Sparrow worked steadily and stealthily on her manuscript, filling in the gaps, adding more detail, and eliminating repetition. She had a problem with commas, but that's what editors are for, right? She thought it was pretty good, and the feedback from beta readers was positive. A week before the final draft was due, she finally told Marga. She was worried that it might cause a tailspin, but Marga took it in stride.

"I'm glad one of us is going to be published," she said, pushing her glasses up.

"Oh, Honey, I couldn't have done it without your support. This book is a result of our efforts together. So, it's really half yours."

Sustainability: Self-Sufficiency in a Balanced Environment came out to local critical success. The newspaper sponsored several book signings that required new tie-dyed togs. Sparrow taught herself how to use a mic after her first event, where people kept yelling "speak up" from the back of the room. She always left time to answer questions and interact with the audience, her favorite part. Her reputation as an expert was growing, so her classes filled up, but instead of adding more, she kept a waitlist. Sparrow knew that keeping time to learn and grow was as vital to her as sharing her knowledge.

The book seemed to strike a nerve. It caught the eye of a book agent who recognized it as a trendsetter and was able to sell it to a national publisher that specialized in alternative books. They were the publishers of her favorite, *The Moosewood Cookbook*, so she didn't hesitate. And the sizable advance didn't hurt.

"I've got some great news," Sparrow said. "Let's go celebrate, and I'll tell you over an expensive dinner and bottle of wine at La Paloma. It's my treat."

They didn't eat out that often, but both of them liked to be pampered when they did. Sparrow chose a dress from her new wardrobe of "professional tie-dye," as she liked to call the more subdued yet still quirky outfits she created. Marga, dressed in black, looked marvelous, as usual. She had an innate grace and subtle style that she didn't even know she possessed. The women were led to a table by the window overlooking the city, which Sparrow requested when she was asked on the phone if the reservation was for a special occasion. Yes, she said, it's a celebration of some good news.

Sparrow waited until their margaritas were served and proposed a toast. "To my new San Francisco publisher," she said, watching Marga's face for any sign of distress.

"What! Your agent got you a deal? Wow. I'm so proud of you, Honey." They clinked glasses and sipped their drinks to seal the good wishes. "Tell me all about it. When is the book coming out? Did they offer you an advance? What can I do to help you?

Sparrow spelled out the details. She was assigned an editor who said the book "needed some work but had good bones," whatever that meant. Actually, what it meant was she had to get a computer and learn how to use it. The book would come out next year in the spring. The advance check was on the way. Twenty thousand dollars.

"It's more money than I've ever had in my life in one clump. It would take me at least five years to earn that much with my classes. But the publishers seem confident that the book will earn that much in royalties and a lot more. It's kinda overwhelming." Sparrow carefully placed her glass on the table and stared at it as if it were too fragile to hold on to.

"We can do this together, Sparrow. I can help you with the finances and taxes like I do for our investments. It would take some of the pressure off you and, you know," she hesitated and pushed her glasses up, "I could be a published author vicariously."

"Would you do that for me? I couldn't do it myself. Would it be okay for you to do that?" Sparrow said, reaching for Marga's hand and waiting for an answer.

Marga thought a moment and then smiled. "Of course, it's okay. I think it will inspire me to start writing again. I feel very jazzed about this like it's the kick I needed to get out of my funk." She stopped and looked surprised at herself. "Oh, Honey, that sounds terrible, like I'm stealing your victory to turn it into my own. I'm so sorry."

"It doesn't sound like that to me at all. What I hear is a loving partner sharing my excitement and joy. It's good for both of us."

The server brought another round of cocktails in response to some secret signal Marga emitted. Sparrow raised her glass and toasted, "To our writing futures."

Little did they know what they were moving towards. Sparrow would publish a series of books, write articles for major newspapers and establish an international educational nonprofit, EcoSchool for Women, with branches in San Diego, Washington State, and Mexico. Marga graduated from bookkeeping to managing every aspect of their business undertakings and Sparrow's career. She had a few poems published in online magazines, love poems. They were one of the first same-sex partners to get married in Arizona on October 17, 2014.

Madrona 1998

Maria hurriedly stuffed clothes in grocery bags and rushed them out to the van as fast as she could, pain shooting up her ankle, leaving her four-year-old daughter crying in the middle of the living room. She returned to the house and emptied the grocery money jar into her purse, saying, "Shh, don't cry, Sunny, it will be alright." Kneeling, she held Sunny in her arms. "He's gone, we're safe now."

Sunny gently touched the bruise blossoming purple and red surrounding Maria's right eye. "Mommy's okay, we're going to be fine," Maria said quickly. 'We are going on a car trip, just you and me. But we gotta leave right now."

Calmed but still sniffling, Sunny asked, "Can Mouser come?"

"Sorry, baby, we can't take the kitty. She'll be fine guarding the yard from squirrels. But you can choose two toys if you do it real fast."

Sunny went into her room while Maria filled another bag with anything they could easily eat on the road. Cheetos, peanut butter, a few apples, and a bunch of grapes, adding two forks, two spoons, a sharp knife, and a roll of paper towels.

"Time to go, baby," Maria said. "Brownie is waiting."

They hurried out to the brown 1972 Chevy conversion van that Sunny named Brownie. Those were happier days, before her husband's drinking got bad, before the flashbacks, and before things got physical. When she was living with a fragile but loving man.

Strapping Sunny into the passenger seat, Maria handed her the pink stuffed bunny and Hot Wheels car she chose for her journey. She kissed her wide-eyed child on the cheek, shut the door, and ran around to the driver's side.

"Goodbye, house of horrors, good riddance Portland," Maria yelled, quickly backing out of the driveway, pointing the car towards the freeway.

"How ya doing, Sunny?" Maria said to the silent little girl. She had seen Sunny run and hide when the chaos began, terrified by her crazy, out-of-control father. The violence was escalating. Marie didn't know what that fucker would do next; she just knew she had to save Sunny and herself.

"Don't worry, Sunny, we're going far away, and Daddy can't hurt us anymore."

"Good," Sunny said, hugging Rabbit close, looking out the window at the trees whipping by.

Five-and-a-half hours later, they left the highway and turned down a road that led to a long shady driveway. A hand-painted sign announcing West Farm was wired to the gate. The sun was low on the horizon, and light flickered through tall, skinny trees. Maria had heard about this women's community in Southern Oregon from a girlfriend and always wanted to visit. Under different circumstances, of course. They pulled in and parked in a small clearing.

"Mama, look at those naked ladies."

Two shirtless women wearing shorts and tool belts were carrying two-by-fours over to a cabin at the edge of the clearing.

"That's because we are on Women's Land, and men are not allowed," Maria said, opening her door and carefully stepping out. One of her eyes was almost swollen shut, and she had some bloody scrapes on her arms. She couldn't put any weight on her left foot.

The women watched Maria limp out of her car, and seeing that she was hurt, they came over to help. The woman with close-cropped grey hair saw Sunny sitting in the van and went around to the open window.

"Hi. My name is Sage, what's yours?"

"Sunny."

"Hi Sunny, how old are you?"

"Four," Sunny said, holding her thumb down and displaying four fingers.

"Four, that's a great age. Can I help you out of the car? Barb is taking your mom into the cabin to make her feel better. We can go with them if you like. Don't be shy, it's alright, you are safe here."

Sunny looked gravely at Sage and nodded her head. Rabbit tucked under her left arm, she reached out her right hand to Sage. They stood in the doorway watching as Barb attended to Maria, who was slumped in a chair as if she had used up the very last bit of her energy.

"This will sting a bit," Barb said, swabbing Maria's cuts with turmeric paste. "We don't want those cuts to get infected." Maria flinched but kept her eyes on Sunny, even putting a weak smile on her face to reassure her daughter.

"I've got some aloe vera for those bruises," Barb said, gently smoothing the cooling gel around Maria's eye and carefully rubbing some into her swollen left ankle. "Who did this to you?"

"My old man."

"You and your little girl can stay as long as you want. It's just me and Sage here right now. Everyone else went down south for the winter, but we don't mind the grey days. You managed to get here on a perfect fall day," she said, hands on hips, looking out the window at the bright sky.

"I was hoping you'd say we could stay," Maria said, attempting a broad smile that came up short when her eye throbbed from the effort. "We are good in the van, but I could really use a bathroom right now. How about you, Sunny? Need to go potty?"

"Sorry, no bathroom," Barb apologized. "We have an outhouse behind the cabin and water from a hose where you can wash up. You need to keep your foot elevated; you've got a nasty sprain."

It wasn't until after a warm dinner of vegetable soup with cornbread, and they were tucked into their sleeping bags, that Maria felt the constant tension she had gotten used to living with ratchet down a notch. Softly hugging Sunny to her, a wave of guilt churned her stomach. How could she have allowed Sunny to grow up in that crazy household? She had to force herself to think of the future. They were on their own now, and no matter how tough things might get, it would be better than living in constant terror. She was only twenty-six years old. She had lots of time to make it up to Sunny.

The following day, the three women and Sunny sat around a small round oak table in the cozy cabin, sipping cups of steaming tea. Sunny drew pictures with colored pencils and paper Barb had pulled from a drawer.

"If we hang out here for a little while, I'd like to contribute, but I'm afraid I'm not up to helping with your construction project," Maria said, widening her brown eyes against the swelling that was forcing them shut. "But I have an idea. How about I do the cooking in exchange for our stay?"

"Sounds great to me," Barb said, looking over at her partner, waiting for a nod of approval before she went on. "We are pretty well stocked up with a basic vegetarian pantry."

"Have at it," agreed Sage.

A variety of foods she'd never seen, like kohlrabi, quinoa and spelt, challenged Maria's creativity in the kitchen. Each day, she consulted *Diet for a Small Planet* or the *Moosewood Cookbook* for ideas. Sunny pulled a chair over to the counter and washed veggies or measured grains while Maria, foot propped up on a chair, supervised. After dinner, Jan hauled water in a small tin basin and heated it on the woodstove for the dishes while Maria read bedtime stories to Sunny in the van, in the light of a headlamp. Once Sunny drifted off, Maria reached for her own book and read herself to sleep.

After a few weeks they relaxed into a quiet routine, but the nights were growing longer, and it was getting too cold to sleep in the van. They were lucky it hadn't rained too much. Maria's wounds were mostly healed, but her slight limp was a reminder of why she had to get away. She needed to put more miles between her and Portland, so she told her hosts it was time for her and Sunny to leave.

"Thanks for everything," Maria said with tears in her eyes. "You were lifesavers, and I'll never forget you." She reached out her arms to enfold her rescuers in a big hug. Sunny squirmed into the middle, getting special hugs and kisses from Sage.

"We'll miss you. Let us know where you end up."

Maria drove east to Idaho and then south, through Utah and into Arizona. They camped along the way in the beautiful canyon country. Keeping south to avoid snow, she consulted her precious copy of *Women's Lands* and saw that they weren't too far from Desert Haven in Southern Arizona, so that was where she headed.

Maria knew that riding in the car for so many days was pretty boring for a little girl, but Sunny wasn't a complainer. She watched the wires on the power poles loop by and searched the landscape for cows. When

Sunny got antsy, she climbed into the back of the van and played with her new crayons and coloring book or took a nap. At night, they cuddled up with their sleeping bags zipped together. Sometimes they had a fire, and Maria held a straightened coat hanger with a skewered marshmallow over the flames and slowly turned it until it was crisp brown all over and gooey in the center. When Sunny tried, the marshmallows caught fire and got black and crunchy.

They were on the road for almost a month and Maria was getting tired. She whooped with relief when they turned into the cactus lined driveway to Desert Haven. Parking the car next to a walled vegetable garden, she saw a wiry woman in cutoff jeans, heavy work boots, and a battered straw hat, picking exuberant greens. The woman looked up, smiled, and went back to her chore.

Stepping out of the van, the two travelers stretched their cramped legs, taking deep breaths of clean air with a hint of creosote. The sky was solid azure. Everything looked clear and bright. Maria said "Hi" to the grey-haired older woman in the garden, who put down her basket and greeted them across the fence, saying her name was JoJo. She looked Sunny up and down. In her flannel shirt and shorts, sneakers, and short-cropped hair, Sunny's gender was not obvious. The child stared back.

"I found you in the Lesbian Land book," Maria said. "This is Desert Haven, isn't it? We need a place to stay for a little while."

"You are welcome to look around and find a place to park your van," JoJo said. "The bathhouse and kitchen are communal areas. If you can afford it, I ask for four dollars a night. Unless you want to stay long-term, and then we can negotiate. "But," she added quickly, "If you don't have any money, not to worry—we can work something out."

JoJo paused and glanced at Sunny. "And no men on the land and no boys over the age of five."

"Oh, no problem," Maria said. "She's a girl. Sunshine. I call her Sunny."

Maria and Sunny slept in their van parked next to the bathhouse the first night they were at Desert Haven. The next morning, they went exploring for a place to settle down for a while. Other than a few rustic structures and old trailers, the ten-acre desert property was crowded with creosote, mesquite, and palo verde trees, saguaro, and thick stands of jumping cholla cactus. Maria reminded Sunny that everything was prickly, so she had to be careful. Even so, Sunny stepped too close to a spiny cholla segment, and it attached to the toe of her sneaker.

"Don't touch it!" Maria said sharply, picking up two sticks and prying the offending cactus off. "It would stick to your fingers just like it did to your shoe." Sunny hugged her arms close to her body and carefully placed one foot in front of the other as they continued to explore the land.

They got to a flat area that looked like someone had cleared a space for something. "What about right here? We could park Brownie and stay awhile." Maria said hopefully. "Let's ask JoJo."

"That's as good a place as any," JoJo told them. "Some women from New Hampshire were here last spring. They cleared this patch for a dugout, but when summer came, they couldn't take the heat and moved on to greener pastures."

"What's a dugout?"

"It's an underground house that uses the earth as insulation against heat and cold. I've worked on two of them so far." She explained how to dig out a hole and use that dirt mixed with cement to construct the walls and how the roof was the most critical piece of the puzzle because it held it all together. She said that building the entrance was crucial because it had to be designed to keep water out. "And, yes, it rains in the desert, especially during monsoons."

"Could I do that here? Build a dugout?" Maria asked. She had never imagined that she could build herself a house. A real home, dug from the earth, what could be better? "Sunny and I can do it together."

A twinkly smile crept like sunrise across JoJo's face. "I'll help you build it."

A few days later, after setting up camp and meeting some of her neighbors, Maria knocked on JoJo's door and said she was ready to build her house.

"Well, let's get started," JoJo said. "I've got plans from the other places we built, but I know where we made mistakes, so this will be the best one yet."

JoJo was a scrap material hoarder. Anything that could be used or reused was piled in a corner of the land, lovingly nicknamed The Yard. Lumber, metal pipe, open boxes of screws, sheets of tin, bags of cement mix, discards from previous building projects, and other cast-off materials scavenged from building sites were scattered under fraying tarps in an order only known to JoJo. She methodically chose what they would need to construct the dwelling.

They worked with shovels and buckets, stone, chicken wire and concrete, wood and nails all winter and into the spring. Some of the land around Desert Haven had been sold, and a few houses were going up around them. Maria was glad that the place she chose for her house was still private.

Building was a communal affair. Many of the winter visitors pitched in as they were able, lifting beams and mud-plastering the walls. Maria grew strong, and her foot stopped bothering her. Even though she was only four years old, Sunny helped by fetching tools and sorting screws. Sometimes, she even made the peanut butter and jelly sandwiches that fueled the crew.

JoJo was a cheerful mentor and their constant companion. Most nights, the three of them shared the evening meal, and when Sunny was tucked in her sleeping bag, the two women talked into the night.

"I always knew I was bisexual, even when I married my husband," Maria said. "I thought I would just live as a straight wife and mother. But then his ghosts reared up, and he turned to drink and became abusive, so I turned to my girlfriends for support. One thing led to another, and I had a series of affairs. When he found out, the shit hit the fan."

"I think I was always a woman-loving woman," JoJo told her. "But back in my day, it wasn't as easy as it is now."

"We make a good team with your wisdom and my desire to learn," Maria said, wanting to acknowledge the age difference between them but also to let JoJo know it didn't matter to her.

Their first kiss evolved from a nightly sisterly peck on the cheek to a lingering longing. The next evening, after dinner, Maria picked up a sleeping Sunny and carefully deposited her on the couch in JoJo's trailer. The two women went into the bedroom and shut the door.

The finishing touches to the roof were on well before the summer monsoons came. Maria and Sunny sat inside the structure while JoJo sprayed water from the hose over the new construction.

"Looks good," Maria yelled out the back window. "No leaks anywhere. JoJo, you are a genius roof designer." She picked up Sunny and twirled her around until they both got dizzy. Plopping down on the ground, the earth beneath her, within the walls she had built with their own hands, Maria felt as transformed as the house was from a hole in the ground. So much had changed in the last six months.

Sunny and Maria were glad to move out of the hot van into the cool underground, even though they sometimes stayed with JoJo. Sunny said she liked to have the couch all to herself while Maria slept in the bedroom with JoJo.

They christened their new home Kozy Kiva, and painted the name on a beam over the front door with red paint. Maria built an open-air ramada for the kitchen and ran a hose from the bathhouse for water.

One night, a few weeks after they settled into their new nest, Maria told Sunny, "I think it's time for me to take a new name."

"Don't you like Maria anymore?" Sunny asked, looking up from the picture of a rabbit she was drawing, her markers spread around her on the table.

"I want to choose a name that has a special meaning, a symbol of our new life, and a connection to the sacredness of Mother Earth. A name that isn't my father's or husband's. A name that is beyond the ownership of the patriarchy. A post-patriarchal name." She knew that Sunny might not understand some of the words she used, but she would get the core meaning and feeling behind her words.

"Okay. Should I change my name too?"

"I think Sunshine is the perfect name for a sunny girl like you, but maybe we can change our last name together." Maria watched as Sunny drew a big yellow sun in the top left corner of the drawing. "Let's decide before the next full moon circle."

Everyone gathered at the Meeting Space while Sunny and Maria put the finishing touches on their outfits for the ritual, fresh flowers in their hair and matching flowing purple shawls. They each carried a tree branch tied with little gifts for everyone. Wolfie presided, calling in the directions and imploring the ancestors to bless the space.

"Gaia, life force from which all other beings sprang, including the earth, the sea, and the mountains, we welcome you. We dedicate this naming ceremony to you.

Everyone whooped and shook noisemakers when Maria revealed her new name, Madrona. The Mother Tree. From that day forth, they were to be known as Madrona and Sunshine Wimminchild.

Sunny was in the habit of waking with the sun and heading straight to JoJo's garden, where she would find the older woman tipped back in a rusted green metal lawn chair, a mug of coffee in her hands, surveying the changes that had occurred in the span of twenty-four-hours. A few more crimson cherry tomatoes, the chard looked wilty, mint was trying to take over. Drops of water still clinging to leaves from the hose spray. Madrona loved to spy on them as Sunny quietly opened the gate and stealthily, for a four-year-old, tiptoed on the crunchy garden path, hoping to surprise JoJo. JoJo would wait until Sunny was right behind her and turn around and say Boo! Then, they would collapse on each other in laughter and love.

Bath nights were extra special at Desert Haven. Madrona filled the outdoor cast-iron claw-foot tub with water, and, with help, she carefully placed a heavy sheet of plate glass over it. When the water got steamy from the sun in the late afternoon, it was ready. In the winter, they could light a fire under the tub.

Sunny bathed first. When she was dried off and tucked safely into bed, JoJo and Madrona had their turn, often soaking together with a bottle or two of wine, enjoying the glorious sunset.

There weren't any other full-time kids on the land, but sometimes visitors brought children. For a few days or weeks, Sunny would have girls her size to play with, but then they would leave, and she went back to the company of grownups.

One of the recurring items of discussion at the weekly community meeting was Sunny's education. Madrona was still flying under the radar, so she didn't want to register Sunny in school. It didn't take much discussion to come to the consensus that it was the community's responsibility. Moon made a chart of whose turn was on what day and posted it in the bathhouse.

After breakfast with Madrona or whoever was cooking and sharing that day, Sunny would go off for her daily lesson. If it was Monday, she and Moon met in the Gathering Space and sat at the splintery picnic table in the shade of the giant mesquite tree to do their sums. Moon had been a math teacher but left her school job because she didn't feel the children were being respected. She said they had more ability than anyone gave them credit for. Her philosophy was if she could make it fun, they would learn, and Sunny was a perfect example. The basic math she learned at four wouldn't be introduced to school kids until third grade, when they were already bored with all the busywork.

On Tuesdays, Sunny's lesson was in the desert with Wolfie, learning about plants and bugs. Sometimes, they would sit quietly for hours, waiting to see which insects showed up. Wolfie made notes and drawings in a notebook so Sunny could remember what she had seen. Then, when she got old enough to keep it herself, the book was ceremoniously turned over to her in a ritual to mark her graduation into a new phase of her education.

"I love going out in the desert with Wolfie," Sunny told Madrona, hugging her book to her slim chest. "Do you think that Wolfie is part wolf?"

"Do you?" Madrona asked.

"Yeah, I think she is because she smells like one."

Madrona suppressed her smile but had a good laugh later with JoJo and Wolfie over Sunny's observation.

On Wednesdays, when May didn't have to go into town for her chef's job, she and Sunny met in the community kitchen and spent the day cooking and baking bread or pizza in the domed outdoor adobe oven she called a horno. Sunny learned about measuring and cutting with a big knife and got to eat as much as she liked. If May had to miss a week, she would always bring a giant cookie from the café to make it up to Sunny.

Whenever she was in town, Madrona went to thrift stores to buy children's books of all levels, some with pictures and some with just words. She liked the ones about animals best. So, Thursday was reading with Madrona.

These were the lessons Sunny always tried to get out of.

"Stop being such a wiggle worm and sit still," Madrona said impatiently.

"I can't figure out these squiggles. I don't have to learn; you can read it to me."

"It says here that girls who don't know how to read will not get very far in life," Madrona said, pointing to some words on the page. "They will always be dependent on their mothers and never grow up."

"It does not," Sunny said, her voice going soft with disbelief.

"If you knew how to read, you would know what it says," Madrona said triumphantly.

Sunny said her favorite day was Friday. That's when she had JoJo all to herself, and they built stuff like a pen for the chickens or plastered adobe walls that had melted after the rains. JoJo was pretty quiet most of the time, but she had lots to talk about when it was just the two of them. She told Sunny about growing up in Pennsylvania on a farm, her animals, and how she didn't want to wear dresses either, but her mother made her.

Sandy and White Rabbit were in charge of gym class on weekends, and Madrona always joined in. It could be yoga or jogging down the road. Sometimes, everyone piled into a couple of cars and drove to the closest schoolyard to shoot hoops.

Hawk filled in when someone couldn't make their shift. She taught Sunny the history of Native American tribes and how they lived in the desert.

Sunny's teachers changed as some women left the land and others moved in. Spider was a weaver who showed Sunny about warp and weft on a Navajo-style loom. Jude found a quarter-sized guitar at a yard sale and taught her to play chords. There were many drawing/painting/sculpture teachers; one ex-kindergarten teacher insisted that Sunny make a color wheel from dyed macaroni. Sunny asked Madrona if they could boil it and have it for dinner.

Most of the time, things were pretty quiet at Desert Haven, but once in a while, conflict erupted at a community meeting, and women would shout or stomp out. Madrona got the willies when people were yelling; it stirred too many memories for her. Disagreements happen; it's natural, but she couldn't reconcile these women using the same bullying tactics and intimidating behaviors that she had escaped from. If it happened, she and JoJo would exchange looks, and the two of them would quietly leave the meetings. Neither wanted to be around the people they loved when they were so angry.

Later, when they lived in New Mexico, and Sunny was older, she asked Madrona about those fights. Their new home was very mellow. There was never a raised voice. Madrona explained that some women had different opinions about how Desert Haven should be run, and they passionately defended their position. In her opinion, if a woman disagreed with how things were going, they were free to leave. She thought JoJo was the most generous woman to allow everyone to crash on her land, and she disagreed with the faction that wanted to set up a land trust and take JoJo's land away from her.

But that's not why Sunny and Madrona left. They moved to a women's community near Solana, New Mexico, so Madrona could study botanical medicine.

The night Madrona told JoJo they were leaving, the moon was full, and the two women were lying on lawn chairs gazing at the sky.

"Remember I applied to go to that school over in New Mexico?" Madrona said, fixing her eyes on one bright star and waiting until a million others came into view in the dark sky.

"Yeah, I remember. I mailed that letter for you at the post office."

"Well, they accepted me. I wrote that I couldn't afford the tuition. They gave me a scholarship, so, I guess I'm going." She looked over at JoJo, who silently watched the sky as if looking for the correct response.

After a pause, Madrona said, "I'll miss you. When I told Sunny, she asked if JoJo was coming with us."

"I can come and visit," JoJo said, not taking her eyes off the sky.

On moving day, the women gathered around Brownie to say their goodbyes. Madrona blinked back her tears because she didn't want to upset Sunny, but Sunny was already bawling and holding on to JoJo.

"I'm sorry, baby, we have to go. It's time to leave now," Madrona told Sunny as she gently pried her from JoJo's arms and carried her over to Brownie. Sunny's legs almost touched the ground. At nine years old, she was really too big for Madrona to carry.

Friends and landmates surrounded Madrona to send her off with hugs and well wishes. May reached inside the van and placed a bag heavy with cookies on Sunny's lap, saying, "Save some for your mom."

JoJo stood to one side, watching the parade of friendship. As Madrona got into the driver's seat, JoJo walked to the other side of the car and reached into the open window, cradling her hand around the back of Sunny's head. "Goodbye, little one. Come back and see me soon." She placed a kiss on Sunny's forehead and backed away from the van. Madrona understood JoJo's remark was for both of them. She waved and whispered, "I love you, JoJo," and shifted the van into Drive.

Mel 2003

Things weren't going so well with Melanie and Andrew. They hadn't even been married a year, and already they were bickering a lot. Mostly over small things. Andy said the strands of Mel's long blond hair clogging the shower drain made him gag. Mel said Andy's habit of cracking his knuckles sent unpleasant barbs of electricity up her spine. Complaining about each other over many glasses of wine with friends, they were told the honeymoon was over. The time had come to adjust to each other's everyday eccentricities and learn the art of compromise, ignoring little things and focusing on the positive.

Good advice, but it didn't work for them. Minor infractions, unresolved, were like children's blocks sloppily placed upon each other. Melanie and Andy each accumulated a precarious tower of resentments.

Their first connection had been words. They met at the university library in the 800s of the Dewey decimal system. Literature. Book snobs, they wouldn't read anything that was on a bestseller list. Recent graduates of NYU, the comfort of the stacks drew them back even though they were out in the work world; Andy was a junior editor at a university press, and Melanie worked in victim advocacy at the city attorney's office.

Their conversational style included dumping the contents of their busy brains and sorting out the jumble of thoughts together. Melanie always felt she learned something—lots of things—after one of their talkathons. They could gab all night and still have things to tell each other at breakfast. Most evenings were spent sitting on the couch holding hands, feeding each other warm buttery popcorn, and watching classic films starring Loretta Young, Cary Grant, or Katherine Hepburn in glorious black and white.

Two years of courtship, meaning Melanie rushed to her apartment every weekday to change clothes and get ready for work, led to the logical conclusion that they could save enough money to buy a house if they joined forces. So, they pooled their resources and left the city for a not-yet gentrified, still affordable suburb in New Jersey. Their 1950s ranch house had original peach tiles in the bathroom that they pretended to like. Both families amped up the pressure for marriage, so they acquiesced with a small ceremony in the backyard, presided over by a justice of the peace. Melanie indulged her mother's need to make a big deal out of simple things, so the wedding party of seventeen people, including the justice of the peace, carpooled to the best restaurant in town to enjoy a lavish celebratory dinner, and her mother picked up the bill.

After the trips to Ikea and calling the plumber a few times, the house was as comfortable as it could be without a major investment in a new heating and cooling system. They noticed that no one was on the street after dark, which Melanie thought was ironic because wasn't it safer in the burbs than in the big bad city? But, of course, there was nowhere to walk to. Their cable package didn't include Turner Classic Movies, so they started watching reruns of *Cheers*.

Melanie was getting restless. She thought it would help if she had a garden, but the crickets ate all of the herbs. Andy wanted a dog, but Melanie wouldn't have any part of it. He gave her a puppy for her birthday, thinking she couldn't resist the sweet yellow lab. When the puppy dug up what was left of the garden and almost died from inhaling a sock, they were able to rehome her to a family with a stay-at-home dad.

They were both so tired at the end of their long commute from the city that they didn't have much to say to each other over frozen dinners and a bottle or two of wine.

Andy took on extra hours at work to cover the car payment. He was stressed and exhausted all the time, so he smoked a little weed after dinner just to relax and then fell into a world of his own. Went to bed early. He lost weight but gained a potbelly.

Melanie got tired of keeping up both sides of the conversation, so she fell silent. She gained weight and let her hair grow out to mousy brown.

They were still surprised that it happened to them. They'd seen other couples drift apart, but they thought that the rope tied around each other's hearts and minds was so tight it would never unravel. Slowly, that tie got caught in the wheels of routine. It stretched and frayed and sagged.

And now it was tattered—an odd collection of strings and loops that neither of them could make sense out of anymore.

One Friday, when Andy was late coming home from work, Melanie found herself being alternately pissed off because the coq au vin she made from a recipe in Bon Appetit was getting cold and terrified that something had happened to her husband because he was always home at 6:30 sharp. She texted an intentionally casual message, slowly tapping out the numbers on her number pad, "What's your ETA hon?" When she got no response after fifteen minutes, she wrote, "CU soon??" and sent it wishing she had been more direct.

At 8:00, she tapped in, "Where the fuck R U?" Too direct. She erased it and instead sent, "I'm worried where R U?"

Andy texted back, "Out wiissh my boss. B home sooon."

At 9 p.m., Melanie was in the city, crying tears of frustration in her cousin's guest room, furious with the inconsiderate lout she had married.

At 9:15, the front door slammed open, the doorknob making a slight dent in the wall, and Andy lurched into his home, disoriented, disheveled, and full of happy-hour margaritas. The lingering odor of food beckoned him to the kitchen, but there was no dinner on the stove. No recently wrapped-up plates of food in the fridge either. He didn't think to look in the trash.

He searched for Melanie, not a difficult task in their compact tract home, and his sodden brain slowly understood that he was alone. With nothing else to do, he fell back onto the bed and passed out. In his impaired state, he thought he got up and went to the bathroom, but instead, he pissed all over Melanie's precious Isaac Mizrahi duvet cover.

The screaming argument the next morning and the consequent weepy reconciliation is what led them to be standing in a large chain-link fenced-in lot in the blazing sun, surrounded by shiny travel trailers at The Vintage Trailer Extravaganza. Their logic was thus: Things had gone from bad to worse. They still loved each other but weren't sure how to mend the relationship. Melanie suggested that they do something that they both loved so that they could re-bond. Camping. They both loved camping. The trailer was a new beginning.

It was adorable. A 1972 fifteen-foot Jayco JayWren, two-tone white and red. The owner gave them a detailed list of all the repairs and restoration he had done. It still needed a little work, but it was mostly cosmetic stuff. All the systems were in tip-top shape. The price was right, and they could tow it with their SUV.

Melanie pulled out her sewing machine and made some red and white gingham curtains. Andy practiced backing up. Melanie made reservations at a state park, and a month later, they were on the road. They were both surprised at how quickly the gas gauge swung to empty. Andy was confused by Melanie's directions on backing the trailer into the small campsite. When he bumped into the metal picnic table and made a dent in the side panel, Melanie called him a fucking idiot. The friendly neighbors who had come out to help faded away back into their tin box homes.

Melanie couldn't get the stove to light and filled the camper with the smell of gas. She opened all the windows to air it out and flapped around a dishtowel adorned with a cunning red trailer applique. The hamburger meat was soggy from the melted ice in the cooler, and it burned to the unseasoned pan. Andy forgot his toothbrush and wanted to use Melanie's, but she said that was disgusting. He said it was no worse than kissing. After arguing themselves tired, they went to bed, back-to-back, trying not to touch in the bigger than a single but not quite double bed.

It was just like home but a lot closer. Melanie tried to calm herself by planning a hike in the morning, but they woke to the loud pitter-patter of rain on the roof and a leak over the dining room table. Andy said it was a good thing that they didn't unhitch the trailer last night so they could get the hell out of there.

They packed up and headed to the interstate, looking for a place to have some breakfast. Next exit, International House of Pancakes—"all you care to eat pancakes for only $3.99." Andy said at least one good thing happened on this godforsaken trip and ordered his second stack of three buttermilk cakes with bacon. Melanie knew she shouldn't, but she couldn't stop herself from reminding him of his pledge to lighten up on the carbs because he didn't want to end up looking like his father. Andy just gave her a long, cold stare and poured extra maple syrup over the warm stack of comfort before him. He dug into his food like a man clinging to a life raft. Melanie virtuously devoured her spinach omelet, eschewing the toast. She vowed to herself to become a vegetarian to counterbalance Andy's destructive food choices. Silence overtook the table, and it persisted during the two-hour drive home, the unpacking, and all the next day.

When Andy returned from work Monday evening, he found a note. It wasn't unexpected. "I guess we both know it's not working. I'll be back for my stuff in a few days." He left the note on the counter and put a frozen burrito on a paper plate in the microwave. He ate it standing over the kitchen sink, looking out at the carport where Melanie's car should have been.

"You can have the couch. I never liked it anyway," Melanie said, running her fingers across the bumpy fabric.

"But you were the one who insisted on orange. You take it."

"I don't want any furniture at all. I don't want any possessions, and I don't want to be tied down," Melanie's voice rose as she struggled to articulate a thought, a concept, an idea that was surfacing in her brain but wasn't entirely clear yet. She walked to the front window and looked out at the neighbor's blank windows, drawn curtains, and pristine front yard. It made her uncomfortable, like she was living on a movie set. Not real. Phony.

"You can have it all. I just want the trailer and the SUV."

"What are you talking about. Of course, we'll split everything down the middle," Andy said. Melanie wasn't sure if he was sincere about being equitable. She didn't trust his words anymore. It made her sad.

"No, really, I don't want anything. I've already quit my job, and I'm ready to hit the road."

"You quit your job?" Andy repeated as if he didn't believe her. "But you love your job."

"Yeah, I did. But it's time for me to move on. I'm done with social work, done with victim advocacy, done with all the emotional pain." Melanie twisted her torso right and left as if she was trying to wring out unhappiness.

"I can't believe you didn't tell me," Andy said, getting up from the table, walking over to the couch. He looked down at it like a foreign object that just appeared in his living room. A big orange boat that drifted up with the tide and could just as easily drift away.

"Well, we haven't exactly been talking lately," Melanie said and instantly regretted her tone. She didn't want to be sarcastic or snide; it just slipped out that way. She hoped that her exit would be as drama-free as possible.

Melanie needed a fresh start with no entanglements. No tentacles enveloping her limbs. She was tired of fighting the octopus that had become her marriage and needed to "find herself." That's how she thought of it, in quotes. "Find Herself." Quotes and capital letters. A quest that she needed to embark on alone. Andy, the furniture, the house, it all had to go.

"You really intend to leave it all behind, don't you? Leave me behind." Andy said, turning away, not willing to share the emotion visible on his face.

"I think it's best for both of us. We are not helping each other anymore. Let's just let it go." Melanie said.

"I don't seem to have a choice, do I?"

Melanie walked into the kitchen, worried that they would get into another fight. She was done with the struggle to hold it together. She looked around to see if there was anything she wanted. Was she just fooling herself about leaving it all? She opened and closed a few drawers, glancing at silverware, ladles and mixing spoons, plastic baggies and waxed paper, Tupperware, and empty yogurt containers. Nothing had an emotional charge. She felt overwhelmed by the sheer amount of stuff.

Andy watched her in the shadow of the doorway.

"So, are we in agreement that I'll get the trailer?" she asked. "That's all I want. I'll sign the house over to you."

When he didn't reply, Melanie didn't know if he was pissed or sad or just trying to annoy her. She never knew what was going on with him.

"Whatever. I won't fight you," he finally said. "Let's get it over with as fast as possible."

Andy backed the SUV close to the trailer. Not very precise, but better than she could do. From now on, Melanie was on her own. With a few instruction booklets and some practice, she knew she could figure it out.

But all the books she had read about how to keep a marriage together didn't seem to help—the instructions were always too vague. They stressed open communication, but what if neither party has those skills? How does compassion work if it's one-sided? Andy pooh-poohed all that "psychobabble," preferring to go on his instincts.

In the course of their relationship, Melanie had learned to distrust her instincts. They led her into an unfulfilling relationship, didn't they? She had to relearn that she was the best authority on herself. Now her instincts were yelling, "go solo," and that's one thing she thought she could do.

Her first stop was her mother's upstate farm, where she planned to practice with the trailer before she hit the road. When she saw the swaths of yellow crocus and purple iris along the driveway, she had to smile. She always loved spring in the Catskills.

Melanie parked where her mother suggested, in a flat area next to the barn. She tried to remember the order in which she should do things: level from side to side on those orange flat Lego things, unhook the hitch, set up the stabilizers, level from front to back, find an outlet for the extension cord, roll out the canopy. If she had been in a campsite, she would have hooked up the water and maybe the sewer. She would learn how to do those tasks another day.

The farm was actually Mother and Steve's. Steve became her unofficial stepfather ten years ago when he moved into the house Mother got in the divorce. Dad got the apartment in the city. Mother didn't want anything to do with it because that's where 'The Bum' fucked that whore." She took the 52 acres with the 1880s remodeled farmhouse and a tidy monthly alimony check. If she married Steve, the checks would stop, and she wasn't going to let The Bum off that easy.

Steve was younger than Mother, but he had lots of grey in his beard, and Mother dyed her hair to an unnatural black, so it was hard to tell who was older. He farmed an acre of garden and did all the maintenance around the property, so apparently, his share was "sweat equity." His extensive guitar collection was housed in a section of the basement he converted into a recording studio. Every day after lunch, he'd say, "See you at happy hour," and disappear down the stairs, shutting the door behind him. He said he was recording his original songs, but he could have been smoking dope and looking at porn for all Melanie knew. No one ever went down to check on him. On the whole, Melanie liked him. He didn't ask a lot of questions, and he never offered advice.

The day after Melanie's arrival, the party of three went into town for a steak dinner. The conversation was mostly about mutual friends and relatives. Small talk, safe talk.

Over her second or third martini, Mother let it slip that she had a "problem fibroid."

"What does that mean?" Melanie asked

"It's called uterine myoma, a fairly common annoying condition that usually goes away with menopause, but mine seems to be hanging on. Don't worry, these things are rarely cancer."

"Oh, shit, I didn't know I should be worried about cancer. Are you okay?" Melanie asked, trying to look into her mother's eyes past the gin.

"Oh, sure honey, no problems. Just a heavy period every month, some cramps, mood swings, that sort of thing. Girl stuff," she said, looking over at Steve, who looked slightly embarrassed in an old-fashioned kind of way. "Now, where the hell is our waiter? I need some food to sop up all this alcohol."

Melanie got back to her trailer at 10:30, satiated with rich food and drink. Her new pledge to follow a more austere diet had flown out the window. Her mother, the perfect hedonist, insisted that everyone join in her excesses. Melanie had always found it difficult, if not impossible, to resist the pressure, so once again, indulgence won. The doggie bag stuffed with rare prime rib and garlic mashed potatoes tucked into the cooler, Melanie made a mental note to get some ice from the house tomorrow. She kicked off her shoes and crawled into bed.

Pulling the covers over her head, Melanie felt a blanket of sadness crush her into the mattress. It was hard to catch her breath, and she was flooded with memories. Searching the house for hidden bottles and pouring the booze down the toilet when she was eleven. The night when she carried her mother over her shoulder to keep her from dancing on broken wine bottle shards. The worst was the time when Mother screamed bloody murder, sobbing that she had shooting pains in her stomach, so Melanie checked her into the hospital, knowing she was just on a four-day binge. She left her there for a week so she could dry out.

Focusing on an old water stain on the ceiling to keep the world from spinning, Melanie decided to leave as soon as possible. The likelihood that this would be the time she got Mother's attention and love was crushed as usual. Melanie felt gored by helplessness, and great belly sobs racked her body. Arms wrapped around her legs, she curled into a ball of pain. She couldn't make it as a daughter or a wife. She was just a failure. Her sobs turned to soft moans, and she fell asleep, a package of misery.

She woke with a start, blinking in the morning sun, her mouth dry as cardboard, and the hint of a headache over her left eye. Sitting with a cup of oolong tea on the dewy trailer steps in the cheerful sunshine, she watched tall grass swaying to a slight breeze. It was a new day, and it was time for a fresh start. And she knew the perfect way to begin her new life. She took the kitchen scissors into the tiny bathroom. Flipping her hair forward over her shoulders, she said goodbye to the long locks that had taken her years to grow out and snipped, a handful at a time, leaving the miniature sink overflowing with golden tresses. It was terrifying. It was exhilarating.

Staring at her image in the mirror, Melanie felt herself transformed from a fussy person with too many needs into a simpler, self-contained being. Someone who needed an easier name. As simple as snipping her hair off, she lobbed the ending letters off her name and emerged as Mel.

Sitting at the little fold-down table, Mel took out her road maps and bundle of highlighters to plan her journey. Mel had joined AAA and matched their campground guide to a large map that featured small highways headed south and west. The general route was marked with yellow highlighter. Green meant places of interest like the Liberty Bell and Graceland. Pink meant people she might want to visit. Many of her old friends randomly sprinkled the map like dandelion seeds puffed westward. She entered addresses into her Palm Pilot and filled her CD case with her favorite albums. She was ready to leave at seven a.m. the following day.

The ritual of folding up camp was soothing and gave her something to think about so she could tuck this visit into an ignored corner of her brain with all the other hurts. Should she be worried about her mother? Mother didn't seem to be concerned, so why should she fret about it. It was just Mother and her drama.

◆ ◆ ◆

One of the things Mel was nervous about was staying awake while driving. Her strategy was to stop every two hours for gas and walk around the truck stop parking lot, sipping tarry vending machine coffee. Her other fear was not handling the trailer on her own, even though she had practiced a few times at her mother's place. After seven hours on the road, she arrived at a KOA campsite southeast of Pittsburg. All the pull-through spots were booked, so she was stuck with a back-in site in the trees.

Following the park map to her site, she pulled up just past it so she could back in. The extended side-view mirrors gave her a lot of information, but they were disorienting. Smoothly gliding backward into her site proved to be a fantasy. In reality, she backed up a little bit and got out of the SUV to see where she was in relation to the electric box, picnic table, and low-hanging branches. Then she climbed back into the vehicle and pulled forward to correct her mistakes, and backed up again. Repeat. Repeat. Repeat.

Other campers watched her efforts with a sort of indifference that said, been there, done that. Finally, a kind grey-bearded man in a Bronco's t-shirt came over and asked if he could help, and she gratefully relinquished the wheel.

He backed the trailer onto its concrete pad on the first try. Mel thanked him profusely, embarrassing both of them. She plugged in the electric connection but decided to forgo the water hookups. The public bathroom was nearby, and she could use it without further mortification.

Dinner was a satisfying can of Campbell's tomato soup with a grilled cheese sandwich, all concocted over the gas stove using thrift store kitchen items she had lovingly collected—the more vintage, the better. She made herself a mental note to refill the gas canister the next day.

After washing her dish and pan in the communal bathroom, brushing her teeth, and admiring her new spiky hairdo in the mirror, Mel locked the trailer door and got in bed with her journal.

She thought about this amazing day of facing her fears. A list was in order:

- Drove by myself for 7 hours. Did not fall asleep.
- Spent all day alone and was not bored. Not even for a second.
- Survived embarrassment of parking fiasco. Next time I may even ask for help.
- Learned that I just have to practice backing up more, and eventually I will get it.
- I love my little home on wheels!! I feel so FREE!

The word "free" deserved and received pink highlighting.

After a week on the road, with help from friendly camping enthusiasts, she felt much more comfortable in her new skin. Her red and white aluminum skin. When the toilet started to smell, she learned how to use the dump station from a large, sweaty man wearing a backward Vietnam Vets baseball cap. When she almost sheared off the awning with a low-hanging branch, the RV repair shop she found in the phone book stayed open late for her and only charged her twenty dollars to straighten out the posts and glue the material back together. People passing her on the highway would point and yell things she couldn't understand, so she'd pull over at the next safe spot and look around the trailer to see if she forgot to stow the stairs or left compartments open again.

The trailer was cute as a bug (that's what the lady with pink hair curlers told her in the campsite in Oklahoma City), and it had stopped feeling foreign and awkward. She was becoming a happy camper.

Sitting at a picnic table in a campground with a glowing lantern was an invitation to small talk with other travelers. The distraction was welcome because she knew it was a temporary connection, and she could quickly wave goodbye the next morning. Everyone was quick to tell where they had been and to share tricks of the road. McDonald's had clean restrooms, and the thermos of coffee she'd make in the morning would stay warm most of the day and was much better than fast food restaurants' poor excuse for java.

Crossing the New Mexico/Arizona state line was a thrill. Mel didn't know that she would fall in love with the desert, the big skies, the weird landscape, and the taciturn shopkeepers. She didn't quite understand why it felt right in her bones. She announced to Red Betty, the name her trailer seemed to embody, that she was home. Now, all they had to do was find a place to settle down for a while.

Every week, she dropped some coins into a payphone to satisfy her mother's request that she check in regularly.

"Yeah, I'm safe. No problems. The rig is doing great. I'm having a great time. No, I don't need any company to keep me awake while I drive. I enjoy the quiet. No, I haven't met anyone along the way. I don't want to meet someone, Mother—I'm just fine the way I am. No, I don't need any money. I've got plenty, thanks. How are you? Are you really okay? That's great. Yeah, thanks, Mother, take care."

Mel's momentum took her barreling towards Tucson. She had been on the road for almost four months, and the idea of staying put was beginning to appeal to her. Surprised to find her simple lifestyle so gratifying, she loved cruising along at her own pace. Eventually, she might look for work, but right now, clearing her head and finding her heart's desire were the two things that took all her attention.

Her AAA book guided her to The Prince of Tucson RV Park. She paid for a week and took some time to get familiar with the town, checking it out as a potential home. She explored the shops on Fourth Avenue near the University of Arizona, and found her way to the campus library. Researching campsites nearby, she read about Desert Haven. The woman at the desk said she should talk to Ruth in the women's studies department because she had some tie to a camping spot for women. She tracked down Ruth, who said the place was out of town, on ten acres of land. And it was women only. Mel figured she qualified.

Following the hand-drawn map, Mel drove right past the driveway. From the road, it looked like an abandoned enclave of old trailers and piles of trash. She backed up on the narrow, rutted lane, mentally patting herself on the back for her recently acquired skills and pulled into the driveway.

JoJo, the owner of the property, saw Red Betty drive by and then back up and turn into the drive. Walking over, she leaned on the open window and said, "You looking for a place to park your rig?"

"I heard I could rent a space here."

"Oh, we don't have anything as formal as spaces. Take a look around, but you might want to park in that level spot under the big mesquite tree over where Juniper's truck is. There's no electric or water except at the bathhouse."

"That'll do just fine. How much is it?"

"Seven dollars a day or forty dollars a week. If you can't afford it, we can work something out. My name is JoJo."

Mel extracted two twenty-dollar bills from her wallet. "I guess I'll stay for a week if that's okay with you. My name is Mel."

She smoothly backed the trailer between spiked cactus arms and low-hanging tree branches. After getting set up, Mel fetched a cold beer from the cooler, pulled her lounge chair from an outside storage compartment, and sat, facing the long view of mountains in the distance. Relaxing into the chair, she stretched and sighed. Until that moment, she hadn't realized how much effort it took to be constantly on the road. It was time to take a breather. She felt like she'd come a long way, both in miles and in attitude.

The desert was dry and hot and soothing. The sky was a brilliant blue. Red Betty was perky as ever. Mel felt full -- and something else. Happy. She had to think about it for a moment because she hadn't felt that way for a long time.

A few women drifted by on their way to a central area, interrupting her reverie.

"You coming to the potluck?" asked one woman.

"Sure, what should I bring?"

"Whatever food you have to share and your own plate and utensils."

Carrying a bag of blue corn tortilla chips, an open jar of Pace Picante Sauce, and her beer, she walked towards a small group of women gathered around a stone-lined fire pit on an assortment of seating arrangements. JoJo waved her over to share the cracked and peeling light blue center seat from someone's van. She raised her glass of wine in salutation, and they clinked drinks.

"Ladies, may I have your attention," JoJo said in a soft but authoritarian voice. "This here is Mel. She's staying with us for a week. Or maybe more, who knows. She might decide she likes it here."

Mel wondered how she had given that impression to JoJo but then realized that, yes, she might stay for a bit. She was briefly the center of attention as everyone was curious about the newcomer, but then the talk shifted to gossip and a discussion about clean-up day.

"I'll contribute to the cost of the roll-away dumpster if someone calls and sets it up," offered a woman in an oversized red AZ Wildcats sweatshirt.

"I can help with the clearing out, Curry, but I don't have any money right now," said a thin older woman with pink hair and a large mole on the side of her nose.

They decided that the following Saturday would be the best day for the community effort and dug into their feast—spicy beans and cheese, assorted cut-up raw vegetables, warm quinoa salad, soybean hummus, a watermelon split in half with a help-yourself large mixing spoon dug into the flesh. The food choices were as eclectic as the women themselves. Mel excused herself after dinner, before the singing began, saying she was tired from the drive.

She soon discovered that the dinner gathering repeated itself nightly. Not everyone came every night, and she had noticed that Juniper, who lived in her truck, hardly ever came to anything, so Mel felt comfortable joining or not, depending on her mood. She didn't have to answer to anyone. There seemed to be no rules.

It was September, and the heat wasn't as intense as summer, but it was still pretty hot. Sunsets were a riot of color, and she always made time to walk down the road, face west, and be awed. Her mini daily ritual. After a week, she gave JoJo a month's rent and joined in the clean-up project.

JoJo and a couple of women were making adobe blocks for a new community building, and Mel asked if she could join them. When her muscles ached from the physical labor, Liv gave her homemade arnica salve. Mel didn't mind the discomfort. On the contrary, she found it exhilarating.

During a foray into town, she stopped at an art supply store where she bought watercolor paints and a selection of papers. She heard Wolfie had been an art teacher and asked if she would give her painting lessons, and they settled upon a modest fee. When Wolfie came on to her, Mel explained that she was straight. Surprised, but with no judgment, Wolfie shrugged and said, whatever floats your boat.

Bright landscapes, abstract designs of splotches of color, and watery shapes filled the trailer walls. Mel didn't care if they were amateurish. She just loved the process of putting brush to paper and being surprised at what emerged.

One night at a potluck, Liv and Curry exchanged angry words in loud voices. Knowing glances around the circle. "There they go again." Mel learned that the women had been lovers but had split up six months ago. They didn't seem to realize that they no longer had to fight all the time.

Mel took her plate back to her trailer. Avoidance was the best policy. Conflict wasn't her thing, and she certainly didn't want to be around people who treated it like sport. She passed Juniper sitting in the shade of her truck, eating her dinner. Juni waved shyly, and Mel waved back, knowing it was a gesture of friendliness, not an invitation to engage, grateful that there was someone else who enjoyed solitude as much as she did.

She finished her dinner alone at her picnic table, counting the stars and listening to the chorus of coyote howls. A sense of peace and expansion filled her heart so sharply it almost hurt. Leaving her marriage had given her inner hermit space to emerge. She felt a profound need to spend most of her time in her own company. No apologies, no accommodation to other people's expectations. She didn't need anyone else to feel complete.

There were a lot of things she liked about living at Desert Haven. The safety she found in women-only space removed a subconscious stressor she didn't even know she had. Living closer to the land kept her aware of the ebb and flow of nature's idiosyncrasies. She could use her body in ways she never had before, and she had ample time to read and daydream. Sometimes, at night, the breeze carried the sweet sound of someone singing a sad song. Somehow, she had been led to the perfect place at the perfect time. She didn't believe that everything happened for a reason, but she did know that some things were just out of her control.

◆ ◆ ◆

Since she didn't have a phone, whenever she was in town, Mel called her mother. In December, Mother mentioned that she was scheduled for a "little procedure" in the hospital.

"You want me to come to be with you? Mel asked.

"Oh, no, it's just a simple thing. Don't worry. I'll be fine. Steve is here."

In January, her mother was back in the hospital, this time for exploratory surgery related to her "plumbing problem." Mel flew home and went directly to the hospital.

She stopped at the nurse's station, saying, "I'm looking for Sally Harris."

The nurse located the room number and, without looking up, said, "Down the hall, 1205."

Her mother looked small and grey in her oversized hospital gown. "Hi honey, you didn't have to come," she said softly and shifted some of the tubes and monitors so Mel could come closer for a peck on the cheek.

"Of course I did. Steve said that you have cancer, Mother."

"That's what they say. They took my uterus and ovaries, and anything they thought might have cancer cells. Maybe they caught it in time. I don't know. Maybe my time is up."

"It's not like you to give up so easily. I'm here for you. I'll help you through this."

Her mother looked away as if gazing out a window, but she stared at the blue-flowered divider curtain. Mel pulled up an armchair, resting her head on the edge of the bed

Mel thought she could feel the cancer taking over her mother's body. She smelled the cells and heard them devouring healthy tissue. Her mother was exhausted. She must have been fighting this thing for a long time. Why didn't she share her struggle? Mel was painfully aware that her mother hadn't trusted her with this important life transition. She reached for her mother's hand, and, at the touch, her mother instinctively withdrew.

Sally was buried in the family plot, alongside her parents and a sister who had died in infancy, behind her grandparents' joint grave and amongst many ancestors that Mel had never heard of. A blank headstone next to Mother was saved for Steve when his time came. Mel wondered if she, too, had a reserved burial plot but didn't know who to ask.

The immediate family went for lunch at the country club, where Mel mingled with cousins she didn't remember and sobbing elder aunts. "She was so brave." "She had such a wonderful life." "Taken from us too soon." Mel removed herself to walk the graveyard and escape from the cloying words and self-conscious proclamations.

Sally's lawyer introduced himself to Mel and asked if she could stop by his office the following day. He wanted to share some details of the will.

Mel took a seat in Mr. James' office at ten a.m. She remembered the time because he had a huge subway clock on the wall behind his desk like he wanted his clients to know exactly how much each word was costing them at $300 per hour.

"First, let me offer my condolences for your loss. Sally was a wonderful woman. I've known her for years, ever since she came to the valley."

"Thank you."

"Are you aware of the terms of her will?"

"No, we never discussed it."

"She was a big-hearted and generous woman. She left the house and land to Steve, of course. Being that you are an only child, the rest of the estate is yours. Minus taxes and my fee, of course."

"Won't Steve need some money to live on?"

"She knew that he didn't need it. He has a sizable income from his music." Mr. James noticed the confused look on Mel's face. "You do know about that, don't you?"

"Not really."

"Steve has been selling chart-topping songs to country stars for years. Do you know Vince Gills's "Know It's Love" or "The Best Day" that George Strait scored with? Those were Steve's."

"It's not my kind of music. So, Steve makes a living selling songs?" She was trying to understand this twist.

"He's doing quite well, actually. So, Sally thought it was more practical for you to receive the inheritance."

"How much are we looking at?" Mel asked, still in shock about Steve's secret life.

"Well, there is still a lot to take care of, but I would say the estate is in the neighborhood of one point three."

Silence. Mel tried to figure out if he meant one point three million dollars or if it was some sort of code. Where would her mother get that kind of money? How could she have not known until now?

"Are you saying over a million dollars?"

"You are surprised," Mr. James said.

"Shocked is more like it. When do I get it?"

"Sally was very thorough, and it's all taken care of. The estate should settle within six months. If you need some money to tide you over until then, I can work something out. Maybe an advance of $50,000? It would come out of the estate, of course."

Mel's brain was on overdrive. What would she do with all that money? What did it mean to have such a huge inheritance? How could her mother have hidden this from her?

"No, I'm fine, thanks. Do I have to stick around for anything, or is it okay that I'm leaving tomorrow?"

"As long as I have your contact information, no problem. Here's my card. Call me if you change your mind and need a little cash."

Returning to her old trailer on the rundown property was surreal. Mel looked around her and thought, I don't have to live like this. I have choices. I could live anywhere. She decided the best thing to do was to do nothing while sorting through her feelings about the money. And her mother's death.

JoJo asked how her trip was, and she said, "Fine." She didn't feel a need to share. Maybe she was more like her mother than she knew.

Mel was surprised when she hit her six-month mark at Desert Haven. Time had passed so quickly, with so little effort. Her only expenses were rent, occasional trips to the food co-op, gas, and art supplies. She bought four new tires and a cell phone. She was still living off her savings. When she got the registered letter from Mr. James saying the estate was settled and Mel could start drawing on the account any time she wanted, she told her curious landmates that the official-looking letter was about a legal thing in her past and dropped it. She filed the letter in a folder marked Important Papers along with her social security card and divorce decree. She didn't need the money now. And besides, it made her think about her mother, and she didn't want to revisit her sadness.

She was starting to understand how much like her mother she was—both introverts, both women who enjoyed their own company and who engaged with life on their own terms. They had chosen different paths to the same destination.

After a year on the land, Mel fell into an easy routine. Rising with the sun, she stood outside Red Betty and took a photo of the sunrise with her cell phone from the same spot every day. It was her morning prayer, giving thanks for a new day. Then, depending on the weather, she either sat under the mesquite that she thought of as her Bodhi tree, at the picnic table she had built, drinking a cup of English Breakfast tea, or, in the winter, she waited until it warmed up before venturing out into the cold air, enjoying her first cup of tea shrouded in a blanket in front of the built-in propane heater. She had constructed a lean-to that extended her awning with two canvas walls to protect her from the sun and occasional monsoon rains. Her outdoor kitchen was a Coleman camp stove and plastic basin fed by a garden hose that snaked over from the bathhouse for washing dishes. After contemplating the state of the desert, Mel put on her sneakers and went for a run down the dusty lane, out into the desert, where the houses thinned out. She had the whole landscape to herself. The only sound, her breath softly keeping time to her footfall, counting 1, 2, 3, 4, over and over in her head like a breathing metronome.

If no one else had used the hot water coiled in the black water hose on the roof of the bathhouse, she would have a nice warm shower. If someone beat her to it, the shower was fast and refreshing. Breakfast consisted of oatmeal with evaporated milk and raisins. Her meals never varied because she found what worked through trial and error and didn't feel a need to reinvent the wheel. Getting the same quantities of the same foods simplified grocery shopping.

After breakfast, Mel did her rounds to see what was happening on the land—any tracks or animal droppings to indicate nocturnal visitors, cactus wren nests being constructed, ripened tomatoes in the garden, new human residents. She was always happy to pitch in with whatever creative and sometimes ill-conceived construction project was underway. If they needed supplies, she went to the hardware store or lumber yard, paying for materials. No one offered to pay her back, and that was just fine.

By afternoon, except for the few months of winter, it was too hot to do much, so that was her sacred reading time. Her tastes were extensive, from Marge Piercy to Thich Nhat Hanh, Mary Oliver to Dan Brown; she was a regular shopper at the feminist bookstore where she would pick up three or four books a week, happy to support a local independent instead of one of those big chains that seemed to be taking over. Since the trailer had limited storage space, she donated an armload to the library every month.

In the evening, she settled in with a beer and the setting sun. If she had been alone all day, she would seek out the company of others, maybe sharing a meal for an hour or so. That was her limit. She was cozy in her trailer at night with a battery-run lantern and piles of books. She wrote in her journal for a half-hour before bed.

Predictable, comforting, and never dull, she loved her schedule and freedom. When women raged about politics and oppression, she had nothing to contribute. She had pared down her needs and became quiet.

Although there was much discussion at the hours-long consensus-driven community meetings about budgeting and splitting costs equally, it was an illusion that JoJo allowed. She was the landowner, the one who got the tax bills and had the bathhouse installed. Her pension couldn't cover everything, so she asked for a little rent that most women could afford, but no one was turned away for lack of funds.

Some of the women who showed up at Desert Haven were desperate for shelter. JoJo felt strongly that it was her mission to provide safety for anyone who needed it. She established a sliding scale that only she understood because it was very circumstantial. She trusted it would work out because it always did. Someone would come into a windfall and pay up for their last six months just when the insurance bill was lying on JoJo's desk under a hand-painted statue of Lakshmi, the serene Hindu goddess of prosperity.

Mel wanted to help. One Tuesday evening after dinner, she walked over to JoJo's and found her sitting on the deck enjoying the last bit of color in the western sky.

"Isn't it beautiful," Mel said.

"It always is," JoJo said. "It's getting a bit nippy. I was just going in— please come and join me." she said, opening the door as an invitation. "Can I get you a glass of wine?"

"Thanks, don't mind if I do," Mel said, accepting a jelly jar of red liquid poured from a two-liter bottle. Not fancy but drinkable, she thought after taking a small sip. Mel looked around for a place to sit and settled on a small wooden chair next to a folding table. The only other perch was an unmade double bed that JoJo flopped down on. Piles of books on the table, muddy tools in one corner of the room, clothing discarded atop the dresser, drawers dangling open, and drawings pinned to the wall gave Mel a claustrophobic feeling. JoJo seemed oblivious to the disorder.

"I've been here for a year, and we've never really talked. Not about personal stuff, anyway," Mel said. "We always seem to be building something or in some damn meeting."

"I could do without those meetings too," JoJo said and raised her glass in a toast of sisterhood.

"Cheers," Mel said and drained her glass. JoJo got up with the bottle, and Mel nodded her head in assent. "All that arguing about a land trust. Sounds to me that you don't want any part of it, yet it gets brought up over and over."

"I just want to do my own thing," JoJo said, fluffing a pillow behind her and resituating herself on the bed, "They can stay as long as they like, but I'm not going to sign the land over to them. I've got other plans. But let's change the subject. Tell me a little about yourself. What brought you to Desert Haven?" JoJo asked, leaning back, settling in for a story.

"I was on the road for a while, just traveling, trying to decide what I wanted to do after my marriage ended. I was at loose ends. Coming here was a chance to slow down and regroup," Mel said.

"You were married?"

"Yup. And I'm straight. I know that most women here are lesbians, even though they might have been married in the past. It's not my thing, but I don't have any problem with it. I just mind my own business."

"Did you go through the South?" JoJo asked, obviously not caring a damn about Mel's sexuality and getting back to the subject at hand.

The two women chatted, mostly JoJo talking and Mel listening, about their adventures, JoJo topping off their glasses when the wine got low. Mel mulled over how to bring up her awkward subject while JoJo talked about hitchhiking across Colorado in 1952. When the bottle tipped up empty, JoJo said not to worry—there's plenty where that came from and reached under the bed to produce another giant bottle of red.

By this time, Mel was pretty drunk and ready to broach the subject.

"You know my mother died last year? When I went back to New York. Well, anyway, I inherited a lot of money," she said in her most apologetic voice. "I see that a lot of women here are struggling, and I just feel like such an oaf with money stuffed in my pockets. I want to help out, but I don't know how. I don't want to stir up any resentment. I just want to continue being invisible. I need to know how I can help without seeming like a jerk."

The long speech exhausted Mel. She got up, discovered she was a bit wobbly on her feet, so decided to sit on the floor rather than tip over. She lowered herself down, her feet splayed out, and leaned back against the leg of the chair she had just abandoned, waiting for a reaction.

JoJo stared at her guest, taken completely by surprise. If anyone came to talk to her about money, it was usually because they were broke and couldn't afford to pay. She looked towards the window at the reflection of the room: her on the bed, Mel on the floor. "Don't feel bad about it," she said. "It's kinda great, actually. Hooray for you."

They sat in silence, each one digesting Mel's outburst.

"I think you are right not to flaunt your money, JoJo said. "Some of these women might be resentful. You said you want to help—what did you have in mind? I'm getting social security now so things aren't as tight as they were but there is always something that needs to be fixed or paid for." JoJo drained her glass, picked up the wine bottle, and said, "Here, looks like you're empty," she said, gesturing with the bottle.

Mel clumsily put her hand over her glass and said, "No more for me." JoJo filled her own glass, splashing a few drops on her leg.

"I don't have anything in mind. What do you need?" Mel struggled to her feet, holding on to the table edge to steady herself. "Can I buy that fencing material you've been talking about? Are the taxes due? Do you have a mortgage? I can pay it off. Any way I can help would make me happy. And I would like to feel happy. Don't be embarrassed to ask; I've got more than enough to live on. But it has to be our secret."

Mel had gotten in the habit of driving into Tucson every Wednesday and Saturday. She never got tired of the twenty-mile trip through unspoiled desert. Shifting sunlight sculpted the saguaro forest into an alien landscape. On Wednesdays, she invited passengers if they wanted to visit the food co-op, bookstore, library, laundromat, or go along on any errand JoJo requested.

Saturdays, Mel always went to town alone. She had to protect her other secret. Mel was happy to be a member of a community of women, but she still liked having sex with men.

She was respectful of the commonly held narrative that men had fucked up society and that women united were the only hope to restore sanity and equilibrium to the planet. One of the few rules at Desert Haven was no men. There was no way she would bring a male lover to the land.

So, she answered personal ads in the back of the local independent weekly paper and got together with men on Saturday nights. Her intention was just sex, pure and simple. No entanglements, no questions. She would meet them in a public place, and if there was chemistry, if they smelled right, she would accompany them to their apartment or home or motel room and get down and sweaty. She carried condoms and always took a shower afterward so the women couldn't smell a man on her (she was sure they could.) She was back on the land by eleven or shortly after and tucked into her bed for the night.

Occasionally, one of her dates was particularly agreeable, and they would decide to meet again. Mel would lay out her rules:

1. Discretion— if they happened to bump into each other in a public space, nothing would be revealed about the intimacy of their relationship.

2. Honesty—they could ask for anything they wanted in bed, but no meant no.

3. The relationship was a Saturday thing only, and not to expect anything more. It would last as long as they were both having fun.

In its purest form, it was the perfection of two people using each other for mutual pleasure with no strings and no hypocrisy. Unfortunately, personalities sometimes got in the way. Even if a man agreed to the rules, he might not be a true believer in non-monogamy and non-attachment. If he wanted more, that was the end for Mel. She loved her double life and wanted to keep it just the way it was.

She knew she was not living transparently because she had two big secrets: men and money. But transparency and honesty were not necessarily the same thing. She was being true to herself, and that was what really mattered.

Daisy 2006

When Daisy came to the land, she created a ruckus— that's the only way to describe it. Even on ten acres of women's land in the desert under huge Arizona skies, she took up a lot of psychic space. She was a big woman who demanded attention, her blue-streaked fuzzy hair rose like smoke from her large head, and her plump brown breasts were always on the verge of falling out of her blouse. She was a twenty-two-year-old loud tease and a nonstop flirt. It was easy to fall in love with her, and many women did. But she wasn't interested in anyone but Melanie.

And Mel wasn't interested.

Mel let Daisy know right away that she was straight and, besides, she didn't want a relationship with anyone. Daisy raised one eyebrow in disbelief, the other one taking on a determined slant. No woman had successfully resisted Daisy. She had a one-hundred percent seduction success record, and she loved a challenge. Mel's adamant resistance made her even cuter in Daisy's eye. It was just another layer of conquest.

Daisy, like most of the residents of Desert Haven, was a transient being. Although she had stayed at many women's lands, the Haven was one of her favorites because it didn't have a bunch of rules, and that appealed to her independent spirit. She didn't need to be told what to do. She had plenty of that growing up with a control freak Mum who was bad-tempered and ordered her around like a servant.

All of Daisy's belongings fit into a custom-painted canvas bag. When people expressed amazement that she traveled the world with everything she owned in one bag, she said, by way of assuring them, that it was a very big bag. Since leaving her Australian home when she was sixteen, she had been to thirteen countries and almost every state in the United States in the past six years. Arizona was especially appealing because the climate reminded her of north Queensland, where she grew up. Dry heat, lots of space, endless bush, big skies. She never could get used to green and humidity, so she always boomeranged back to the desert.

Not being particular about her living quarters, Daisy was quite content in her orange three-person dome tent. She scrounged up some necessities from what others left behind, including a queen-sized mattress that took up almost all of the tent's floor space. The backpacking stove in the community kitchen heated her tea water, and she ate five or six Jif crunchy peanut butter and strawberry jam sandwiches a day. The twenty-two slices of Wonder Bread per loaf lasted her two days if she ate the heels. She didn't care for vegetables, so this diet worked quite well for her. Cheap, easy, dependably good-tasting, and moderately nutritious. She had saved up enough money from her last waitressing job to be able to coast for a while.

It was the vernal equinox, one of Daisy's favorite celebratory occasions. She politely knocked on Mel's travel trailer door to ask her about the upcoming ritual since Mel had been at Desert Haven for a few rotations around the sun and could tell her what to expect.

"It's 2006. Do you really think it is appropriate to observe pagan ceremonies?" Mel said. Daisy couldn't tell if Mel was kidding or being grumpy, so she just grinned, distracted by how cute Mel looked in her short shorts and Kiss t-shirt, her blond hair sticking out in all directions.

"Okay, tell me why you are so excited," Mel asked. "Honestly, I don't know much about it."

"I love that day and night share equal space in the 24 hours we call a day. Darkness and light are in perfect balance. The sun will cross over the equator from my southern homeland and join me in the northern hemisphere. It's a great time to assess where you've been and look forward to the future," Daisy said.

"All days are meant to be celebrated," Mel said and stepped down two stairs to be on the same level as Daisy. Daisy didn't know if she should be insulted or impressed by her friend's ability to dig right into the existential core of any conversation, even if she disagreed with her.

"But tonight is a perfectly level playing field," Daisy said, ignoring Mel's comment. "The marble of your life can slide any way you tilt it. Anything is possible." After a meaningful pause, she added, "Even that you would be extra nice to this girl who loves you."

"Don't count on it," Mel said. This particular type of exchange happened fairly often over the past three months of Daisy's residency, always in a teasing but insistent way. "Daisy, I can't figure out if you persist out of habit or you're not listening. I'm not interested so let's not let it interfere with our friendship."

Daisy didn't like the direction this conversation was going, so she quickly changed the subject. "How many do you think will be here tonight?" she asked. "I do love a party."

"Let's see, there are six of us living here now, right? You and me, JoJo, Earthling, Carrot Top, and Madrona. Oh, and Juniper. She's so quiet I always forget about her. That makes seven. And Sunny, Madrona's daughter, but she'll be in bed by then. Liz, the shaman, will be here. Maybe another dozen from town. I'm cooking up some kale and onions from the garden. I'm tired of winter roots; I want something green that grows above ground."

"I think I'll make a stack of jam sandwiches," Daisy said.

Mel raised her eyebrows and suppressed a smile. "Daisy, you are the most unpretentious woman I have ever met, and that's the main reason I can tolerate your company longer than anyone else's. You don't have an ironic bone in your body. I'm going to go cook now. See you later," she said, turning to climb back into her trailer.

"I don't have time to slave over a hot stove, I have to make my costume," Daisy told the receding figure.

Cars started arriving around five o'clock and the visitors gravitated to the "teepee circle." Very tall poles staked in a twelve-foot circle, leaning inward and tied at the top, delineated the ritual space. There was no covering, just poles. A stone fire ring sat in the center. On one side, a few splintered picnic tables and an assortment of weathered chairs were strewn about. Some women brought folding chairs slung over their shoulders, and all had a dish to share. By six o'clock, the fire was roaring. Food was set out on the tables covered with pink and orange floral bedsheets. As usual, it was an eclectic assortment of foods, from homemade and homegrown to deli containers of things called salad that had mayonnaise as the main ingredient.

Daisy set herself up as the unofficial hostess, greeting everyone warmly with smothery hugs. "Hi, ladies. Welcome to Desert Haven. Happy Equinox" She recognized some of the women from the monthly moon circles, and there were some new faces.

Subtlety was not her strong suit as she eyed each new arrival hoping that someone would spark her interest. Mostly it was couples. Not that it ever stopped her before. But she wasn't attracted to any of them. This was very unusual for her. She wondered if her crush on Mel was interfering with her usual carefree self. Well, she wasn't going to let it keep her from enjoying the festivities.

Her costume was a playful depiction of the equinox. She had found some discarded white and black clothing in the bathhouse and cut them down the middle. Since she didn't sew, she stapled pant and blouse halves together, black on the right, white on the left. She felt very clever, but to her great annoyance, she was reduced to explaining the symbolism. Mel was the only one who got it and watched with amusement as Daisy tried to pantomime equinox.

As the sun dipped below the horizon and the sky lit up in a kaleidoscope of colors, the women stood holding hands in a circle. Liz in the north, a purple scarf with golden threads wound around her grey braids, welcomed everyone. She invited them to consider the cycles of the seasons as the cycles of their lives. When she started the chant, *We all come from the Goddess, and to Her we will return,* a chorus of voices joined in. The circle moved to the right in step with the song, paused at the end of the chant, and then stepped left, signifying the change of seasons. A colorfully painted talking stick made the rounds, each woman speaking in turn. When everyone had their say, the circle was ritually closed. Women bowed to each other, hands on their hearts, murmuring Blessed Be.

Then the drums came out. As seriously as Daisy took the ritual, she put the same amount of vigor and intensity into the musical celebration. Mel quietly stepped away and was gathering her serving bowl when Daisy grabbed her hand and tried to pull her into the dance. Mel pulled free and said, "Goodnight," and walked towards her trailer.

"Oh, come on, darlin', the evening's just beginning."

"Not for me. I'm done with people for the day, and that includes you, Daisy."

"Why won't you just dance with me. Is it because I'm black?"

"Oh, don't be ridiculous."

"I won't take no for an answer. You know how much I like you."

Mel reached the door to her trailer, mounted the steps, and said again, "Goodnight," shutting the door.

"You're missing out on all the fun. Especially me!" Daisy rested for a moment on the steps, elbows on knees, chin in hands, wondering why her charms weren't working their magic. She usually didn't have this much trouble. How could Mel resist her? Maybe she had a sexual wound from her past that Daisy could help her heal. Perhaps she was asexual. It was very mysterious and intriguing. It made her even more determined.

Daisy stood, straightened her costume, and turned back to the dancing and drums. It didn't look like anyone was going to be her sweetheart for the night, but she would still have a great time twirling and stomping under the moonlight.

The next morning when Mel got back from her run, she found a note stuck between the screen door and frame. "I guess I came on pretty strong last night. Forgive me?" It was adorned with so many hearts pierced with arrows it looked like Cupid had run amok.

The reply, written in red marker, was placed on Daisy's pillow that afternoon.

"You are forgiven because I like you, but I'm getting tired of the game. Would you prefer if I was angry at you? Would that make it easier?"

Damn, Daisy thought. She's tough.

Lacy pulled her VW camper van into a clearing next to Daisy's tent two days later. Before she stepped a foot on the ground, Daisy was at the driver's window.

"G'day! Cool van. What year is it? I had a '63, but the taillights were smaller. Where are you from?" she asked. Not waiting for an answer, she kept going, "Do you know anyone here? How long are you going to stay? How come you have a shaved head?"

"Whoa girl! Slow down. I'll be here long enough to answer all of your questions. Now, what is your name? I'm Lacy," she said, extending her hand.

"No worries. I'm Daisy." Her hand was grasped in a firm, sturdy shake. Once down and release. Not one of those fancy up and down girly shakes. This one gesture elevated the newcomer in Daisy's esteem from a possible conquest to a potential friend. Maybe even both. She appreciated a woman who offered her strength as a greeting.

"First things first—where is the bathroom?"

"That building over there with the blue door. Says Bathhouse." Daisy watched the newcomer stride across the dusty path, her long legs stretched from cut-off denim shorts down to her red shit-kicking cowboy boots. Even her tie-dye t-shirt seemed to exude confidence. The message was, here I am, eccentricities and all. Fuck you if you don't like it.

Daisy checked out the van to learn a little more about the new arrival. An orange trail bike and a pair of skis on the roof rack. Oregon license plate. Rainbow bumper sticker. Ethnic fabric curtains at the windows. When she opened the side door to look around, Daisy saw a small sink and fridge unit behind the passenger seat. Instead of two rows of seats, two benches faced a table. They probably converted into a bed, Daisy thought. Boxes of gear—pots and pans, hiking boots, and books, lots of books—were neatly piled in the back storage area. A stack of poster board signs lay on one bench, and Daisy looked them over.

Racy Lacy, Sex-Educator
There Are No Stupid Questions
Freedom from Ignorance
Sex: It's Fun and Legal
Just Say Yes
Let's Talk About Sex

"Seems like you have an interesting hobby," Daisy said when Lacy returned.

"Seems like you are pretty nosy," Lacy said and burst out laughing. "And you seem unapologetic about it too. I like that in a woman."

That night they shared a meal watching the sun burst into a million hot colors in the sky. Daisy contributed a stack of Jif and jam sandwiches, the crusts cut off for this auspicious occasion. Lacy opened a can of Campbell's vegetable soup to round out the meal.

"This was the most perfect dinner. Now, all we need is a little weed to help the digestion," Daisy said dreamily. She wasn't at all surprised when a fat doobie appeared, pulled out of a little leather pouch hung around Lacy's neck. The two women sat back in Lacy's folding chairs, puffing in silence, appreciating the cooler night air and infinity of stars. When the spirit moved them, they softly shared their stories with each other.

Lacy said she earned a small but sustainable living driving around the country offering her expertise as a sex educator to anyone brave enough to hire her. Her BS degree in counseling gave her legitimacy. She gave workshops at Gay Community Centers or in people's houses. Sometimes she was booked for a party as entertainment, and occasionally she had private sessions. As a sex-positive human being, she felt her mission was to free all women from their inhibitions. If people made love, they wouldn't have time to make war. Her voice got a little more insistent and passionate as she talked.

"It's my social responsibility. And I'm good at it," she said without a hint of false modesty.

Daisy said, "I feel the same way, but I'm doing my part by sharing my love with one woman at a time. As many of them as I can, of course. Spread the gospel, as it were. So, is that why you came to Desert Haven? To teach these lesbians a thing or two about sex?"

"Are all the women here gay?"

"Most of them. Except for one beautiful, stubborn gal who refuses to see that I'm the best thing that will ever happen to her. I'll introduce you to Mel tomorrow; she lives in that red trailer over there, the one with the lights on. She reads most of the night. Why she would rather read than snuggle down with me is a mystery. I'm kinda hooked on her, but she says she's straight."

"I can see it would be pretty hard to resist you," Lacy said with a wink that went unseen in the darkness. "But seriously, if she says she's straight, she is straight, so get over it."

"I never let it stop me before, and every one of my so-called straight girls didn't mind letting me make love to them. Most of them were pretty fast learners too. Some went back to their boyfriends, and that was that. But this one, she doesn't seem to have any sexual charge at all."

"So, leave her alone," Lacy said with a sigh of exasperation.

"But I love her. I mean, really, who is she to break my record?"

"Sounds like you are more interested in the conquest than the woman. Have you ever heard of sexual compulsion?"

"No, doctor, I haven't, and I'm not compulsive. I just like to sleep with girls. Mel is haunting me!"

"Because you can't have her. Like I said, leave her be. Being straight is just as valid as being gay. It's the way she was born; she can't help it." Both of the women contemplated this information in a restless silence. Lacy was done being the expert for the night, and it was slowly dawning on Daisy that she might be right.

Lacy spoke into the quiet, "So, you must be a good lover after all that practice."

"I've been told so."

"Let's find out."

The sun was lighting up the eastern sky but not yet poking its head over the horizon when Lacy eased her arm out from under Daisy's neck. She knew that the feeling would come back as soon as she shook it but didn't want to bounce the van, so she slid the door open as quietly as she could with one hand and slipped out, stepping over the condomed purple dildo on the floor. She quickly assessed the proximity of cactus and other prickly things that might poke her naked body. Vigorously wiggling her fingers and swinging her arm wildly about, she winced as the blood returned. Walking to the Bath House, still shaking her arm, she was startled when a woman seemed to appear out of nowhere. And then another. Lacy went over to look and discovered that they had come from a tiny hobbit house dug into the ground. The name painted over the door said Kozy Kiva.

"Hi," she offered. "I'm Lacy. I just got here last night."

"How ya doin' Lacy? I'm Earthling, and this here is Carrot Top. You might want to cover up once the sun comes out, it's pretty brutal."

"Yeah, thanks, I'll do that. See you later. I'm on my way to the loo."

Back at the van, there was still no stirring inside, and Lacy desperately needed some caffeine. She returned to the underground house and found the two women boiling water on a camp stove outside under a canopy.

"You got a cup of coffee to spare? My van is occupied right now, and I don't want to wake up my guest."

"Sure, pull up a chair," Earthling said. "You might want to sit on that cushion so you don't get splinters." Carrot Top chuckled at her partner's joke.

The women could have been twins – fifty-something, short hair that looked like it was cut with pinking shears, frayed jeans shorts, and faded concert t-shirts (Indigo Girls on Earthling, Suzanne Vega on Carrot Top), Birkenstocks. Their barrel-shaped bodies could be called "stocky." Besides the images on their shirts, the only difference was Carrot Top's unnaturally reddish-purple hair.

"You missed the solstice circle if that's what you were aiming for," Carrot Top said, keeping her gaze on Lacy's face to cover her uncomfortableness with the naked stranger.

"No, I'm just on the road, doing my thing. Didn't even know that the season had changed."

"What's your thing?" Earthling asked.

"I'm a sex educator. I give workshops on safer sex, healthy relations, negotiating skills, that sort of thing." The usual silence greeted her pronouncement. After an awkward pause, some people said, "That's cool," or something to indicate that they weren't embarrassed even if they were. Some people changed the subject. Once in a while, someone wanted to argue with her. Talking about sex was odd and challenging for almost everyone she met, which was exactly why she did what she did.

Carrot Top asked where Lacy came from, and they chatted about their origins. After a few minutes, Lacy shifted the conversation and inquired about Daisy.

"You better watch out for her, she's a sex addict."

"Too late. She's sleeping in my van. Tell me about Mel."

"Oh, Mel is a mystery. She keeps to herself mostly. Rumor is that she's straight, and I would believe it. She seems kinda stuck up," Earthling said.

"Oh, honey, she's just shy," Carrot Top said.

"I don't think she's shy, I think she's got some kind of secret that she's not sharing. Where does she get all that money? She thinks she's so slick, giving JoJo money to run this place on the sly, but everybody knows it comes from her."

Carrot Top added, "She's never had a girlfriend or, really, any friend, except maybe Juniper, in the year that we've been here. That's strange. Why would she move to a women's community if she just wanted to sit in the shade of her trailer and read all day?"

Lacy sipped her coffee and tried to picture Mel. She couldn't see her trailer through the lush creosote bushes but determined to stop by once she washed and put some clothes on.

"Where you been, darlin'?" Daisy asked, stretching her short frame beyond the confines of the little camper bed. "I missed you. And you don't have a stitch of clothes on. What are you doing wandering around naked as the day you were born? Advertising your workshop?"

"Just chatting up some of the natives. Let's have a bite to eat and go meet your friend, Mel," Lacy said, slipping into her shorts and T-shirt.

They breakfasted on Jif and jam sandwiches, washed down with two glasses of Tang.

"Damn," Lacy said, "I didn't know they still make this stuff.

"It's good, isn't it. This container says it makes six quarts. Want some more?"

"Uh, no thanks. I'm going to pay Mel a visit. You want to introduce me?"

"No, you go ahead. I don't think she wants to see me right now. I kinda made a pain in the ass of myself." Daisy thought a minute and then said, "Maybe you can find out if she's really straight and if that's why she resists me. It's hard to believe, isn't it?"

"Obviously. I couldn't resist you, could I?"

Mel was sitting in the shade of an old mesquite tree. The branches hung almost to the earth like a live green tent. "May I join you?" Lacy asked.

"Sure. Have a seat," Mel said, picking up a pile of books and magazines from the spare webbed lawn chair. She returned to her perch and waited to find out who this new person was.

"I came in yesterday. My name is Lacy, and I know you are Mel. I just thought I'd say hello."

"Hello," Mel echoed. Lacy waited for her add to the conversation, but she seemed content with her two syllables. They sat in a silence Mel seemed comfortable in until Lacy said, "I hear you are a straight girl."

"Who told you that?"

"Daisy seems to think that's the only explanation for how you can resist her seductive charms."

"She said that? Well, she's sort of right. I'm straight, but I'm also not interested in having a lover. And besides, it's nobody's business but my own."

"I understand. But I'm curious why you want to hang out with a bunch of lesbians?" Lacy asked.

"I like being in the company of women; I like female energy. And I feel safe in an all-women space. I don't have to be afraid of being raped or harassed. Daisy can be a pain in the ass, but she's not violent or scary. I guess I needed a break from the patriarchy, and this place offered me a sanctuary of sorts. How about you?"

"I'm a refugee from mainstream culture too but in a different way. I found my calling in sex education; I believe in freedom from the bonds of propriety and shame. Everyone deserves to have the kind of sex life they desire, and I love starting tough conversations."

"You sound like an evangelist. You going to hold a tent revival of earthly pleasure?"

Lacy laughed and said, "I'm not here to advocate for an orgy, although it wouldn't be a bad idea. Do you think the women would be interested in a little workshop? It's a chance to ask questions and share."

"Sure, just post it in the Community House, and they will probably come. Especially if there is food."

When Lacy climbed back into her van, Daisy was dozing. Lacy carefully fitted her back against Daisy's soft belly for some spooning time.

"What did you learn about the mysterious Mel?"

"I thought you were sleeping," Lacy said. "I learned that she's a bona fide heterosexual woman. Yes, some women are born that way, and she is one of them. She's also asexual because she seems to be just keeping her own company. So, give the girl a break and focus your amorous attention on someone who will return the affection. Like me."

"I guess I get it. The girl likes dick, and there is nothing I can do about it," Daisy said.

"Yup, that right. Now let's take a nap. After."

"After what?"

"After we have sex," Lacy said, pulling Daisy's hand to her mouth and sucking the tips of her fingers.

Later, after their nap and a solar shower, the women sat cross-legged in Daisy's tent making invitations.

Everything You Want To Know About Sex
But Were Too Embarrassed To Ask Workshop
Brought to you by Sexologist Lacy Macy
Tonight at 7 in Community House
Snacks will be Served
Donations Accepted But Not Necessary

"Is that your real name? Lacy Macy?" Daisy asked.

"The Macy part is what I was born with. I made up Lacy cause I like the way it rhymes."

Daisy busied herself cutting the crusts off Wonder Bread slices to make triangular-shaped jam sandwiches she called "hors d'oeuvres" while Lacy distributed the invitations. She met a few women in the Community House, and they said they would be sure to come to the event. It was still pretty hot out, and they hoped it would cool off by then.

Lacy dressed in her favorite black leather harness over a white undershirt and purple satin boxer shorts. She finished her outfit with her red boots. Daisy was inspired to rummage through her costume box. Any occasion for dress-up was okay with her. Her pink ankle-length net tutu was the same color as the angel wings she attached to a low-cut black camisole. Lacy smiled her approval. "You sure know how to strut your stuff," she said. "Let's get over to the room and set up some of these posters and the donation bucket. And your fabulous refreshments, of course."

Carrot Top and Earthling were sitting on the legless couch in the Community House munching on jelly sandwiches at seven o'clock. Mel slipped in quietly and stood leaning against the back wall, arms crossed, watching a few more women come in and find seats.

"Thanks everyone for coming tonight. I'm Lacy. I just got in last night, and already I feel very welcome," she said, smiling in Daisy's direction. Eyes followed her gaze and a few heads nodded knowingly.

"We'll be talking about sex, gender identity, gender expression, and sexual orientation in terms of intersecting continuums. Sometimes these are tough subjects, and I want to give everyone permission to speak their truth. The ground rules are no interrupting and no shaming. And there is no such thing as a dumb question. Okay?"

Murmurs and head nods.

"Okay, we are in agreement." She held up a poster divided into four fields. "I want to give an overview of the continuums. The first one is sex. Most of us think of sex or biological anatomy as binary, you are either born a male or a female. But research shows that many people are born with internal and external mixed messages. They are what we call intersex. At birth, babies are assigned the sex that matches their obvious external genitalia, but that is not the only thing that determines a person's sex. Mother Nature isn't perfect, and neither are we." She noticed some puzzled looks but didn't stop to address them. She would allow a discussion after she laid down the basics.

"The next area is gender expression or the way one presents to the world. The range is from masculine to feminine, with androgynous being somewhere in the middle. Some of us know this as butch-femme territory." She paused and looked around the small room for Daisy. She found her sitting in the back near the empty snack tray. Their eyes met, they both grinned.

"When I was coming out as a butch, I thought I was only supposed to go for girly girls," Earthling said, slinging her arm over Carrot Top's shoulder. "It took me a while to understand who I was attracted to."

"Exactly," Lacy said. "The most important thing is to trust yourself and ignore what's fashionable at the time."

Turning back to the poster, Lacy continued, "Next, we have gender identity. It differs from gender expression because this is an internal state, a psychological sense of the self. One can identify as a man, a woman, or both. Or neither. This is the basis of the transgender or two-spirit controversy that the Michigan Womyn's Music Festival's womyn-born womyn policy excluding trans women has brought to the fore."

Lacy heard someone say, "Once a man, always a man."

"Hold on to your comments and questions. I know this stuff can be difficult. We'll have time for discussion later." Lacy said, turning to her chart. 'And lastly, we have sexual orientation, or who we are attracted to both physically and emotionally, with male on one side and female on the other. Bisexuality is on this sliding scale. A lot of us have varying degrees of attractions during our lifetimes, but some people are firmly on one side or the other."

"That's right," Daisy said, standing up and moving across the room with purpose in her step. Heads turned to follow her crossing the room. "Some people are just straight, and there is nothing wrong with that." She stopped in front of Mel.

"I'm sorry," she said softly.

The two women looked into each other's eyes as if seeing the other for the first time. Mel nodded and reached out, briefly embracing Daisy's hand.

Daisy slowly, deliberately, turned to the room and said, "I confess that I have been known to be pushy, maybe even to the point of being obnoxious. I guess I was thinking pretty narrowly. But, thanks to Lacy, I have a bigger picture of how many unique identities go into making us human. I seem to be more fluid than most, but that's not the only way to go. I get it. Thanks, Racy Lacy Macy. You are the best teacher."

A huge grin lit up Lacy's face. "And you are the best student."

Giving some space to let Daisy's interruption sink in, Lacy paused, surveying the room.

Then, as if remembering an important omission she said, "Hey, I don't want to avoid talking about the trans issue. It's complicated and seems to be pulling communities apart because there are so many strong feelings one way or another. In my opinion, the best thing we can do is respectfully express our opinions and live and let live."

"You mean you would let men who think they are women move to the land?"

"I mean that we are all directed by our inner compasses. I think a woman is someone who knows through their own interior process that they are a woman, regardless of the anatomy they were born with. Remember I said it's a continuum? Some people reject the whole concept of gender binaries, and choose to define themselves as non-gendered or non-binary. Would you turn them away?"

"I see what you mean," JoJo said from the back of the room. "It's all a bit arbitrary. And troublesome. If we are all here because we don't want to be controlled or defined by society, then how can we reject someone else in their struggle for authenticity?"

"But I came to women's land to get away from men," Earthling said.

"I understand," Lacy said. "But it's not black and white. It's nuanced. I feel that being open to how people gender themselves, or not, is essential to liberating all people from the tyranny of labels and boxes. And besides, who am I to judge?"

In the next two hours, the discussion, sometimes heated or, as Lacy called it, "excited," went in many directions. Sex toys, yea, or nay. What was kinky? What was normal? Can polyamory be a viable ethical choice, or is monogamy the only genuine lesbian relationship possibility?

Lacy brought up bondage, dominance, sadism, and masochism, saying, "I know that BDSM can be a touchy subject, but I believe that consenting adults have the right to determine their own erotic pleasure."

"This conversation is triggering to me," Juniper said in a shaky voice. Everyone turned their attention to the woman who rarely spoke. "I have a history of sexual abuse."

Earthling slid nearer on the bench they both sat on, being careful to keep a respectful distance, and said, "Oh, Juniper, I didn't know. I'm so sorry." She turned to the group and said, "I think we need to change the subject."

After a compassionate moment, Carrot Top broke the silence by saying that she became a lesbian when her husband brought another woman into their relationship for a threesome. The women fell in love, and Carrot Top left her marriage.

"I knew I was different when I was three years old and had a crush on my girl cousin," JoJo said. "And that was sixty-six years ago."

"You win," Lacy laughed. Looking around the room, she said, "It's getting late, and I think we are all getting tired. Thank you all for coming, and thank you for sharing your truth. If you take away one thing from this workshop, I hope it is that you are the one who determines how you want to be touched and who may do the touching. I think hugs all around would be an appropriate closure if you give permission, of course."

Giggles, hugs, even a few tickles as the women exited to a bright night sky, the almost full moon illuminating the clouds. Lacy collected her posters and upended the donation bucket. Three folded twenties along with crumpled singles and assorted change spilled out on the table. Daisy glanced over and said, "Oh, those twenties would be from Mel. She's rich."

Lacy wrapped her arms around Daisy, pulled her close for a long, slow kiss.

"You, my dear, were magnificent," Lacy said. I think we make a great team, don't you?

"Damn straight. I could help you, like the magician's assistant, wearing beautiful outfits, handing you props, and making refreshments."

"No, Daisy, I don't mean like that. You could co-teach with me. It's just a matter of presenting some facts and letting them talk. Once in a while you have to correct misconceptions or referee a fight, but mostly it's stuff you already know. You are the most sex-positive woman I've ever met."

"You mean all my experience seducing women might be a professional advantage?" Daisy said, grinning at the compliment.

She paused, smile turning serious, and said, "Lacy, I have to thank you for helping me break that crazy obsession I had with Mel. I think that she and I can be friends now and that's great. I was pretty inappropriate, wasn't I?"

"Yes, you were," Lacy said. "Want to be inappropriate with me?"

"Is that a term for sex that you forgot to mention in your talk?" Daisy said and slid her hand inside the back of Lacy's shirt.

Lacy asked, "Your tent or my van, your choice."

"Your van. My guess is that you've got some interesting toys with my name on them.

Maya 2010

Maya walked down the bustling tourist street in the swampy heat, trying to take everything in, charmed by the bilingual cacophony. She zigzagged around the grinning, mustached men blocking the sidewalk, beckoning her to spend money in their overflowing shops. "Come in, come in, everything is almost free for you, lady," and jumped back when a fishmonger lewdly wiggled raw jumbo shrimp at her saying, "They slept in the sea last night, you can eat them today."

It was spring break in a Mexican beach town. The bars were filled with puke-over-the-balcony-drunk-show-me-your-tits, college students from across the border. Mestizo women in traditional long skirts and bright-colored blouses worked the crowd with a kid or two in tow, selling four-packs of Chiclets and little hand-painted head-bobbing turtles. Maya couldn't believe she was in Puerto Peñasco, or, as the Americans called it, Rocky Point, on the Sea of Cortez.

Just a few hours ago, she had her thumb out, hitchhiking on an Interstate entrance ramp, trying to get from Phoenix to Tucson. A minivan stopped. A blond head poked out the window and hollered that she and her girls were going across the border for the best party of the year. "Come with us," she yelled. Maya knew they thought she was around their age, high school, with her blond ponytail and slender frame, even though she was a decade older.

Although caught by surprise, the idea appealed to Maya. She was on her way to meet her friend Crow at Desert Haven, but that was not until next week, so a little detour would be fine. Besides, she'd never been to Mexico before. The side door slid open, and two girls in the back seat slid over to make room for her. Tossing her Hello Kitty backpack on the seat and climbing into the van, Maya immediately recognized the sweet smell of weed lingering in the air. One of the girls passed a bottle of fancy vodka. Maya knew she had made the right decision.

At the border, the bored Mexican agent glanced inside the car and, seeing a bunch of pretty Anglo girls, just waved them through. Maya, never having been to another country, expected it to be a bigger deal. They pulled into the congested street and followed a slow line of cars through Sonoyta. Every other business was a farmacia or dentist. Older model cars were parked in front of half-finished houses with rebar poking out of the top floors, and families sat on metal folding chairs in tiny front yards. They passed fields flapping with escaped plastic bags caught on dead plant stalks as if they were a type of foreign crop.

An hour later, the driver pulled into a parking space in the old port section of town. Jumping out of the van, she led her entourage down the street and up a flight of stairs to a rooftop bar packed with revelers. She knew where the action was.

"Let the party begin!" The girls ordered tequila shots, shrimp cocktails, beer, and more shots and paid with American dollars. Nobody seemed to notice or didn't care that Maya wasn't taking a turn paying. The girls disbursed, blending into other groups. Maya didn't know anyone, but they were all pretty much interchangeable, so she didn't care. Joints and a hash pipe passed by. This crowd was serious about getting fucked up.

Most of the time, Maya kept to the company of women, so she had little experience with testosterone gone wild. She was fascinated by and very wary of the young males released from social controls by liquid courage. One boy after another bought her drinks and tried to feel her up. She took the drink and moved out of reach of the clumsy paw, no hard feelings.

After a while, she had enough booze to coast on a lovely high, so she migrated to a portside railing to watch pelicans swoop by at eye level. Claiming a white plastic chair, she tipped back against the wall, her feet propped on a low table crowded with empty salt-rimmed glasses, orphan lime wedges, and tortilla chip dust. From her perch, Maya observed the chaos and cacophony, entertained as only an intoxicated outsider could.

A bespectacled, sweaty youth wove his way over to her, clutching a damp paperback. "Hey, you wanna make out?" he asked as if the answer might be yes. When Maya shook her head, he turned and wandered over to a group of girls and presumably asked the same thing. He was shooed away by a wave of bare-chested surfer dudes who swooped in like a clutch of hungry seagulls assessing the female desirability and availability. A very sunburned guy in low-slung pants and flip-flops spied Maya sitting alone. She did not turn her gaze away, so he took it as an invitation.

"Hey, pretty lady, howyadoing? Have a drink?" he said, more of a command than a question. He sat down next to her and picked up an empty glass from the table. A quart of Cuervo Gold 1800 appeared from a large pocket in his cargo shorts. "Don't worry about germs—tequila sterilizes all it touches. Here ya go." He said, handing over a pint glass almost a quarter full of golden liquid.

Maya accepted the glass and took a sizeable sip, not knowing if it was all hers or if she had to share. "What's your name?" she asked.

"Bart. Like Black Bart, but I'm white. White Bart, yeah, I'm White Bart," he said and fell in on himself, laughing at his hilarious witticism. When he noticed that Maya didn't appreciate his joke, he said, "And what's your name, Miss Frowny Face, Miss Not So Funny, Miss Prude?"

"Maya. It's Maya."

"Drink up, Miss Maya Face," Bart said, pushing her elbow up to get the glass closer to her mouth.

"Hey, don't touch me, you fucker." Maya said it in a low voice, one that did not betray fear or anger. It was an assertive voice, expecting compliance.

"Oh, don't get that way. I just wanna have some fun with you. Don't you like me?" little boy Bart asked and put on a sad puppy dog face.

Maya relaxed and took another swig of her drink, figuring Bart knew the rules. So, she was off guard when he wrapped a muscular arm around her shoulders and pulled her face up next to his. "Just a little kiss," he said as he covered her mouth with his sand-blasted lips, poking his thick tongue into her mouth, sliming her with his saliva. Maya pushed her hands against his sweaty chest but couldn't escape his grip. She bit down on his tongue. He bellowed in indignation and pushed her away, toppling her from her chair onto the pebbly tarpaper roof. Her scraped thigh and the palm of her hand burned, but she quickly sat up and watched Bart intensely to see what he would do next.

His enraged eyes reminded her of a wounded bull. "What the fuck. You stupid cunt, why did you do that."

"I think she was trying to tell you something," said a low voice behind him. Bart turned and looked up at a stocky woman wearing a red bandana headband, a sleeveless sports jersey over a white undershirt, and turquoise beach shorts. Formidable biceps and an advancing, threatening stance persuaded him to get the hell out of there.

"Crazy bitch," he muttered over a retreating shoulder.

Maya still held the glass and was amazed that not a drop had spilled. She emptied it. Not quite sure what to do next, she laughed. Nervous and drunken laughter. Grateful guffaws. She laughed so hard tears squeezed out of her eyes. Blinking to focus, she saw her companion was squatting in front of her, enjoying a good laugh at the asshole's expense. The two of them leaned in on each other, arms on shoulders, and roared.

"You girls okay?" a waiter asked, checking in on them.

"We'd be better with a couple of beers and double shots of your best tequila," BD said.

BD was the way she introduced herself, and when Maya asked what it stood for, she said, "Just BD." Maya thought, big dyke, bulldagger? Her gaydar was flashing.

They clinked glasses, nodded like conspirators, and threw back the shots. BD stifled a cough. "First drink of the day sometimes goes down a little rough. It looks like I've got some catching up to do."

"I didn't need any rescuing, you know," Maya said in her pretend-I'm-sober voice. "I had the situation completely under control. But it was nice of you to come on over." BD just smiled.

They both agreed that bullshit-boy was in way over his head and that they had handled much worse than an icky kiss. BD offered to get the bad taste out of her mouth and, with consent, gently nibbled on Maya's lower lip. She softly made her way to a full-on smooch that led to a long, deep kiss.

"Where you from?" BD asked, lighting a cigarette and sitting back to look Maya over.

"Lots of places. Was born in Colorado, but I've lived all over. How about you?"

"I'm strictly LA. Came down here on business, and I found a sweet deal, so decided to stay for a while."

The rooftop was getting even more crowded. Two boys were trying to squeeze behind their chairs when one drunkenly tipped into BD. She jumped up, yelling, "Watch it, asshole," and they skittered away. She turned to Maya, "Let's get out of here. I have a great place on the beach we can hang out."

Maya tried to remember what the girls she came down with looked like. Shorts, tee-shirts, blond ponytails. They seemed to have vaporized. Or blended in with everyone else. The part of Maya's still-working brain realized that she had nowhere else to go. She said, "Okay."

BD's quad was parked in a sandy lot next door. It looked like a Tonka toy, only really big: a wide motorcycle with four knobby balloon tires. Maya climbed on behind BD and held on tightly as they roared through town and down a long dirt road.

◆ ◆ ◆

Maya woke up slowly in a huge bed with cream-colored satiny sheets. The clock on the bedside table said it was 2:30 p.m. Sitting up, she took in the brilliant seascape through the floor-to-ceiling windows. A naked woman was lying on a wrought iron lounge chair on the balcony. Her breasts, released from the binder, fell to her sides over her rounded belly. Her body was brown and solid. Maya sort of remembered who she was.

Her head felt underwater and thick at the same time. Her eyebrows ached. She carefully rose and went to pee in a bathroom that was bigger than most of the houses she had lived in. Washing her hands, she noticed her right palm stung and saw a red, raw, scabby scrape.

She slid open the Arcadia door. "Wow, this is some view," she said, stepping across to look over the railing, shielding her eyes from the glaring sun. The pool ten stories below glowed a phony turquoise and was surrounded by palm trees wearing grass skirts of untrimmed fronds. A few uninviting faded aqua lounge chairs were scattered around. There wasn't a human in sight. She remembered the woman's name was BD.

"Where are we? This place looks deserted."

"Welcome to Escondite, the Hideaway. Luxury condominiums built for rich gringos, but then the American financial crash happened, and nobody was buying. Eight loco owners rent the units out to unsuspecting tourists on a website with very little information. There are no restaurants or shops, maintenance is rare, and the best part—very little security. Mi amigo Jesús is a guard here, and he lets me know when renters are coming so I can stay invisible. Want a tour?"

"Maybe it would be a good idea to put some clothes on," Maya said, turning around a little too quickly, sloshing and crashing her booze-soaked brain into the side of her skull. "Fuck, and maybe some food to sop up all that tequila."

BD grinned and handed over a bottle of brown liquid. "This will cure what ails you."

Maya knew food was the better choice, but she took a long pull on the tequila bottle and puckered her face from the nastiness. It would make the pain go away, but at what cost?

Back in the condo, BD produced a packet of Bimbo vanilla wafers. Maya scarfed down a dozen along with her second drink. The throbbing in her head was subsiding. Once released from stabbing pain, she was able to notice her surroundings. The room was large and beige in a Holiday Inn kind of way. Sun streamed in across the floor up to the kitchen. There was a door to the bedroom. She had an inkling of a night of passionate lovemaking. The partial memory excited her, and she suddenly wanted more.

Simultaneously self-conscious, shy, and turned on by desire, she looked down. White lines crisscrossed her tanned feet, and it looked like she was still wearing sandals. She watched her feet walk into the bedroom where BD was already propped up on the pillows in the middle of the big bed as if she had read Maya's mind.

"Come back to bed, Bebé," she invited with the confidence of one knowing that she would not be denied.

The next time Maya woke, it was dark out, and she was alone. She stepped out on the balcony to appreciate the silver crescent moon hovering over the black sea. A breeze ruffled the surface of the water, and lights from the pool area reflected off the ripples. Her stomach rumbled from hunger and rebelled against the alcohol. Maya could hold her liquor better than people twice her size, but BD was twice her size.

The condo door slammed open, and BD, plastic bags slung over both arms, carrying a pizza box, clomped in. She wore cutoffs, a Harley Davidson t-shirt, and worn huaraches on her pudgy feet. Maya wondered how she managed to sneak out without causing a disturbance. It seemed that everything BD did was large and noisy.

"Got some food for us, Bebé," she said, laying the pizza on the kitchen counter. Maya grabbed a piece and took a big bite, scalding the roof of her mouth.

"Hey, hey, slow down, there's plenty of food. You won't starve."

The cheese was gooey and greasy, the crust thick and soggy, and the pepperoni spicy, hot, and tough, but she ate it with relish. "Hunger is the best sauce. That's what my grandmother told me," Maya said.

They demolished the whole pie standing in the kitchen, licking each other's fingers and scooping up the crumbs. "What else did you get?" Maya asked, surveying the plastic bags lined up on the counter.

"Don't you worry about a thing. We are all set for days," BD said, pulling out Styrofoam boxes and containers. "I got some tacos, fried fish, guacamole, and some nice steamed vegetables. I even got some Chinese takeout. All we have to do is heat it up. And look, chica, I got you cornflakes!"

Maya looked puzzled. "Cornflakes?"

"Yeah, don't you remember? Last night, you said they were your favorite breakfast, along with chocolate milk. BD pulled a carton of TruMoo from one of the bags. "Who loves you, Bebé?"

Maya's eyebrows shot up, and she unconsciously took a step back. "How long do you plan on being here?" All these boxes said it would be a while. A one-night stand was in her realm of possibility, maybe even two, but she had to get to Desert Haven. Crow would be waiting for her, and they had plans to hit the road for the summer.

"We can stay as long as we want. It's no problem. My man Jesús has access to the condo calendar and will let us know when someone is coming. Then we just move to another place, the cleaners come, and the owner will never know. Jesús takes care of me, and I take care of him." BD put two fingers together, placing them against her lips, inhaling loudly, indicating how she took care of Jesús.

Maya walked to the window and gazed at the sea, letting this piece of information sink in. She had no idea where she was, had no transportation, and was on the tenth floor of an almost abandoned high-rise with a woman she barely knew. BD seemed nice enough, but what the fuck? Was this a dangerous situation? Should she be scared? It didn't feel that way, but maybe she was still too drunk to know what she was feeling. How was she going to let BD know that she wanted to leave without seeming ungrateful? She had to be diplomatic and not piss off her hostess. Or was she her jailer? It was confusing. Maya just knew one thing—she needed to keep it light. No big confrontation.

"What the matter, Bebé? Something bothering you?" BD asked as she came up behind Maya.

"Well, I was just thinking about my friend up in Arizona. The one I'm supposed to meet at Desert Haven pretty soon."

"What's Desert Haven?"

"It's some acreage out in the desert owned by an older woman named JoJo. She lets women camp on the land. I'm going to meet my friend, and we're going drive up to Oregon and stay at another lesbian land, West Farm, for the summer."

"I'd really like it if you'd just hang out with me a few more days," BD said softly and slid her arm over Maya's shoulder, turning her around. The kiss was tender, tentative, careful. Maya acquiesced. They stood in the light of the waxing moon, high tide slapping the beach, holding on to each other.

Two days later, BD was dressed and checking the pockets of her fishing vest to make sure she had everything she needed. Maya ran into the bedroom yelling over her shoulder, "Wait a minute, I'll get some clothes on. I want to come with you."

"Chica, I'm so sorry, I can't take you with me. It's business. Just tell me what you want, and I'll bring it for you. Anything you want. Why do you want to leave? We have everything we need. Here, Bebé, have a line—this is the best coke ever."

Maya looked at the empty food containers, beer cans, and tequila bottles overflowing the tall kitchen trash bin and spilling over on the floor. She tried to remember how long she and BD had been in the condo. A bottomless baggie of pot and lines of coke sat ready on the glass coffee table. The only times they had left the condo was to swim in the warm sea at high tide or walk the shore when it ebbed, exploring the tide pools for surprising creatures. They rarely saw anyone on the beach, and no one was in the condo complex except Jesús, who they could hear patrolling the halls occasionally. Maya's pockets were full of shells and sea glass. To her astonishment, she found a whole seahorse. "I didn't know they were real. I thought they were like unicorns." The days blurred together.

BD announced the place was a fucking pigsty, and it was time to move to another condo. Maya, in the grips of a sensuous fog, had forgotten there were other units in the building. BD took her hand and led her through a maze of halls. The elevator came, and they stepped on. They sampled a few unlocked units, chose number 504 with a view to the south, and returned to the tenth floor to get their stuff.

While BD gathered up clothing from the bedroom floor and packed the drugs into a backpack, Maya searched the fridge for something edible, sniffing and discarding some Styrofoam boxes with questionable contents. She found a soggy cheese crisp that didn't look too bad if she scraped off the browned guacamole. Taking the food and a bottle of water with her, she stepped out on the balcony to feel the sun on her skin. The shock of the heat floated a thought to the surface of her muddled mind, but it was still out of focus. How long had she been there? A week? Longer? She vaguely remembered saying that she needed to go a few times, but BD would hand her a pipe or pour a drink or kiss the bottoms of her feet. She couldn't quite figure out what she needed to do or how to do it. She chugged the liter of water, telling herself that it would clear her head.

In the middle of the move, on the elevator clutching her backpack and sandals, the feeling of dropping suddenly brought Maya back to herself. Her forehead cooled, her eyes opened a little wider, and her senses woke up. She had to get back to her life. When the doors opened on the fifth floor, BD stepped out and waited for Maya.

"I forgot something up in the room. Go ahead. I'll catch up with you."

"Okay, Bebé, don't be long."

Maya pushed the button for the tenth floor, and the car rose. When it stopped, she waited a few minutes and then pushed the button to the ground floor. Slipping on her shoes, she quickly walked in the direction of the lobby, having no idea what she was going to do. It was all very impulsive, yet she knew it was the right thing to do. Her head was floating above her shoulders on a short string, and it kept bobbing along with her footsteps.

She saw the quad in the circular driveway, but Maya didn't know how to drive it, and besides, she would need a key. There was a guardhouse at the gate, and she sprinted over to it. Empty. Not a soul in sight. The road seemed to dead-end at the high-rise, so it was apparent there was only one way to go. She could see a string of brightly colored houses along the road in the distance, maybe a quarter of a mile. Heart thumping, fuzzy-brained, she ran/walked down the sandy road, looking back over her shoulder. No BD. She probably hadn't realized that Maya was gone yet.

Maya had just reached the houses when she heard the roar of the quad behind her. She ducked behind a wall and waited until it passed in a cloud of dust. Listening to the sound fade in the distance, she knew that this was a long road. Shifting the weight of her backpack, she kept walking, knowing she would have plenty of warning if the quad turned around and came back.

The elation of escape was wearing off, and it was replaced by fear. What the hell did she get herself into? What if she was caught? She had no reason to suspect BD would be violent or try to restrain her, but she wasn't thinking straight.

She was there by her own free will, wasn't she? Well, yes and no. The alcohol, drugs, and sex had her in such a stupor that her usually logical mind had taken a vacation.

If it was a vacation, why did she feel so uneasy? Think, think. It felt like a dream, a hallucination. She had been spirited away. She was brainwashed. It was the Stockholm effect, and she fell in love with her captor. But wait, she wasn't in love, she was in lust. And the sex was amazing. She had been lulled into a state of nonbeing. Or something.

BD took really good care of her; she was kind and generous. And hot. Why leave? What else was going on that she needed to get to? The rest of her life seemed very vague and unimportant.

She could just go back and say she went for a stroll and lost track of time—BD would never know.

But it was pretty boring in that room. No books, no one else to talk to. She did the same jigsaw puzzle three times. She'd fit in the very last piece, stand back to admire her work, and then pick up one corner, letting the whole thing come apart in her hands.

Maybe she would feel more grounded if she could move around more. Being in a building all day, not touching the earth, felt unnatural. It was very creepy. BD was creepy. A spider holding Maya in her web.

She kept walking, just putting one foot in front of the other, and the effort seemed to help land her back in her body. Sweat trickled down the side of her face, and she wiped it with her shirttail. There were more houses. A street veered off to the left, and she took it. Another street. She turned right, and she was walking parallel to the main road.

Good, she thought, this way BD won't sneak up on her. The air was hot and humid but not unbearable. She wished she had thought of taking a bottle of water with her. She flashed on a chilling thought. What if BD took her wallet? She kneeled and dug through extra pairs of underwear and T-shirts. Thank Goddess, the wallet was still there, and her money was inside. She had to get back to Arizona. If hitching didn't work, at least she could catch a bus. If there was a bus and if she could figure out how to get to the depot. Her head was starting to clear, and she felt shaky. Just keep walking towards town.

BD was probably pissed that she just left like that without saying goodbye or anything, but what else could she do? This way, there was no confrontation, no hassle. It was safer.

The longer she walked, the more people she saw. She could ask somebody how to get back to Arizona. When she thought she heard the sound of the quad going back to the condo on the main street, she wondered, for a fleeting moment, if she had hurt BD's feelings.

Two women were getting into a parked car, and Maya heard them speak English. She asked if they knew where she could catch a ride back to Tucson. They said there was a shuttle service; did she need a ride?

They dropped her at the office, and she waited inside just in case BD was still roaming the streets looking for her. Her stomach growled, and her head was killing her. A few shots of tequila would ease her pain. Maybe she shouldn't have just left like that. It wasn't so bad, was it?

"Get real," she snapped at herself, but she said it out loud, to the surprise of the ticket agent sitting behind the desk. To cover up her embarrassment, she asked if she could buy a bottle of water.

It was just a thing that happened, another adventure, and now it was over. She had to focus on getting to Desert Haven and hope that Crow was waiting for her.

Crow 2010

Crow didn't have to consult her map for the most direct route from Arkansas to Arizona; this was her twenty-second trip across the country, and she knew it by heart. She liked her routine and didn't see any reason to change it. The same diners, same rest stops, and same cheap motels every year. Although everything cost twice as much as the year before, or so it seemed.

But lately, she had been thinking that this could be her last trip West. At nearly seventy years old, the driving took longer because she needed frequent stops. Sometimes to pee, but sometimes because her eyelids got heavy, and she was afraid to nod off at the wheel. She used to pride herself on driving twenty hours on caffeine and candy bars, but the time, a few years ago, when she snapped awake driving on the median scared her shitless, so she swore that she would stop every few hours to keep her head clear.

She needed stretch breaks too. Sitting for hours at a time was murder on her hips. Especially her left side, the side that was never quite right since that horse bucked her ass-over-head. She was only trying to do a good deed, rounding up her neighbor's stray cows that meandered into the woods. She would have held her seat if she was younger. Experience was outmaneuvered by inattention and slow reflexes.

So, Crow was thrilled when Maya's saguaro-cactus-wearing-a-sombrero postcard arrived announcing that she would be at Desert Haven the first week of March, and if Crow's offer was still good, she would be happy to ride along to Oregon. Another driver, for even half the trip, was a blessing, and Crow had planned to stop for a week or two at Desert Haven anyway. After double-checking that Maya could drive a stick shift, they made a plan. This way, she would have at least one more year at the Land Dyke Festival at West Farm up in Oregon. Connecting with old friends and meeting new ones was the motivator keeping her on the road. Maya was one of the latter, a young woman newly enchanted with the idea of living on women's land and full of energy. Crow could be her mentor.

Besides, Maya was kinda cute. Crow instantly chastised herself for the thought. It was not that she would make any moves on her—she had at least forty years on that child. All she needed was some company for the long hours on the road.

The rolling hills of Arkansas, the insistent green, were familiar and comforting to Crow as she slowly left her country home for the long journey. Going the speed limit seemed to enrage other drivers, but she didn't care. It was easy. Slow and steady wins the race. After moving to The Pines in rural Arkansas from New York City thirty years ago, Crow couldn't bear to spend more than two days in a city before the pollution and hurried pace drove her batty. All those people milling around, driving themselves into an early grave with stress and addictions. Nope, it was not for her. The smartest thing she ever did was to drop out and move to lesbian land.

Crow settled in with a Mountain Dew in the cup holder, a Chris Williamson CD in the player, and the freedom to let her mind wander. Reminiscing kept her company on the road, and the older she got, the further back her memories strayed.

Carol. She was called Carol when she was born. Carol Levy, a nice Jewish girl from the Lower East Side.

Her newlywed parents came to America in 1928 in search of a better life. The family story told at every holiday and extended family gathering was how they got off the boat at Ellis Island after a very long journey and stood in a long line, grouped with other Ukrainian refugees. It was overwhelming: the enormous chamber, officials shouting instructions in English, a tongue they didn't understand, babies crying, the roar of dozens of languages. They held on to each other, terrified to be separated in the crowd in the vast hall. Until Mama couldn't wait any longer and had to find a toilet. Papa wanted to go with her, but she was afraid to lose their place in line. She reassured him she would only be five minutes even though she didn't know where to find a place to relieve herself in this maze of a building. And besides, they hadn't moved more than three feet in the last hour.

Of course, everything that could go wrong did. The restroom was on another floor, down a long hall. She could not find someone who spoke Russian or Yiddish and was too shy to ask an official because they were all men. When she finally located the women's room, a long, slow-moving line snaked out the door. She tried to explain it was an emergency to no avail. Just as she got to the front of the line, it happened. A puddle grew on the floor around her boots. She didn't know if anyone noticed because she kept her head down while she frantically cleaned up. Would they still let her into America if she smelled like a wet baby?

When she got back, Papa wasn't where she left him. Mama panicked and ran ahead of everyone towards the big desk. She saw Papa talking to a man in uniform, waving his arms wildly. As she got closer, she heard him saying, "My wife will be here soon. Please don't make me step aside." She had gotten there just in time. A little damp but somehow respectable enough to pass scrutiny of the immigration authorities. The recitation of this oft-repeated story was always met with comfortable chuckles.

Her parents told their children how they used their meager savings on a one-room apartment in New York's Lower East Side. Papa labored at the shipyard, and Mama sewed ladies' garments in a factory on 28th Street. Mama was clever at saving something, even a penny, from every paycheck.

They took night classes to learn English. Speaking Yiddish, Russian and Ukrainian was fine in the neighborhood, but they had ambition. They wanted to go to City College and become teachers. When Mama got pregnant with their first child, Davy, she quit school and took on piecework jobs at home, making flowers for ladies' hats.

By the time Carol, their fifth and last child was born in 1940, Papa, who was exempt from the draft, taught history at PS 15, and the family settled into a crowded but cozy three-bedroom second-floor apartment over a laundry.. Mama had a knack for making any place a home. She sewed curtains and trained the children on how to keep the kitchen clean.

Thinking about her mother always made Crow smile and sometimes tear up just a little bit, even after all these years.

Crow remembered her first day of grade school. Mama tied a flowered smock over her dress and walked her youngest to school. Then she went to her new job as a clerk at the corner store, a position she held for the next twenty years to pay for her kids' education. Even though it meant she wasn't home after school, the big kids looked after their baby sister, all sitting around the kitchen table together, doing homework. When Mother came home, she smelled like sugar and had five pieces of penny candy in her pocket.

Picturing herself in that cozy apartment on Ave C with six other people, Crow thought about how the neighborhood had changed over the years. In the sixties, the hippies came and brought drugs and free love. They turned the Lower East Side, a working-class immigrant neighborhood into a gentrified East Village.

Unlike her siblings, Crow never liked school. It was all sitting and talking. She would much rather be outside, riding her bike, exploring. Even though she was told not to go north of 14th Street, boundaries meant nothing to her. She would never forget when she was so late for dinner—she must have been around twelve years old—her mother called the police. But they didn't bother looking for a lost kid in Manhattan. Crow had ridden her bike to the Bronx, more than ten miles away. When she arrived home at two a.m., hungry, exhausted, nursing a scraped knee through a rip in her dungarees, she knew she was in big trouble.

Mama was sitting at the kitchen table, ashtray overflowing, face red with anger, eyes sorrowful with fear. She leaped up, grabbed her errant daughter in a smothering, relieved hug, released her, and slapped her face hard, saying, "Never do that to me again." Crow slunk off to bed with a stinging cheek, no dinner, and a determination to never have kids. She didn't want the heartache from being a parent.

Looking back, she was amazed that no one bothered her on her excursions, maybe because she looked like a feral child; she was a dirt magnet with a wild mop of untamable dark curls. Neighbors knew she would help them move or deliver small packages of unknown items to earn a few dollars. Before long, she decided that school just wasn't her thing and stopped going. The truant officer regularly stopped by the corner store, but Mama told her that there was nothing she could do; that child had a mind of her own. So, her mother signed the papers to let

Crow drop out of school when she was sixteen, just to get the truant officer off her back.

By then, her brothers, except for Davy, who enlisted when the war broke out and died at Iwo Jima in 1945, were putting themselves through college or were working. Crow had enough money saved up to get a little pad of her own just down the street on 6th Street. Every Friday night, she and her siblings gathered at her parents' apartment to light the Shabbas candles, recite the blessing and enjoy Mama's cooking.

Crow always thought that she was very lucky to be young and on her own in New York in the nineteen fifties. First, the Beatniks came with their poetry readings, bongo drums, and bohemian attitudes. They morphed into hippies. Head shops popped up on every corner. She could walk down Bleeker Street smoking pot, and no one noticed or cared. Kids escaping the conformist Midwest, looking for freedom and love were Crow's tribe.

The first time she kissed a girl, Crow was sitting at the bar at Walter's Place. She wasn't sure if the person next to her was a boy or a girl, but she didn't care because the person was buying. After many shots of Cherry Herring and beer chasers, they leaned into each other and made out until Walter said people were staring at them and told them to leave.

She and...what was her name? Annie? Marcie? Even after all those years, Crow thought, at least she should remember her first girlsex. They never saw each other again, so that might explain her lapse of memory.

She found a few underground bars in the village where girls in men's suits and short, slicked-back hair danced with femme women in tight dresses and high heels. There always seemed to be some sort of drama going on. Cross-dressing was illegal, and the cops had nothing better to do than harass homosexual women and men. The scene was way too hectic for Crow. She liked to slip under the radar. Go the speed limit and don't attract attention.

Crow eased off the highway and found a shady spot in the rest area. After walking around the van a few times and stomping her feet to readjust her hip, she climbed into the back and stretched out on the bed for a few minutes. Everything about the conversion van pleased her: the brown and gold patterned curtains, compact mini kitchen, and even the portapotty. What good luck she had finding the perfect vehicle. It had everything she needed, including a huge, well-insulated cooler that kept ice for up to three days if she didn't open it too often.

She grabbed a few Chips Ahoy cookies and a frosty Diet Coke and situated herself in the open side door surveying her fellow tourists. Travelers, like her, nondescript, ordinary. That's what she had turned into, a regular overweight wayfarer, doing her own thing, not getting too involved in the world. No one even looked twice at this radical separatist lesbian. She had turned into background.

Crow got back on the road, sliding a Holly Near into the CD player, and singing along until her thoughts settled on Rita. Her first real girlfriend.

Crow was just a punk hanging out with dopers and other dropouts, occasionally attracted to women, having little flings but nothing serious. Crushes that didn't amount to much. Besides, she didn't want to complicate her life. But when she started in with ebony-haired, green-eyed Rita, she was a goner.

A hand-drawn flyer tacked on a light pole on Christopher Street caught Crow's eye. It advertised "An Automatic Happening" at a gallery a few blocks away, featuring "music, dance, art and YOU." She wasn't much of a gallery-goer, but anything new and unusual caught her attention. Curious, she squeezed into the crowded room and found a space against the wall where she could see the action. A person dressed in cardboard tubes spray-painted silver marched awkwardly around the room, offering a tray of Baby Ruth candy bars. Crow recognized Perez Prado's "Cherry Pink and Apple Blossom White" playing loudly through giant speakers. As soon as the record ended, someone picked up the needle and started the song again. A person wearing a drum major jacket, holding a baton, gestured to the crowd to dance and began twirling in the center of the room.

Crow thought it quite amusing, even if she had no idea what was going on. The colorful crowd danced or swayed to the music as if in a group trance. But one dancer moved her body in perfect synch with the Latin sounds. Hips swaying, big red lipstick smile, Rita zeroed in on

Crow, playfully tugging her hand, pulling the mesmerized introvert onto the dance floor. When the song abruptly changed to a slow dance, they moved into each other's arms, so close that Crow could see beads of sweat dripping from the beautiful woman's ear lobes, could smell her flowery perfume, could feel her tender curves.

"Rock Around the Clock" replaced the soft music, and the two women stood apart. Surprising herself with her forwardness, Crow asked the beautiful woman for her phone number. She took the scrap of paper that said Rita with a string of numbers and stashed it in a shirt pocket over her heart.

The next day, she invited Rita out for a drink but was shut down when Rita said she didn't drink. "Do you want to walk around Thompkins Square Park instead?" was all that Crow could think of. Their two-month courtship was all about walking. They went to Queens and back across the 59th Street Bridge. The Williamsburg Bridge took them to Brooklyn. They even spent fifteen cents to ride the Staten Island Ferry and walked around the borough, amazed at how rural it was.

The anticipation of sex was almost unbearable. Crow chuckled, remembering her constant state of arousal. She couldn't sit still, always looking for ways to distract herself. That's how she got her name, Crow. Rita said she was a girl mesmerized by bright, shiny objects and flitted from thing to thing. Crow knew she had met the most dazzling person and wanted to own her.

After they finally had sex and knew they were right for each other, Rita moved into Crow's tiny apartment six months after they met. They were like two bugs in a rug, if that is how you describe the ultimate nesting. They slept curled into each other, ate breakfast and dinner together, walked and talked, and were deeply in love. They were only apart when Rita's receptionist job separated them Monday through Friday from eight to five. She'd put on her plaid dress and four-inch heels and click off to work, looking like all the other girls in the office. She jokingly told Crow about the men who tried to hit on her until she realized that it made her girlfriend jealous and stopped.

Crow's family wanted to know why she never came around, and when they suspected she had a lover, they wanted to meet him. Crow could not even imagine telling them that she was in love with a woman. She knew, at the least, they would shun her, and she couldn't bear the thought. She lit the Shabbas every Friday evening before sunset to usher in the Sabbath out of habit, but she no longer felt a need for Judaism.

Rita was experienced in keeping a low profile, but she knew some other lesbian couples, so they started to hang out together. Picnics and house parties. Nothing overt. Rita went to church on Christmas with her Catholic girlfriends. Crow lit Hanukah candles for eight days, using the menorah her mother had given her when she got her first apartment. They plugged into the gay underground and heard horror stories about police raids on homosexual bars where men and women were beaten and humiliated. They even heard that men gang-raped lesbians to "cure them."

When Rita came home crying in a rage that she had been fired for suspicion of being "a security risk," they were both devastated. A receptionist in a law office that had a few government contracts could not risk anyone's security. She knew it was because she had refused advances from the head personnel guy but was not about to challenge it. Rita lost her job, and they were powerless to do anything about it.

Crow was getting restless just thinking about those times. She needed to move around a little, so she pulled the van into a rest stop for lunch and a pee break. All these memories kept her company, but some of them retained a sting. She checked her watch and saw that she was making good time. She could drive for another three hours before the Motel 6 in Oklahoma City. Two cream cheese and banana sandwiches and another Coke were enough to carry her through to dinner at the diner. Days were getting longer, and she wouldn't have to worry about driving in the dark.

Back on the road, she needed a distraction, so she turned on the radio and found some awful country music to wail along with. At least it kept her from feeling sleepy like she often did after a meal. When she wasn't singing, she talked to herself, commenting on the scenery and her excitement about being on the road.

That night back at the motel, after a hamburger at Denny's, sleep was elusive. Memories of Rita flooded her brain. She was haunted by the memory of telling her ex that it was all going to be alright when it didn't turn out that way at all.

They had been in Thompkins Square Park when they saw the assault. Three men were punching and kicking a skinny young guy yelling "fucking faggot" and "stupid fairy." Rita grabbed Crow's arm and said, "Let's go," but Crow's instincts impelled her forward. She yelled as loud, and with as much authority she could muster, "Get the fuck off him," and charged the group. Rita screamed, "Crow, stop, let's go." The three thugs were distracted from their victim, who took the opportunity to run as fast as he could out of the park.

"Stupid bitch, you want some too?" A hard punch to her gut knocked the wind out of Crow. She fell, holding her stomach, unable to speak or move.

Rita gasped, catching the attention of the men. Crow saw them sizing her up, young and pretty and with a butch girl. Advancing on Rita, Crow's attacker cooed, "Hello sweet thing, how about a little action." We'll show you a real fucking not like your lesbo girlfriend here." Crow watched in panic from her position on the ground, but it all happened so fast, it was a blur. Rita had a knife in her hands. She darted forward, slashing a cheek and stabbing an arm. The men were so shocked at seeing their own blood, they scrambled away, holding their wounds and yelling impotent curses over their shoulders.

"What the fuck just happened?" Crow said, trying to stand. "Are you okay?"

Rita glared at her and, without a word, turned and walked briskly down the path towards home. Crow was dazed and needed a few minutes to collect herself. By the time she limped home, Rita was gone. Crow looked in the bathroom, and the special shampoo was missing from the tub edge. She opened the closet door, and all that was hanging on Rita's side were a few crooked wire hangers.

Crow sat on the edge of the bed, holding her ribs, and looked around the small apartment for a clue. She didn't understand. Was it because she had put her gentle, sweet, knife-wielding Rita in danger by trying to protect the stranger? And then she couldn't even protect her girlfriend? Was she such a failure as a lover and a friend? Was it because Rita had exposed a hidden part of herself, and now she couldn't face Crow? Why didn't she stay to talk it out? Crow curled up in a ball, ignoring the pain in her belly, and sobbed herself to sleep. After all these years, it still hurt to think about it.

After that, she quit the hippy scene. She moved back into her old room in her parents' apartment. Her mom and dad were surprised but happy to have her back home and didn't ask any questions. She learned to cook a few simple meals and pitched in where she could. Crow didn't know how easy it would be to slide right back into her home community. Fear was no longer a constant companion. Fear of being an outlaw and pervert, of being outed, and the constant fear of violence. She hadn't realized how treacherous her former territory was and the stress she had been under. And she needed to let her heart heal.

Crow was still a kid, only twenty years old, although one with a lot of life experience. She loved the feeling of being normal again. She got her GED and went to college for a degree in early childhood education. Hanging out with preschoolers seemed like the right thing to do.

Remembering that comfortable time, Crow was finally able to drift off to sleep with thoughts of bright, bouncy four-year-olds in her head.

In the morning, a little tired and fuzzy-headed from a restless sleep, she packed up, ready to hit the road, but she had the odd feeling that something was missing. She looked in the bathroom and shook out the sheets to make sure she hadn't forgotten anything. Then it came to her in a wave of sadness. It was Bo, her traveling companion of the past ten years. Bo, who died four months ago. Big Bo, the goofy Sheppard mix-and-match who seemed to be her shadow. Bo never needed a leash, she just walked close by, matching her gait to Crow's, sitting when Crow stopped, and scanning Crow's face for clues what to do next. Her tail was like a feather duster that could clear the coffee table with one sweep.

When her landmates came to tell Crow that her dog had been hit and killed by a logging truck, Crow felt a long black gloom cover her. She stayed in bed for days until friends lured her out of her cave with food and songs. They held a lovely funeral, complete with a headstone that said, "Bo, she is in the big Shadowland now."

She and Bo used to have long conversations in the van. Now, she had no one but herself to talk to. And the ghost of an old girlfriend.

Walking through the lobby on her way to the vending machines, Crow nodded to the clerk, who looked surprisingly like John Waters. "A Payday and some Cheetos should be a balanced breakfast. Chocolate and cheese food, lots of vitamin C," she said. John looked right through her.

Back in the van, Crow took a soda out of the cooler and noted with pleasure that it was still icy. After filling up at the Shell station, she turned the dial, looking for an oldies station. "Every small town in America has an oldies station. It has to be there," she said to Bo or Rita or herself. She didn't know anymore who she was talking to.

"I'm running down the road trying to lighten my load, got seven women on my mind," Jackson Browne sang.

"A lot more than seven, Jackson, my friend," Crow said to the radio, faces and names floating across her mind like airplane banners across the cloudless sky.

After Rita, she allowed herself casual flings. It was surprising how many willing women she met in chemistry or history class while working towards her degree. They weren't lesbians, they told her, just experimenting. That was fine with Crow. She wasn't ready for another heartache, and besides, she was tired of the lesbian scene. By then, she had met Joseph, a nice guy who didn't ask too many questions. They were both going to be teachers; they were from the same neighborhood, and being with him was easy. They planned on getting married after they graduated and were waiting to have sex until it was legal.

Joseph was handsome in a frail sort of way. Pretty almost. He had long blond hair, a close-cropped beard, pale aqua eyes, and was the whitest person she'd ever met. At the beach, with his hair hanging down and his slim figure, he could easily pass for a tall young girl. Crow brought him home to meet her family, which meant that they were engaged, at least to her family. He wasn't the nice Jewish boy they had hoped for, but at least she wouldn't be an old maid. Mama loved feeding him because he could eat half his weight at each meal. "That boy has a hollow leg. You better learn to cook to keep him happy."

The day after they graduated, two families crowded into the judge's chambers in City Hall to witness a tiny woman in a huge black robe conduct a simple civil ceremony. Crow's married sister and mother fussed over her, coaxing her hair into an overblown French twist and making sure she had something old and something blue.

Crow went through the motions and did her life like she was supposed to. She went for extra training and got a job at a Montessori school while Joseph taught high school math. Since she was married, her doctor could prescribe her the pill, a fact she didn't mention to Joseph, and he didn't seem to notice that she didn't get pregnant. It was easy for Crow to orgasm when she held his slight frame and fantasized he was female. She thought it was pretty sexy, so she asked him if he ever fantasized about someone else, and he said, "Absolutely not. That's the same as cheating."

If college classes were full of available women, Crow found the single ladies in the Montessori school to be a treasure trove. It was the liberated seventies, and no one wanted to be left behind. The afternoon trysts piled up, and so did the guilt and shame. Crow was living a double life and didn't know how to escape. The quicksand of lies and deceit were swallowing her up.

Crow pulled into a rest stop to move her body and give her mind a rest. Memories of what she came to call The Black Period were still disturbing. It was the only time in her life she felt hopeless. Walking briskly around the perimeter of the parking lot, she tried to shake off the sadness that she still carried after all these years. At least she and Joseph were able to divorce amicably. They stayed in touch for a while until he married and moved to Florida.

She went into the lady's room to pee and peered at her face in the distorted metal mirror over the sink. Old. I look old, she thought. But maybe it was just the funny mirror.

She was standing at the vending machines in the breezeway, looking over her choice of snacks, trying to decide if she would treat herself to a Snickers bar or peanut butter and cheese crackers, when she heard part of a conversation behind her. Turning, she saw two older white men in red ball caps talking to a young black man wearing short shorts and a sparkly tee shirt.

"What's a little fag like you doing out here all alone, anyway?"

"Yeah, how about a blow job? Let's get you into the men's room."

"Speak up, gay boy, can't you talk?"

Crow turned toward the men and heard herself growl, "Shut the fuck up, you fucking bullies." Her face glowed hot with rage. "Get the fuck out of here and leave him alone." she roared and planted her feet firmly to ready her stocky body for what might come next. No one moved.

"Get over here," she ordered the young man, and he moved to her side, slightly behind her. Fire shot from her eyes as she imagined blood trickling down the bully's arms and bellies from the searing cuts she visualized inflicting. The sheer force of her fierce and awful power seemed to drive the men away. Crow glared them into their pickup, and when they were out of sight, she spoke.

"Are you okay?"

"Yeah, they didn't do anything to me, but oh my God, they would have if you didn't come along. You saved my butt, probably my life. Holy shit, I was so scared I didn't know what to do."

"Me too," Crow said, feeling the shaking starting in her solar plexus and radiating to her limbs. "I was scared shitless, and I wasn't going to let it stop me this time."

"This time?"

"It's a long story. Hey, what's your name."

"Jeremy. I'm kinda stranded here. I was with this guy, and he sort of dropped me off and drove away, the bastard."

"What, he just left you?"

"My boyfriend," he said, gesturing his fingers from each hand into air quotes. "We met a few weeks ago at this rave, and he said he would take me to California with him." Jeremy looked at his bright red polished toenails and shook his head. "That was pretty dumb of me, wasn't it?"

"Yeah, it was. But the question now is, what are you going to do?"

"You wouldn't be headed to California by any chance, would you?"

Crow looked at him in wonder, threw her head back, and laughed. She laughed at the naiveté of this young person, at his escape from danger, at herself for having the guts to faceoff with those morons, and at relief for having survived. But most of all, she laughed at finally feeling like she evened a score and redeemed herself.

Jeremy giggled along and said, "What are you laughing at?"

"Just blowing off some nervous energy. I'm not going to California, but I can take you as far as Tucson if you want. Can you drive?"

"I can, and I even have a license. And I can help pay for gas. While he was shoving me out of the car, the boyfriend forgot he left his wallet on the car seat, so I helped myself. It was the least he could do."

Jeremy climbed into the driver's seat, saying he would take the first shift. His skills at maneuvering the van impressed Crow as she relaxed into the role of passenger and listened as he related his story. He told Crow that his conservative, small-town Kentucky parents kicked him out of the house when they found out he was gay. "I was sixteen. I don't know why it took them so long to figure it out."

He went to Louisville, where he found work at burger joints during the day and partied in gay bars at night. "There were lots of pretty boys, and I was considered a little exotic, being black and all. It was such a good time," Jeremy said, pausing, running his hand through his curly hair. "But that's all over, and now my new life is about to begin."

"I was out on my own when I was sixteen," Crow said. "It was rough, but I survived it. I've had a good life, but complicated."

"Those are the best kind," Jeremy offered.

"When I was your age, no one was out of the closet. Except maybe James Baldwin."

"Who's that?"

"A writer you should read. *Giovanni's Room*. All those books were underground back then. *The Well of Loneliness* was passed around like it was a religious text." She noticed Jeremy's brows raised in questioning but skipped the explanation.

"I was a teacher. I had to be discreet, or I could lose my job. My last girlfriend and I met when I was forty. She was the old maid gym teacher at fifty-one, a lanky country girl. When we moved in together, everyone thought it was great that two unmarried women would have roommates to keep them from feeling lonely until they met the right man. The thing was, I had already been married, and it was a disaster."

"To a man?" Jeremy asked. "Why did you get married?"

"Because I couldn't figure out how to get out of it. It was expected. Lots of gay people got married, and some even had children. Luckily, I escaped that fate."

"You mind if I smoke," Jeremy asked.

"I'd rather that you didn't. Unless it's weed."

"I've got a few joints in my wallet. Hold the wheel while I get them out."

"Sure thing, kid," Crow said, thinking that inviting Jeremy along had been an excellent idea. She had run out of weed back home and was hoping to score some in Arizona. If not there, she knew there would be plenty when she got to Oregon.

"This is good shit," Jeremy said, lighting up. "Be careful, or it will knock you on your ass."

"We'll see," Crow said, squinting her eyes against the smoke. "I was smoking pot before your mother was conceived." The drug mellowed them out, and they drove along in contented silence. After about fifteen minutes, Crow started telling her story where she had left off.

"We had a nice life, me and Jan, but city life finally got to us. All the hiding and secrecy. AIDS was killing all the gay men, and the government wasn't doing a damn thing to stop the epidemic. They called it the gay cancer. It was a scary time. We went to rallies and marches, trying to make a difference, but it was discouraging. We decided to drop out and find a place that we could just be ourselves. We subscribed to a couple of underground lesbian magazines, the kind that came in a plain brown paper wrapper, and we read about women who moved out to the country to create lesbian utopias. We ordered a book, *Lesbian Lands*, that gave contact info for places all over the country."

"Places with no men?" Jeremy asked.

"Yep, a little bit of heaven on earth. Present company excepted, of course."

"Of course," Jeremy said and teased out another hit from the roach. "Ow! This one's dead," he declared and stumped it out in the ashtray, shaking his singed fingers.

"We spent summer vacations scouting out places on the East Coast, and after a few years, we settled on The Pines in Arkansas. I'd never even heard of Arkansas before we decided to move there. Remember, I was New York City born and bred. Jan had grown up in Kansas, another place I never heard of," Crow said and chuckled at her own joke. "Her family had a small dairy farm, so she knew a hell of a lot more than I did about country living. There were four other dykes living there at the time, so we had a real nice community."

Crow twisted in her seat and carefully climbed into the back of the van. She pulled a small box out of an overhead compartment and rifled through it. Back in her seat, she handed a snapshot to Jeremy. "This was us back then." Jeremy flicked his eyes from the road to the photo showing two women in flannel shirts and short hair, arms around each other, grinning at the camera.

Crow pointed to the photo and said, "The trailer behind us is where we were living while we built our one-room house. Now it's twice the size with a big, enclosed veranda."

"Nice. What happened to Jan?"

"It's getting late. How about I tell you after we take a little sleep break. Motel or sleep in the van?"

"Van's okay with me."

They eased into a truck stop and looked around carefully for potential gay-bashers. "You be careful in the men's potty."

"Yes, ma'am."

"And watch who you are calling ma'am." Crow went into the restroom and splashed some water on her face. Mopping herself dry with paper towels, she thought about how fast the trip was going with someone to share it with. It boded well for when she met up with Maya. Things always seemed harder doing them alone. And she'd been alone for a long time now. Of course, she had her farm-family at The Pines, but damn it, she still missed Jan.

Back in the van, they locked the doors and wished each other sweet dreams. Crow stretched out on the bed, Jeremy put the passenger seat back, and they slept until dawn. A magenta morning sky greeted them. "Red sky at night, sailors delight. Red sky in morning, sailor take warning," Crow pronounced.

"What does that mean?"

"Rain today, but I'm sure we will outrun it. No worries."

"How about a few peanut butter and banana sandwiches and a Coke?" she asked. They sat at a picnic table, eating their breakfast, an old dyke, and a black gay young man, watching squirrels doing their push-pull routine. Noses twitching, eyes darting, they tiptoed close, hoping for food crumbs. Any movement would scurry them away.

After finishing their meal, Jeremy lit up the other joint. They observed the wind in the trees for a while before getting back on the road. Crow behind the wheel relaxed to the steady rhythm of the tires on the pavement.

"So, what happened with Jan?" Jeremy asked as if no time at all had passed since he saw the photo.

"Well, we both cashed in our pensions from the school and had enough money to buy building materials for our house. We joined the Women's Land Trust. It wasn't far from Fayetteville, so we figured we could always find some sort of work, but we planned to raise our own food and be as self-sufficient as possible. After getting a roof over our heads, we built a pen and got two goats, Bright Eyes and Trouble. You know, milk, cheese, that sort of thing."

"You know how to milk a goat?" Jeremy asked. "You certainly have a lot of talents."

"I had to learn all my talents. We were determined to make it work. Lesbian land is a haven, and we felt it was our sacred duty to preserve one little corner of Mother Earth from destruction by corrupt corporate capitalism and greed." Crow paused and looked over at Jeremy to see if he had a reaction, and when he appeared not to, she went back to her Jan story.

"Jan and I lived happily for almost 20 years. "We used to make this trip together every year. We'd do the festival circuit and gatherings on different women's lands. Lots of women did. Do. Our favorite was Land Dyke Festival in Oregon. That's where I'm headed after my stop to pick up a friend in Arizona.

"But I digress. Jan started to change. At first, it was just some odd things she said. I didn't think much about it at the time. Then, I noticed things were misplaced. The butter was in the bathroom, that sort of thing.

I thought maybe she should go to a doctor to be checked out, but she wouldn't hear of it. She would have fits of anger at the silliest little thing, or she'd be silent for three days at a time. Things were going downhill fast, and I was getting scared. I wanted her to find out what was happening, but she would become enraged and storm out if I mentioned it.

"One day, she couldn't get out of bed and said she had a blinding headache. I panicked and called 911. They ran all sorts of tests in the hospital over the next week and diagnosed her with an inoperable brain tumor. The doctor, a nice woman, Dr. Chen, said they could do radiation to shrink the tumor, but the prognosis wasn't good. Jan got so upset that they had to medicate her to keep her from hurting herself."

"Could you have them do the radiation without her permission?"

"I wasn't next of kin, and we never had any papers giving me legal rights to make any decisions. They contacted Jan's sister, who she hadn't spoken to in more than fifteen years, who never forgave her for being a lesbian. She said to stop all treatments and let her go in peace. I had no fucking rights at all and had to watch it all like a bad movie. Jan said she just wanted to come home, but the truth was I just couldn't handle her. She was erratic, and she was still strong. It wasn't her fault, it was that damn tumor."

Crow blinked back tears and told herself, "No crying and driving." She took some deep breaths to calm herself and went on. "They transferred her to a nursing home. I stayed with her, sleeping in a recliner at her side. She died thirteen days later."

"Wow, that's heavy. I'm so sorry."

"That was almost ten years ago, but it seems like yesterday. Thank the Goddess we held the house with rights of survivorship, or her evil sister would have tried to steal my house. I had the community's support, and they helped me through it the best they could. I couldn't even go to the funeral." Tears were streaming down her face; Crow pulled over to the side of the road and sat slumped over the steering wheel. "Oh, shit, I didn't know I'd get so emotional telling you all this. Sorry."

"Crying is good. Sometimes, I miss my parents, and I cry like a baby. But then I just move on."

"You are a sensible young man, Jeremy. My dog Bo died last year, so here I am, alone again. Except for you, that is. Thanks for hearing me out. You are a real good listener."

Jeremy nodded silently, looking at Crow as if searching for an answer. "So, how do you get through the day?" he asked.

"I'm a little lonely, but I have a great support system of friends all over the country, so I really can't complain. I'm healthy for an old lady, and I can still get around pretty well, although I am slowing down. How about you? Are you happy?"

"I think I am. I was pretty bummed about being stranded, but thanks to you, now I'm feeling hopeful. It's like this is a new beginning for me. You've had your ups and downs, and you survived. You are my role model."

"Jeez, kid, you make me sound like an old lady."

Jeremy unbuckled his seat belt and stretched across the seat to give Crow an awkward shoulder hug. She noticed tears glistening in the inside corners of his eyes.

At the Greyhound bus station in downtown Tucson, Crow got out of the van and gave Jeremy a long hug, one that had to last him all the way to California. They exchanged contact info, but both of them knew this was probably the extent of their relationship.

"Bye, kid, be safe."

"You too, Crow. Thanks for everything."

She watched him walk into the station, turning back at the door to give her a finger wiggle wave. Crow climbed into the van and consulted her map to make sure she knew the route to Desert Haven. She wondered if Maya was waiting for her or if she would be there first. Who would be on the land? Hopefully, JoJo had recovered from that stroke or whatever it was that she had last year. This getting older wasn't for sissies.

Crow never knew who would be on women's land when she arrived, but it didn't matter. They were all family.

Alyson 2013

Alyson excused herself to go to the lady's room. Her four companions were deep into strategizing and their third round of drinks, so they didn't notice when she left. These after-work meetings can wear a girl out, she thought, especially when the fate of The Tucson LGBT Community Center is at risk.

She made her way slowly to the back of the dimly lit restaurant, noticing the flow, who was moving, and where they were going. Excellent, no one waiting in the small hallway. Two doors confronted her, one with a stick figure of a person and the other with a stick figure of a person wearing a skirt. Cautiously, she pushed open the skirted door, whispering to herself, I hope it's a single, I hope it's a single. One toilet, one sink, lock on the door. Big sigh of relief. Potential confrontation avoided.

Her face in the mirror always gave her a little surprise of pleasure; she saw a woman with long eyelashes smiling back at her. She was by no means invisible. At six feet four, including her two-inch pumps, Lucile Ball red hair, and a form-fitting dress exposing modest cleavage, Aly made a statement. Passing might have been a goal when she first dreamed of leaving her male identity behind, but as she grew into her womanhood, there was just too much of her—loud booming voice, big belly, manic dancer when the beat moved her. She tolerated glaring looks and tried to ignore insults like being called "he-she" or strangers asking if she was a boy or girl. As long as it didn't get violent, her policy was to ignore the uninformed idiots. And besides, some of those straight men liked a little dick in a fancy package.

She had waited to go to the bathroom so long she thought the stream of pee was never going to stop.

Two thoughts: Good, now I have room for another cocktail, and hey, you said you weren't going to drink anymore, clashed in her brain. Both of them were true. She was attending three AA meetings a week and was sticking to the program. Except for today. Her first slip. Oh well, it's too late now, might as well enjoy it. Checking her lipstick, she made her way back to the table.

She heard the passionate voices of her companions defending their points of view from halfway across the room. Those queers were a noisy bunch. Sliding into the booth next to Richard, she heard him say, "I vote we take the tobacco tax money. Why not. If we don't, someone else will."

"I see you all haven't gotten very far in this discussion since I left," Alyson said, which prompted a jumble of voices talking over each other to explain what she had missed.

Richard interrupted, "Come on guys, sorry Aly, guys and girl, we no longer have the luxury of turning down grant money of any sort. Who cares where it comes from. We will make it clean by magically turning it into programming for homeless trans youth. And besides, all those kids smoke, so they bought the cigarettes and paid the tax into the fund to support smoking cessation programs for youth. A sick circle."

Richard's husband, Rick, chimed in. "What do you think, Aly?" Four pairs of eyes turned to her.

"As one of the two trans people at this table, I will boldly represent all trans youth when I say they are wondering where their next meal is coming from, and they don't give a shit who pays for it. Our most important job is to keep these kids safe. If their parents kicked them out, or if they ran away because of abuse or toxic bullying, they are on the Tucson streets, and they need our help. They have nowhere to go. What do you have to say, Micah?"

Micah looked surprised to hear his name. With a slight build and personality to go with it, he always seemed to be trying to disappear. But that didn't mean that he wasn't paying attention. "What exactly do you propose to do with the money, Richard? And how much can you get?"

"Well, we have to look at the parameters of the grant, but my idea is to work with the food co-op to serve an evening meal, seven days a week. Once we have the kids gathered in one place, the hope is that we can introduce them to support services in a non-threatening way."

"Oh, you mean like the Salvation Army. Pray over the poor little lost lambs," Clark said.

"Don't be such a sarcastic bitch," Rick came back at him. "Have you got a better idea? How can we reach out to these kids and let them know that they are not alone?"

"Now, you two, no more bickering," Richard said. "We have to make a move on this money. The deadline is Tuesday. That only gives us four days to get our shit together."

Rick, always supportive of his mate, said, "Yes, director dear, you always know how to bring us back on task."

"I wish someone was having this conversation about finding services for me when I was a young'un," Alyson said. "I just thought I was a freak of nature, the one that God forgot. Being on the street isn't something I would wish on anyone. Let's have another round and figure this thing out."

"No more booze until we come up with a plan," Richard said.

The promise of more alcohol was the mother of invention. The five coworkers quickly bounced ideas off each other until they agreed on how to write the proposal.

After their celebratory drink, Rick said he didn't want to break up the party but needed to get up early in the morning. Richard got up to go. Clark was meeting some friends at a club. Alyson said, "group hug," putting an arm around Micha as they all squeezed into an awkward huddle.

Alyson was back in her studio apartment by nine o'clock. Her impulse had been to move over to the bar to keep the party going, but she was trying to be good. Old habits were hard to break. She kicked off her size fourteen heels and stretched out on the futon couch, head and feet propped up on armrests. Tipsy but not enough to get the spins. That was good. She hated when everything seemed tilted and wouldn't stop moving. Her tummy growled, and she wondered what was in the refrigerator but then decided that eating would just kill her buzz. She didn't want to waste the booze that The Center had paid good money for. She enjoyed being back in her old favorite place: Whogivesashit.

The melodic ring of her cell phone roused Aly out of her reverie. Or had she dozed off? She picked up the phone and looked at the screen. Dian. Shit. If she didn't answer, she knew that Di would just keep calling.

"Yessss."

"Aly, is that you?"

"Yesss."

"Why do you sound like that? Are you drunk?"

"No, Dian, I am not drunk, but thank you for caring." Aly tried to keep the annoyance out of her voice and calm herself down. Why did Di have to check in all the time? Just because she was her sponsor, she didn't have to be such a self-righteous bitch.

"Should I come over? Do you need some support?"

"No, Lady Di, I'm good. Just relaxing after work." Attempting to change the focus away from her drinking, she said, "And you, how did your day go, Darlin?"

"Okay, I'm coming over. I know what you're doing, Aly."

"I'm not doing anything. Calm down now. I just went out with some work folks for a business meeting. I might have had one cocktail, but nothing to be alarmed about."

"What about your program? What do you think sponsors are for? I'm coming right over," Dian said and hung up the phone. End of conversation.

Well, damn, that didn't go well, Aly thought. How was she supposed to do her job if she couldn't meet with the staff, even if it was over cocktails? It was fucking embarrassing. I'm sorry, we will have to meet at Denny's. I can't be trusted in a place that serves alcoholic beverages. Isn't there anywhere a trans woman can just let her hair down? An alleged alcoholic trans woman, that is.

Things were going so well she didn't want to fuck them up. Working at the LGBT Center was amazing. She felt like every day was an opportunity to save a life. Not everyone could say that. She loved her job, her coworkers, and having her own apartment. No more living on the street for this girl.

Just a few drinks, enough to relax but not get all kinds of sloppy. It was no big deal, but Di was going to make it into one. Aly was not about to throw away five and a half months of sobriety. It all still counted, and nobody could take that away. No more "hitting bottom," whatever that was. Turning tricks on the Avenue? Her mother refusing her calls? She had lots of "bottoms," no pun intended. But for some weird reason, the one that hurt the most, the one that sent her over the top, or to the bottom, was being denied her womanhood by that bunch of man-hating dykes out at Desert Haven.

Just the memory of it was enough to drive her to drink. She must have been pretty fucked up when she walked into the dimly lit Rusty Spur, surveying the room, looking for some company and maybe a bit of cash. It was only six months ago, but it could have been a lifetime.

She remembered zooming in on one dude. He looked like every other working-class guy bellied up to the bar. Blue baseball cap pulled down low, flannel shirt, gnarly hands. But there was something that seemed different. Aly tentatively perched on the barstool next to the stranger, hanging her oversized purse on the hook under the bar, and caught the bartender's eye. He wordlessly reached into a cooler to fetch her regular drink. Setting the Milwaukee's Best on the bar in front of her, he popped the tab and mutely waited with crossed tattoo arms for the money.

Diving into her purse, searching for her wallet, she looked up to see her neighbor's hand wave towards a stack of bills on the bar. The barman removed two dollars, dropped a quarter, and returned to the soundless ballgame on TV.

"Thanks." Aly tipped the can at her companion and took a refreshing swig of beer.

"No problem."

"I'm Aly. I've never seen you here before."

"I've never been here before."

"And you are...?"

"Stormy. You know, like every silver lining has a cloud. That's me, Stormy."

Aly quickly assessed her new companion: high voice, no Adam's apple, small wrists. Once they got to talking, Aly realized that Stormy was a butch lesbian, not a guy. She was a likable drinking buddy who didn't say too much and kept the beer coming, so Aly was happy. By asking questions, Aly learned that Stormy was a mechanic who worked on esoteric foreign cars. That explained the grease under her fingernails and rough hands. There wasn't a lot of business in this cowboy town for Lancia repairpersons, and Stormy said that suited her just fine. She didn't like to work too much anyway. She preferred drinking with pretty ladies.

Alyson was an experienced small talker and right in her element in this unpretentious, sleazy bar where the Christmas lights were still strung, and the newest song on the jukebox was from the disco era. She liked Stormy's easiness, and they were developing a great bar friendship that was soon interrupted by last call. Two a.m. already! They were just getting warmed up. And besides, Aly wasn't looking forward to having to figure out where she was going to stay the night. She had worn out her welcome at most of her friend's houses. Couch surfing wasn't for sissies.

Even though Aly was indirect about her situation, Stormy figured out that she needed a place to stay. "Come on out to the women's campground with me. I've got a nice travel trailer out there. You can crash on my couch."

Aly had heard stories about Desert Haven, a nest of dropout lesbians, stoners, and back-to-the-landers living on property owned by an old lady named JoJo. They were a bunch of misfits. Didn't sound so bad. And, besides, a couch was a lot better than rolling up in a dirty blanket down by the river.

"Where's your car?" Stormy asked.

"Don't have one."

"So, I guess we'll take mine," Stormy said. Tipping her glass back to get the last dregs of beer, she pushed the remaining bills toward the bartender.

He mumbled, "Have a good night," as they exited.

"Can you drive, okay?" Aly asked.

"No problem. I do this all the time," Stormy answered, helping Aly into the passenger seat of her vintage Volkswagen bus pickup hybrid.

"Cool car," Aly said, admiring how clean and shiny it was.

Navigating the VW along twisty roads, headlights snaking through the quiet desert, Stormy drove with one hand on the wheel and the other holding a Marlboro with a precariously long ash. Aly rolled the window down and sipped the fresh air. She was wasted. Stormy had matched her drink for drink, but if she wasn't worried, why should Aly be.

At Desert Haven, the only sounds were their loud whispers as they searched for Stormy's trailer in the dark and fumbled with the door. The place was basic but homey. A kitchen against one wall next to a dinette and a fold-out couch with peach and turquoise plaid upholstery on the other side of the room. Photos of exotic landscapes cut from National Geographic taped to the walls. A short hall with doors to the bathroom and bedroom. Stormy said, "Don't try to use the bathroom; the plumbing isn't hooked up. There's a toilet in the bathhouse."

Reaching into a cupboard, she pulled out a pint of Yukon Jack. After clinking glasses in a toast to their new friendship, they downed their shots, hugged goodnight, and quietly went to separate beds.

Morning came soon, and sunlight scorched Aly's eyes even though they were squeezed shut. She lurched to the window and closed the curtains. Outside, people were up and bustling, saying "Good morning" and "Beautiful day." Peeking out, she saw women gathered in a fenced area that appeared to be a garden. They wore straw hats and shorts. No shirts. Aly remembered the pre-boob feel of cool air on a bare chest.

Snores from the bedroom assured Aly that her hostess was still in the land of nod. Having to pee, Aly remembered about the bathroom, so she straightened her clothes the best she could and tiptoed out to the bathhouse, staying out of sight of the bare-chested amazons. Her head felt hollow, and her hair hurt. Back on the couch, she pulled the sheet over her face and fell back asleep. It wasn't the most comfortable sleeping arrangement, but at least she was safe.

By the time the two women woke up, it was late afternoon. They agreed that the best way to avoid a hangover was the hair of the dog that bit them, so they cracked open a couple of Bud Lights and sat outside in the shade of the trailer, enjoying the slight breeze. Aly hadn't done her hair or makeup and was getting a bit of a five o'clock shadow, but hell, she was among women. No need to spruce up for the male gaze, as it were.

The trailer was nestled in a patch of tall jumping chollas that, at this time of day and with the light just so, glowed as if internally lit. The distant mountains turned a dusky blue-grey as the sun sunk low on the horizon. Hummingbird wings whirred as the tiny birds darted about catching mosquitos. Aly leaned back, tipping the chair against the trailer, and sighed. She felt cozy.

A few women walked by and looked at them, but no one came over to chat.

"These girls aren't very friendly, are they?" asked Aly.

"They mostly keep to themselves except when the moon is full, and they come out to howl."

"Oh, werewolves?"

"No, Goddess worshipers."

Stormy went to fetch them a few more brewskis, and when she returned, she found four women standing in a semicircle, staring at her new friend. Aly was sitting straight up in the lawn chair, beer in front of her chest as if for protection. She was wide-eyed and frowning at the same time.

"What exactly is going on here?" Stormy asked, walking over to the barefoot bald-headed woman. "Curry, have you all met my new friend Alyson?"

"Alyson, my ass. Al is more like it. You should know, no men on the land. It's one of the basic agreements," a tall woman with a scar across her forehead said.

"I never saw any agreements, and besides, Alyson is my buddy, so fuck off. I came here to be left alone, and I don't need anyone telling me who I can hang out with."

"I came here to be with my women-born-women sisters," JB said, arms akimbo.

The other women joined in a chorus along the same lines, bolstering their collective bravado by the minute. "I don't want to see your weenie. You are making me feel unsafe. We don't want your kind here. You stink of the patriarchy."

Stormy said, "What's wrong with all of you? This is no way to treat a guest." She held the trailer door open for Aly. "Let's go inside and finish our beers in peace,"

Aly towered over her antagonists as she stood. Shaking inside, she hoped she looked regal and composed on the outside. "Yes, let's," and mounted the stairs.

Aly's shame, anger, and frustration mixed with a two-beer and no-food buzz. She dropped into a chair, covered her face, and cried into her hands. Stormy stood patiently next to her, hand on her shoulder, mumbling words she hoped were reassuring. After a few minutes, Aly sat up, patted her tears away, and sighed deeply. She said, "I'm alright."

Stormy asked quietly, "Are you really a man?"

Her sincerity touched Aly. She answered as calmly as she could, "They put an M on my birth certificate, but that never really worked for me. I began transitioning three years ago, and now I am a woman. It's that simple." She paused, listening to her own words, and said, "I wish it was that simple."

Stormy sat and waited for what was going to happen next.

"I have to fix my face," Aly said, picking up her purse and squeezing into the tiny bathroom. She wiped her eyes with a tissue and applied powder and lipstick, staring at her face in the mirror.

Why did this particular slam hurt so much? She was used to the stares, the crude remarks, the rude questions. But these women were outcasts just like her. They had dropped out of a society that didn't have a place for them, and now they were rejecting her. It was like being tossed out of a leper colony for being too diseased.

"I need to leave. Do we have any of that Yukon Jack left? I could use some fortification before I run the gauntlet of that bunch of harridans. Will you drive me back to town now?"

"Hey, I'm sorry. I didn't know any of this woman-born-woman shit. And I really didn't know about you. I guess I'm kinda oblivious."

"My life is a mess, but this tops it all. Please pour me a stiff one. No pun intended."

Stormy tried to apologize for the harsh treatment her landmates had dished out on the ride back to town through the saguaro forest. "I just don't get it. I get mistaken for a guy all the time, and I just let it go. Who cares what gender you are or how you look? I thought we were all in this together."

Aly knew it wasn't Stormy's fault; neither of them was thinking clearly last night. Aly wasn't welcome at Desert Haven. It was a battle she didn't have the energy to fight.

Stormy dropped her off at her friend Kenneth's house. Aly knew he could help her figure some stuff out, specifically, how drinking was messing her up.

"You look like something the cat dragged in," Kenneth said. "I have no sympathy for your sorry state. I have twenty-three years of sobriety, and I know I would have died if I stayed on the drink."

Kenneth had been trying to bring Aly to an AA meeting for years. Before, it was just annoying. Today, it made sense. She might not be an alcoholic, but drinking surely didn't make things better. It usually made them worse, like the cesspit of shame and rage she was floundering in due to her recent encounter with a tribe of man-hating vipers. Kenneth said they might just be man-fearing because he, unlike his guest, was a feminist.

That evening, they walked into the Thursday night Pink Triangle AA meeting in the community room of the Metropolitan Community Church, holding hands so Aly wouldn't flee.

She sat on a hard folding chair in a circle with nine other queers, her eyes downcast, feeling very out of place. She listened intently as people recapped their sorrow-filled stories. Especially when Dian told how she realized that she drank to cover her feelings of rejection when she came out as trans. When it was Aly's turn, she said she might be an alcoholic; she wasn't sure. It was her first meeting, and she didn't have anything to say except she was impressed with how brave everyone was to tell their truth. She was informed that one of the program's pillars is to have a sponsor, someone further along in the program, as a special support person. The meeting ended with something they called the serenity prayer. Serenity, she thought, now that's a concept.

Kenneth steered them over to the coffee and donuts for the after-meeting social hour. Everyone seemed nice, but Aly had trouble remembering why she had even come to the meeting, except for Kenneth's encouragement. She had heard some horror stories at the meeting. Surely, she wasn't as nearly as bad as some of these folks had been. So, she drank a bit. No big deal. Right?

But maybe she could lay off the booze for a little while just to see what happened. She obviously needed something to help her get her shit together.

Between bites of a chocolate donut with rainbow sprinkles, Kenneth introduced Aly to Dian, saying, "You two seem to have a lot in common."

"Oh, just because we are beautiful alcoholic trans women in a cruel transphobic world. You think?" Di laughed loudly and nudged Aly into cracking a small smile. The smile broadened as she understood that Di was right. They were allies. Di's radiant confidence was melting her resistance. It was just an outermost layer, but something shifted; they both felt it.

"I think that it might be a good idea to try out the program," Aly began cautiously. "And I guess I need a sponsor."

"Are you asking me to be your sponsor?" Di asked, grinning. "It would be an honor."

Di, of the big hair and heart to match. Di, who had been in the same place three years ago and was now determined to save every trans sister who walked through the door. Di was wise and willing to share her hard-fought-for truths.

It was Di who volunteered at the LGBT Center and recommended Aly for her job. She believed in Aly's recovery so strongly that she lent her money for the deposit on this apartment. Aly didn't have a quarter of Di's confidence and clarity, but she was working on it.

And now Di was about to walk through her door and drag her sorry ass to a meeting and save her life again.

JoJo 2014

"What's up with JoJo? She's holed up in her house with the curtains shut. Has anyone seen her today?" Liv looked from face to face, hoping for a clue from the four women sitting with her at the picnic table under the Mother Tree.

"I dunno," Maya said. "I guess I haven't seen her either. Maybe she's sick or something. Think we should knock on her door and find out?"

"I hate to bother JoJo if she's asleep," Liv said.

"Out cold is more like it," Curry said more or less under her breath.

Grumbles of agreement and argument.

"Now, don't start that again, Curry. JoJo likes to drink, but she's not a drunk. And besides, what she does is none of our business."

"Why are you always defending her, Liv? If JoJo fucks up, we are fucked. She owns Desert Haven, and if she doesn't take care of business, we can't stay here. Somebody's got to be the grown-up."

It seemed to Liv that she was the only one on JoJo's side. The others said that Liv was too accommodating, too caring, just because she had empathy for the older woman. But was it possible to be too caring? Wasn't her positive attitude a good thing? Or did she have her head in the clouds? But it did get more complicated when JoJo gave them daily reminders of her dysfunction, like not coming out of her house.

"I think we have to come up with a plan," someone said.

"What if we offer to help her with her problem. Tell her we know about all those empty wine bottles she dumps behind her house."

"Remember when we confronted her after she slept out in the rain last February. She could have died from hypothermia. Didn't do a damn thing."

"Yeah, she told us she was a pluviophile and laughed it off."

"What's a pluviophile?"

"It's someone who loves rain; they find peace of mind during rainy days."

"She's never found peace of mind," Curry said.

No one disagreed.

"Let's just leave her be. The woman wants privacy."

"But it's finally cooling off, and we're going to have a spectacular sunset. JoJo loves to watch the day end. Can't you smell the creosote? Maybe we'll have rain soon."

"We have amazing sunsets almost every night in the desert. It will be okay if she misses this one."

Liv stood, stepping from side to side, one foot to the other. "I don't know. What if something is wrong? She had that stroke a few years ago. She could have fallen and broken a hip. It could happen, you know."

"I don't think it's likely. She's pretty spry," Curry said.

"She's spry for a seventy-eight-year-old, but she's getting up there. And besides, have you seen how much stuff is crammed into that house? She could have tripped over a pile of books or something and can't get up."

"We've been through this before. Remember when we couldn't find her for a few days, and it turned out she went to Colorado for a rammed earth workshop and forgot to tell anyone. I don't think we have to worry."

"I think we should at least knock on the door and see that she's okay. What do the rest of you say?" Four women looked in four directions, none willing to take sides. They had been through this before: Curry and Liv, old friends, ex-lovers who habitually disagreed with each other. No one wanted to get in the middle.

"Oh, come on now, we can't just sit around while JoJo could be lying in a pool of blood."

"There you go with your vivid imagination. It's fine, don't worry," Curry said.

"You don't know that. Why are you so damn stubborn? The reason we are all here is to watch out for each other, and we are not doing a very good job of it right now," Liv said and slapped the table with her flat hands for emphasis, arousing startled looks but no reproach.

"Who says that's the reason I'm here. Don't tell me what I think. Just because it's important to you doesn't mean it's important to everyone else."

"Why are you always so fucking negative all the time. You have no compassion."

"Calm down. There's no reason to get all personal. And besides, I'm not negative; I'm just being realistic."

"You are pissing me off now." Liv looked around the table for support, but she knew it wasn't there for her. The others followed the conversation but dared not chime in. They were just biding their time until the two women stopped bickering.

"I'm going over there to check up on my friend because I don't have any judgment about her drinking and how she chooses to live. I just want to be reassured that she is safe."

Liv rose to her full five-foot-two-inches and strode off across the clearing, making every effort to remain focused on her task and not give any mind to damn Curry. That woman could be so fucking annoying. At least Liv had the good sense to dump her years ago. But, of course, if it weren't for Curry, she wouldn't be living in this community.

If she hadn't lusted after Curry's tall sun-browned, curvy naked body in the shower at the Michigan Women's Music Festival; if she didn't go to Curry's "Lesbian Intergenerational Cohousing Communities Workshop; if they hadn't had hot sex for the next four days; if Liv hadn't left a message on her mother's answering machine that she wasn't coming home; if she didn't climb on the back of Curry's motorcycle at the end of the Festival and head west to Desert Haven, she wouldn't have found her home on women's land.

◆ ◆ ◆

Liv hesitated in front of the house, shaking her hands and feet to rid herself of Curry's negativity. Before climbing the two splintery wooden stairs, she paused to feel for JoJo's vibes, but nothing came to her.

The screen door hung from one hinge at an odd angle off to the right. Faded orange paint peeled off the front door like shaggy tree bark.

Rosemary and thyme grew wildly in broken pots in front of the windows. It didn't look very inviting, but in a way, it fit right into this ramshackle collection of trailers and tents called Desert Haven. It was a haven for misfits and outliers, that's for sure. A safe space that accepted all women.

JoJo said that she knew what it was to be an outsider: a tomboy in the conformist 1950s, a motorcycle-riding, leather-chaps-wearing, woman-loving outlaw. She didn't like rules and wouldn't impose any on the property she owned and shared. So, everything was free-flowing and chaotic. She said it suited her, and if you didn't like it, you didn't have to stick around.

Liv took a long, centering breath and knocked on the front door, trying to peer through the dirt-fogged window. "JoJo, wake up. It's me, Liv."

A few more knocks turned into pounding, but still no response. Liv hated to barge in, but now she was concerned. Maybe something really was wrong. She carefully opened the door a crack chanting, "Minx, kittykittykitty, Minx," trying to locate JoJo's cat.

Liv closed the door and surveyed the dimly lit room. "JoJo? Are you here?" Frayed dun-colored bedspreads covered three broken-down recliners piled with books and papers overflowing to the side tables and down to the floor. A *Time Magazine* from April 10, 1995, on top of a pile caught Liv's eye. A dramatic drawing of Christ rising from the dead with the headline, "Can we still believe in miracles?" on the cover. Why would JoJo save a twenty-year-old magazine? Was she religious? Did she believe in miracles?

"JoJo?" Crusty pots and dishes crowded the kitchen counters. She located Minx on the edge of the sink, gnawing at a greasy frying pan handle. The cat turned her golden eyes toward Liv, crouched down, and went back to the pan.

"JoJo? Hello?" Liv edged down the hall, glancing into the large storage room filled with crushed cardboard boxes overflowing with discarded clothing and papers. The smell of mold. She continued a few steps to the bedroom. "JoJo? Are you okay?"

A pile of rumpled blankets, crunchy things on the floor, the bedside lamp on. "JoJo?" Liv got closer to the bed and saw the face of her old friend. Hollow, downcast, not-quite-shut eyes, sunken cheeks, hair limp. She was grey. Her skin had lost all color. "JoJo!"

Liv touched a shoulder. It was otherworldly, stiff. She leaned in to see if she could discern breath from between the blue lips. Stillness. The odor of urine. JoJo's wrist felt like bones already buried in a box deep in the ground. No pulse. "Oh, JoJo."

The old woman was disappearing. Liv felt absence, cold, void. How long had she been lying here dead? Liv perched on the edge of the bed and sensed a heavy fog of grief and remorse descend over her. What if she had been here an hour ago? Could she have saved JoJo? Why did she listen to Curry and not come in sooner? What was supposed to happen next? Should she call 911? What would JoJo want?

Did JoJo know she was going to die? Did she not want to bother anyone? Was she afraid in those last moments alone? Liv sobbed her guilt and pain and gently stretched out on the bedcovers next to JoJo. What's going to happen to the land now? Will they have to move? Who was JoJo's next of kin anyway? She never talked much about her family. Even though they lived side by side for the past six years, Liv knew little about JoJo's private life. She was always there as a benevolent parent, on the sidelines, watching, never the center of attention.

Liv cradled JoJo's rigid hand. Think. What exactly did she know? She remembered one night when they were both pretty drunk, JoJo told her stories of her life back in Columbus, Ohio. She said her given name was Jane, or Alice Jane, maybe. Something that just seemed too sweet and ordinary for a little girl who wanted to keep up with her older brothers. How many brothers did she have? Liv remembered JoJo told her that she hitchhiked out west. When? It was a long time ago. She was a science teacher before she had the motorcycle crash and went on disability. Did she get a big insurance check from the accident and buy the land with it? Was that right?

She moved to the land and offered space to other women through the lesbian grapevine. Pretty soon, women started showing up. JoJo never made plans for the community, so it was logical that she didn't plan for her death either.

The light was fading, and Liv suddenly felt uneasy in the house. She stared at the water-stained Rorschach test ceiling tiles, hoping an answer would magically appear. Leaning over, she scrutinized JoJo's face, looking for clues, but all she saw was a dead woman. Planting a kiss on her friend's forehead, she whispered, "Thank you."

The last sunrays crossed the bed as Liv rose and pushed the burlap curtains aside to look out the window. The women were still sitting around the table, probably still arguing. They didn't know yet that everything had changed.

Sunshine 2014

Sunny compared the address scribbled on a scrap of loose-leaf paper with the numbers on the sagging adobe duplex. This must be the place. Scooping up the pipe and baggie of weed from the passenger seat, she wrapped them in a bandana and stuffed them into the glovebox. No sense inviting someone to break the truck window to steal her stash. She grabbed her ancient faded blue sweatshirt even though it was a warm fall day. Best to have her security blanket when she was going somewhere she'd never been before.

The screen door rattled when she knocked, so she opened it and pounded on the front door a few times. Glancing up and down the quiet Tucson street, she noticed a tiny old man, or maybe a child, sitting on the shabby front porch of a house across the street. They watched each other while Sunny waited. After a bit, the door was flung open by a plump grey-haired woman wearing a red Guatemalan blouse, cradling a longhaired calico cat.

"You must be Sunshine! Come on in. I'm Junebug, but everyone calls me JB. This is Candy," she said, nodding to the cat in her arms. Turning to the open door, JB yelled, "Honey, she's here."

Sunny sidled her lanky frame past the floor-to-ceiling shelves crammed with double-stacked books and multicultural knickknacks lining the entry hall. She saw Hawk across the room excitedly twisting the fringe of her serape, working her way through a maze of couches and folding chairs piled with newspapers and half-eaten snacks.

"Sunny!" Hawk cried and squeezed the younger woman in a bear hug. "I haven't seen you since you were a sweet little girl. Do you remember me?"

"Hawk! Of course I do. I love learning history because of you. I'm so glad that you found me at West Farm. When you said that JoJo passed away and there was an issue with the land, I just had to make the trip down here from Oregon." She quickly added, "And to see you too."

"Have a seat. Just push some of that crap over, don't worry about it. Jeez, it's so good to see you. How long has it been? How old were you when you and your mom left Desert Haven?"

Sunny cleared a little space for herself on a chair and wrapped the sweatshirt around her shoulders, tying the arms like the ends of a scarf.

"I was nine when Madrona and I moved to Solana. I should have been in fourth grade, but I had to go into second grade with the seven-year-olds since I didn't go to school when I was on the land. I caught up pretty fast though, especially math." Sunny hugged her sweatshirt closer, even though it was a little warm in the room. She felt compelled to tell Hawk her story as if she owed it to her mother. "But then Madrona got pissed about the propaganda they were teaching me, things like the Pledge of Allegiance, and pulled me out. I was homeschooled for the rest of the time."

JB came from the kitchen with two handmade porcelain mugs of steaming dandelion root tea and offered one to Sunny. The grassy green aroma and the warm familiarity of the older women brought back memories of her mother and the women of Desert Haven circled under the tepee frame, next to the Grandmother Tree, the sacred space. Tea always preceded a ritual, and it seemed like there was always some sort of ritual or celebration going on.

"How did you end up at West Farm?" JB asked. 'We were lucky that Liv stopped in to see us and said that she had seen you there. That's how we knew where to find you."

"After Madrona died, I went up to Portland to see if I could find my dad. I didn't know him, and I wanted to see what he was like. Madrona hated him so much but I thought he couldn't have been that bad. Anyway, I had to find out for myself." Sunny said, burrowing into her sweatshirt, shaking her head to clear a memory. She made herself go on, "I found out that he was an asshole, just like she said." Sunny sipped her tea slowly and got quiet. The women respected her moment, and sat comfortably in silence.

What she didn't say was that when she found him, he was living in a squat with a bunch of homeless vets. He was surprised to see her and asked if she had any money. When she said no, he said she could stay there with him and the guys for a few days. She could put her sleeping bag on a stained mattress in the corner.

She didn't tell the two older women that after she sat with the men and listened to their incoherent talk fueled by cheap alcohol and fury, she quietly left and lay down on the mattress, trying to figure out why she was even there. Eventually, she drifted into a restless sleep. Just as light was starting to creep into the uncovered windows of the stark space, her sleeping bag was yanked off, startling her awake. A weight fell across her body, and bony fingers grabbed for her breasts, moving like spiders over her body, trying to insert themselves into her pants. Vile alcohol breath. Rage and adrenaline filled her. She punched and punched again, making solid contact with her attacker's eye socket and nose. She tasted his blood dripping into her face. "Get back, you fucker," her voice roared, an enraged lion. She pushed him off and leaped up, grabbing her sleeping bag and backpack. As she ran out, she heard her father cursing her, calling her the awful names she remembered him calling her mother.

Sunny drove south on the Interstate, stopping to wash off the smell and horror at the first rest stop she saw. Looking in the distorted metal mirror, she saw her mother looking back at her. "I told you he was rotten. Now you know," the image said, not shaming but using the opportunity as a teaching moment, just like Madrona did when she was alive. Tears of grief and loss burned Sunny's cheeks, splashing on her T-shirt on top of blood splatters. She pulled the shirt over her head, stuffed it into the trash can, and dug through her backpack for something clean.

When she got out her wallet to buy a Coke, she discovered that the two hundred and thirty-two dollars she had was gone. Insult to injury. She just hoped she had enough gas to get to southern Oregon.

West Farm didn't seem much changed since she was there with her mother years ago. The same hearty land dykes, the same petty squabbles, and huge communal gardens. Only this time, she was a grown-up. Sorta. She was twenty years old, with no mother and no father. She had an avocado green Mazda pickup truck but no money for gas. She was a hard worker, and she was looking for a home. No one had to explain women's land to her; it was all she had known. She felt comfortable in the company of independent separatist lesbians passionately creating their own culture, leaving the mainstream for a life of freedom and honest labor. A young woman named Sunshine Wimminchild would always be welcome.

"I was at West Farm for around two years. I liked it there. I insulated an old wooden outbuilding that sat on a ridge and ran electricity to it. It was cozy. Never leaked. And that's pretty darn important in a rainforest." She felt she was talking about herself too much, so she asked, "Hawk, why did you leave Desert Haven?"

"JB moved in with me, and some of the new women objected to our exclusivity. It caused all sorts of fuss," Hawk said, laughing and reaching over to pat her partner's thigh.

JB added, "Things have changed since you and Madrona were there. I want to say we were very sorry to hear about your mom's passing. We heard she stuck to her guns and refused to take the medical monopoly's poison."

"She did high-dose vitamin C infusions instead of chemo," Sunny replied. "We hoped it would work, but I guess the cancer was all over by the time she finally went to a doctor. In the end, she smoked a lot of dope and got some pills from some friends for the pain. She didn't suffer too much."

"Well, the whole thing made me mad. And sad. Madrona was a sweet person," Hawk said, trying to comfort.

Wanting to change the subject, Sunny asked, "Can you tell me more about why you left?"

Hawk told her that there were just too many changes. Younger women showed up with different ideas like open relationships and cell phones. They wanted to set up all kinds of rules. Hawk and JB felt like they didn't fit in anymore: they thought the youngsters had no respect for the ideals that had brought them to the land to begin with. The last straw was when a so-called trans woman wanted to move in.

"Women's land has been and should remain space for women-born women only. No men," JB said, slapping her hand on the coffee table, perilously bouncing books and teacups.

Sunny remained silent. She was looking for refuge after the foul encounter with her father, and being in a place without men suited her just fine, but the trans issue was tricky. One of Madrona's meditation friends was a trans woman. She was a member of the caretaking team as

Madrona got weaker and sicker. Being trans didn't make her less compassionate.

"So, you said that there was going to be a memorial for JoJo," Sunny finally said to break the silence. "I hope I made it in time. What's happening to the land now that JoJo has passed?"

"You don't know? Oh dear, I guess I was hoping that you already heard it through the lezzie grapevine," Hawk said, looking over to JB for support. She hesitated and then blurted out, "JoJo left it to you. I didn't want to say anything to you on the phone because it's kind of a touchy issue. Some of the women are trying to fight it already."

Sunny carefully placed her cup down and sat back in the chair. JoJo left her the land. She struggled to understand.

"But wait, I thought it was a land trust."

"Nope, that was never JoJo's idea, and she didn't change her mind. She told me she wanted to keep it in the family, and you are the closest to family that she ever had." Hawk paused, watching Sunny's reaction. "You want something to eat, dear?"

"Oh, no, I'm fine. But thanks."

"There was a split over the land trust issue, you know," Hawk continued. "That was the origin of Wildflower. A few women pooled their money and made a down payment on four acres on the east side. They got legal papers to ensure it would be there for all women, with no individual ownership. The board of the land trust was responsible for the stewardship of the land."

JB cut in, "But that's not what JoJo wanted. She didn't like thinking about the future. She was a be-here-now kind of person. Very serene and present."

Hawk bobbed her head in agreement and continued, "So, she made a will but didn't tell anyone about what was in it. She could be very secretive. After JoJo had the heart attack, Liv called, and a few of us old-timers went over to clean out her house. We found the documents in with some old bills and letters. It was notarized and everything. Let me tell you, we were as surprised as you are."

"When did she write the will?" asked Sunny as she was beginning to grasp the situation.

"About three years ago."

Sunny felt a chill of guilt. She hadn't seen her since JoJo visited Solana the year Sunny turned sixteen. She assumed that JoJo was there to see her mom, so she didn't make much of an effort to hang out with the two older women. Why didn't she spend more time with JoJo? Why didn't she stay in touch?

"Was there a letter or an explanation anywhere? Why did she leave it to me?"

"It was just like JoJo to do things her way. Sorry, we don't know anything more than we told you," Hawk said, reaching over to pat Sunny's shoulder. They lapsed into silence, making space for Sunny to let this information sink in. Candy appeared and took the opportunity to spring into Sunny's lap, snuggling in.

Sunny absently petted the purring ball of fluff, wondering what was going on in JoJo's head to leave her this enormous burden. What was she going to do with acres of Arizona desert with a bunch of women living on it? Were they going to fight her for it? Would she have to make decisions about who could stay? How was she going to be responsible for a property when she didn't even have a credit card or bank account?

"I love Desert Haven, but I don't want to be in charge of anything. I don't know about paying taxes or whatever else you do when you own land. Maybe a land trust is the right way to go. What do you think I should do?" She looked from JB to Hawk with a bit of panic in her eyes.

JB carefully placed the cups on the tray and stood. "I'll wash up," she said, adding, "I don't want to intrude," and made her way to the kitchen.

"I sort of had the same thoughts when I found the will," Hawk said, moving from the couch to a chair across from Sunny. "It's a big responsibility. One thought is that you could sell it and get the money."

"But what would happen to the women who are living there?" Sunny said, burying her head in her hands. She disappeared for a moment in the darkness of her mini cocoon. "I don't know what to do," she said, rocking side to side.

"You've got a good heart, Sunny. It's a big decision, and I don't envy you. JB and I never owned any property, and we try to keep things simple. The thing is, you don't have to decide right now. Marga and Sparrow paid the land taxes for next year. You have some time to think about it."

Sunny felt a calm come over her like she had been struggling to swim in a riptide and had finally landed at the shore. No need to panic, she told herself. I have time to figure this out.

JB stood in the kitchen door, tea towel in hand, looking into the living room, and saw the two women, one barely an adult and the other well on in years, sitting across from each other, holding hands. She leaned in to hear Sunny say, "I wonder what Madrona would do?"

After a respectful pause, JB quietly returned to the living room and stood behind Hawk's chair. "That's an interesting idea," Hawk said. "What would Madrona or any of the other women do? The memorial is on Saturday at Marga and Sparrow's place, and women are coming from all over to pay their respects. It will be a great reunion and an opportunity for you to get some opinions."

"And everyone has an opinion, as we well know," said JB, widening her eyes and grinning. Hawk gave her a look, so she said, "Sorry to interrupt, I just couldn't resist."

"I don't think it's a good idea to bring it up during the memorial," Sunny said, dusting cat hair off her hands as Candy jumped down and headed to Hawk. "If you think some of the women are mad at me, it will make me feel terrible. And it would be a distraction."

"Sunny is right," JB said. "I heard that Curry and a couple of women are boycotting the memorial because they wanted the land to go into a land trust. We've got to keep the focus on celebrating JoJo's life. It's a party, not a community meeting."

"Those meetings! I'll never recover from them," moaned Hawk, scooping up Candy and hugging her close. "Endless hours trying to get everyone to agree. You had a vote when you were a child, didn't you?"

"I did, and I took the responsibility very seriously," Sunny said. "It was kinda stressful, but it made me feel like I was a part of the community. Like my voice was heard and my opinion respected."

"Powerful," Hawk said, head nodding in a soft rhythm.

"They gave me a voice, and I'll give them theirs. But not at JoJo's memorial," Sunny said, smiling with relief. "Can I stay with you for a few weeks while I visit the women who are still on the land or live in town and see what they think I should do?"

"Stay as long as you like. Candy approves," Hawk said, waving the cat's paw.

"We couldn't have asked for nicer September weather," JB said, turning to the back seat to include Sunny, as Hawk hunted for a parking space on the crowded block. The rusted iron gate with EcoSchool for Women painted in bright yellow letters was ajar, and purple balloons bobbed above it in the slight breeze. "We haven't been here since Summer Solstice. When did we get too lazy to show up for rituals anyway?"

"Getting old, darlin'," Hawk said. "I see Teagan and Alice are here. That's their Lexus. They still like living the good life."

"We have a good life!" JB objected. "It's not fancy, but it suits me."

The courtyard was festive with small white tables and chairs set up around a large round central table crowded with bright-colored pottery bowls and earthenware pitchers of iced herbal tea.

"I'm glad we brought our fall fruit salad," JB said, moving a few dishes to make a place for their bowl. "They said not to bring food, but you know lesbians." She shrugged her shoulders, looking for confirmation from her companions.

"Hawk, JB, great that you could come," Marga said, coming up behind them.

"Wouldn't miss it for the world. How you doing, Marga? Do you know Sunny?"

"Sunshine, Madrona's daughter?" Marga said, turning to Sunny. "I haven't seen you since you were a wee thing. Sparrow will be glad to see you. She's around here somewhere, being the perfect hostess."

"Sunshine!" A small woman with close-cropped grey hair limped quickly toward her, arms outstretched. Sunny wasn't sure who it was until she got close enough to inhale the familiar earthy scent.

"Wolfie, you are still here!"

"Oh yeah, I'm in an old ladies' home but still kicking," Wolfie said with a grin, but it quickly faded. "Say, did you hear that Mel died?"

"No, when did that happen?"

"Sometime last year. You know she and Juniper moved out to some property in northern California, on the coast. I heard that uterine cancer got her."

"Oh, that makes me sad. We should say a few words for her today too."

Sunny took a deep cleansing breath as she saw two women making a beeline for her.

"Hi Sunny, I'm Crow. I didn't get to the Haven until you were already gone, but I've heard about you. This is my friend Maya. You might have met her at West Farm."

"Of course, I remember you, Maya. You ran the 12-step recovery groups."

Hawk interrupted, saying, "Come and say hello to Moon," steering Sunny towards a grinning purple-haired pixie. "She said she was your math teacher, but I don't remember."

Sunny recognized many of the older women that had visited them in New Mexico over the years, but she didn't know any of the baby dykes buzzing around, greeting people and filling glasses.

"Who are those younger women?" she asked Sparrow when she finally came around for a hug.

"Oh, those are some of my students from EcoSchool. They're here on paid apprenticeships, and they live in the dorm," she said, pointing to a two-story building on an adjoining lot.

"It's pretty amazing what you've done here," Sunny said, glancing around at the grounds.

"Anytime you want to stay with us for a while, you are welcome. JoJo would have wanted that for you."

Sunny didn't have a chance to reply because a piercing two-fingered whistle cut through the chatter.

"May I have your attention," Eagle bellowed. "Please find a seat. We are about to begin, but you can continue visiting after the memorial. If you have something for the altar, you can add it later." Sunny saw a long series of tables against the house draped in rainbow tie-dyed tablecloths. Framed photos of JoJo were interspersed with vases of flowers and other meaningful objects, like JoJo's battered straw hat and her tool belt.

"First of all, I'd like to thank Marga and Sparrow for hosting this celebration of JoJo's life." Hoots and hand wiggles. "I have a message from Sky. She is with us in spirit even though she isn't able to travel anymore." Eagle paused, and all the quiet chattering ceased. She began speaking softly but could easily be heard.

"JoJo was an inspiration to so many of us and the reason we are all together today. I know that we didn't all live at Desert Haven at the same time, but our network extends far beyond a single place. The one thing we all have in common is our love for JoJo. She was a strong woman who never imposed herself on anyone. She was my oldest friend, and I miss her. She taught me to follow my heart."

Eagle wiped a tear from her wrinkled cheek with the back of her hand and raised her other hand, holding a battered hiking staff over her head. "This was JoJo's. I remember her telling me stories of all the places they had been together. Today, it will be our talking stick. Hold it when you have something to say and pass it on when you are done. Blessed Be."

Silence held the group suspended. No one wanted to break the sacred moment of acknowledgment that JoJo was gone. Some heads bowed; some eyes scanned the crowd for familiar faces. Forty women gathered together to say goodbye to their friend, mentor, and, in one case, benefactor.

Sunny wept to hear the stories. There was so much she didn't know about JoJo, but none of it surprising. JoJo was a surprise, always.

Sky 2015

Sky balanced the metal tray on the seat of her walker. She carefully put the cup of nettle leaf tea and the latest *Lesbian Farmwomyn* magazine on the tray and shuffled out to her screened porch, door slamming shut behind her. The air smelled green and humid. A sigh of contentment and relief escaped as she plopped herself into the white wicker settee, aware of the protesting crackle from the elderly couch. Sitting on the porch of the house she built amongst the tall pines and quaking aspens of Northern Arizona on an autumn afternoon never failed to thrill her secretly, quietly. All the years of sweet memories she and the house shared made it easier to accept her loneliness.

But, today was a good day. Sunny called to say she was sorry that Sky couldn't make it to JoJo's memorial and asked if she could drive up to Prescott for a visit.

It will be good to see her, Sky thought. Those young dykes are the future. Sky remembered when Sunny was little, maybe four years old the first time that she, Madrona, and JoJo stopped by on their way to Colorado. They came for a few weeks every summer until Sunny and Madrona left Desert Haven and moved to New Mexico. Sky counted out on her fingers, adding the years, and figured that Sunny must be about twenty years old now.

Blowing across her teacup to cool the hot green liquid, Sky took a sip and picked up the magazine. Headlines screamed, "The Last MichFest," proclaiming the demise of the Michigan Women's Music Festival. Thousands of women had been flocking to the six-hundred-fifty acres of isolated land for a week-long women-only music festival and camping event every August for almost forty years. And now it was closing and going away. It just didn't make sense. Sky read the articles hungrily, trying to understand. Contributors accused or commiserated, and everyone had an opinion about why and how this could happen. They all took the controversy personally, and Sky thought, well, they should. It was personal.

Watching leaves rustle in a gust of wind, she considered the way Michfest perfectly bisected her eighty-year life. At forty, she was an uptight, closeted woman who was afraid even to say the word lesbian, much less do anything about her feelings. And then there was Dorothy.

Sky wasn't always called Sky. Her given name, which sounded so strange to her now, was Kathy Green. That person, Kathy Green, MSW, worked at a nonprofit agency in downtown Prescott, providing services for recent immigrants. She was a career social worker and had worked her way to a supervisor position with her eye on the next step up the ladder when the director retired in a few years. One of her jobs was to prescreen potential employees, so she was the first person to interview Dorothy Horowitz for the position of client liaison. It was June 14, 1975. Ten a.m. Their meeting was casual yet professional. Dorothy wore a sharp blue blazer over a starched white and navy-blue striped blouse and tan trousers. Brown penny loafers completed the picture of a job interview costume assembled by a dyke. Kathy thought that Dorothy looked exactly like one of those fabulous women in lesbian magazines she secretly bought at a bookstore in Phoenix.

She recommended Dorothy be hired for the position. Their jobs dictated that they work together on several projects. They took to eating lunch at the same time in the staff room and going for cocktail hour together on Friday nights at one of the bars on Whiskey Row. They laughed at the same jokes and were very guarded around the rest of the staff. But they had nothing to hide because Kathy was hiding from herself. Dorothy might have been interested in more from the relationship, but she was patient and allowed their friendship to grow.

They were a symphony of contrasts—Dorothy with her close-cropped hairstyle, Kathy with long flowing auburn curls; Dorothy always trim and tidy, Kathy ruffled and fussy. If it weren't out of fashion in the 1970s to call them butch and femme, they would have fit into that stereotype. After a time, they were spending every weekend together, going to a movie or a potluck with Dorothy's friends. One Saturday night, they went to a Cris Williamson concert in a church basement with sixty other women. Slowly, Kathy was introduced to an underground community she had only guessed (and hoped) was there. It was the most logical thing when the two women became lovers—it was an extension of their deep closeness.

Sky jerked awake when the magazine fell off her lap and flapped to the floor. It seemed that every time she sat down nowadays, she would drift off. She thought it might be something to do with her asthma and not getting enough oxygen to her brain. She probably wouldn't die from it, but she might sleep through the rest of the days she had on Earth. And there was no one to wake her up, no one living on the land with her. Her isolation would be complete if it weren't for the rooftops she could see from her perch. New houses were popping up like weeds in her pristine paradise. At least she had the first twenty-five years of privacy before the real-estate boom. If only the Los Angeles Times hadn't run an article on how Prescott was "One of The Best Places to Retire in the US." Of course, it wouldn't hurt when she went to sell the place.

No, not sell. Where would she go? To some sterile room in an old folk's home? Not for this independent gal. Hadn't she bought this land as a refuge where she could survive the collapse of the corrupt and violent patriarchal society? Sky felt a rush of joy mixed with a tug of sadness, remembering her passionate desire to follow her heart and re-create herself.

The doorbell's melodic tones interrupted Sky's reverie. Startled, she thought, is it four o'clock already while she rose as quickly as she could, teetering to the front door to greet her guest. Sunny stood in the doorway, sweatshirt tied around her shoulders, looking all grown up.

"Sunshine, how nice of you to come to visit. I hope you can stay awhile."

Sunny smiled shyly. "Thanks, Sky, it's great to see you."

"Let's sit on the porch. Do you mind if I hold on to your arm? I was so excited to greet you that I didn't grab my walker. Sometimes I forget I'm not young anymore."

Depositing Sky on the couch, Sunny excused herself to use the bathroom. When she returned, Sky waved the magazine at her.

"Can you believe that MichFest is over? It's such a great loss."

"Madrona and I went a few times," Sunny said, sitting in a matching wicker chair facing the expansive view. "She loved being surrounded by all that woman energy. Said it was healing."

"I was at the very first Festival with my first and only true love. I still have the flyer; it's there on the wall right inside the door. Would you bring it to me, dear?"

Sunny reverently handed the relic to Sky, who took the gold-framed 8 ½ by 11-inch lavender flyer and read, "To help create a physical/psychological space for three days where women can retreat to the country to experience women's energy, especially women's music." Sky's fingers traced the words as she continued reading, "An alternative to the mass-produced patriarchal culture." She paused and said, "It's hard to describe how exciting and revolutionary it was. They created a safe space for women to change the world.

"I'm not sure why it's closing down," Sunny said. "Something about trans women?"

"There are two factions that are unable to come to a peaceful resolution and a lot of blaming and angry voices out there. It's a complicated issue of who's rights are 'righter.' I understand both points of view. I believe that women-only space is vital. Some women feel that the uniqueness and importance of lesbian culture is disappearing into a generic category of "queer." and they are fighting for their right to remain separate. And at the same time, I have difficulty with excluding people who identify as women. They have their own struggle, and I don't think that should add to that. There is plenty of space for everyone. Humanity is evolving, society is evolving, and life is always evolving. I have friends in many different communities, and I treasure the diversity." Sky paused to catch her breath. "Does that make sense?"

"Madrona taught me to accept people where they are at," Sunny said, remembering how adamant her mother was about including everyone at the table. Literally. "She welcomed friends and anyone who had nowhere else to go. Our house was a gathering spot."

"She was a good woman and she taught you well, Sky said, staring intensely at Sunny as if she could see Madrona in her face. "I wish more people thought like her."

"Thanks. I guess I'm proud of my mother's legacy," Sunny said, basking for a moment in the pride and a sharp pain of loss. She noticed the last of the setting sun glinting off the glass of the poster and thought that Sky wasn't done reminiscing. She said, "I bet you have some good stories about MichFest."

"It was where Marlin and I got our post-patriarchal names," Sky said, seeming eager to share a fond memory. "We had joined a feminist baptism ritual to free ourselves from our father's names and become truly independent women. It was very trippy and genuine at the same time. Twenty women chanting, induced into a trance-like state, imploring the Grandmothers for guidance. When we left the circle, we proudly carried our new names and identities. I became Blue Sky, and Dorothy was Marlin.

"Marlin was flat-out excited about three days submerged in women's culture, but I was timid. You see, I was just coming out and learning about feminism. Marlin was light-years ahead of me. For twenty dollars, we got three vegetarian meals a day, a campsite, workshops, concerts, and security. Even then, it was a deal. I remember exactly what Marlin said when we walked through the gates. 'Thank the Goddess, I'm home!' She pulled her T-shirt off over her head in one graceful movement. That was my Marlin."

Sky's unfocused eyes flickered and landed on Sunny's attentive face. Tucking a stray lock of silver hair behind her ear, she said, "Oh, my dear, I'm so sorry for boring you with all these old recollections. I seem to be time-tripping today."

"Oh no, you aren't boring at all. I love hearing about women's herstory. You were so lucky to have been at MichFest in the beginning."

"And now it's the ending. So many things are ending. JoJo's death shook me up and sent me down memory lane. I've been thinking about the past, and of course, about my Marlin."

"What happened to Marlin, if you don't mind me asking."

"I love you asking," Sky said, wanting to talk about her late partner, thrilled to be able to tell their story.

"Marlin and I were inspired by being in a community of women for three days so we decided that was how we wanted to spend the rest of our lives. It was a radical decision and the best one I ever made. We quit our jobs, got a van, and traveled to women's lands for a few years. That's how we found Desert Haven and met JoJo. We never found the perfect place, so we ended up back in Prescott, buying this land, building our house, and starting the Goddess soap business. I carved the figures for the molds, and Marlin was the production department of one."

"I remember your Goddess soap. Madrona loved it. Remind me what your label said."

"Aphrodite, Artemis, Demeter, or Hekate, come clean with the goddess of your choice."

The sun dipped below the mountain, and the air was getting cool. A great horned owl hooted from the tallest pine, waking to the dusk, searching for their next meal.

"Many women lived on this land over the years. See that flat spot over there near the fence? Marigold lived there in her bus for three years until she fell in love with her pen pal and moved to The Pines in Arkansas. And Wolfie was here for eight or nine summers, living in a yurt near the goat hut until she broke her hip and couldn't navigate the rocky terrain. That's when she moved to assisted living in Tucson."

"Wolfie was at the memorial and told me to say hi to you," Sunny interjected. "She said to tell you she's still limping along."

"Aren't we all?" Sky laughed, and her face lit up remembering Wolfie.

"To think that Marlin and I built this house with help from our sisterhood. We moved tons of rocks and earth to terrace the hillside for a kitchen garden behind the house. We built fences to keep deer from eating our vegetables, pens to shelter the goats, and a glorious mansion of a hen house to keep our darling chickens safe from coyotes and foxes at night.

"My mother planned the gardens and orchard for us. She lived in town and came out to help until she got dementia and needed care. She loved joining 'the girls' as she called our lesbian friends for potlucks and summer construction parties. She made the best lentil soup." Sky paused, taking a moment, and said, "I miss her too."

"But I digress. Marlin...it started with a slight pain in her left side, difficulty digesting food, and shortness of breath, all things that could be attributed to getting older. After all, she was seventy years old. But it got worse quickly, and one night, I just couldn't stand her being in pain anymore, so I grabbed our Medical Power Attorney papers and packed Marlin into the car, driving her to the emergency room. After a long night of waiting and many tests, she was admitted to the hospital. We got the bad news, the horrible, terrible news the following afternoon. Stage four ovarian cancer. Prognosis...two to three months.

"When the doctor figured that she couldn't convince Marlin to undergo procedures that would possibly extend her life a few more months, she gave us a prescription for painkillers and a referral to hospice. Marlin died three weeks later. That was almost five years ago. We had thirty-five glorious years together."

"I'm so sorry," Sunny said, reaching over, gently touching Sky's hand.

Blinking back tears, Sky said, "Let's go in, it's getting cool out here. I'll show you your room, and we can have a bite to eat."

Sky gathered up her teacup, held on to the walker, and did the balancing act back into the kitchen, refusing Sunny's offer of help. Damn this arthritis. Damn these swollen knees. Damn you for dying, Marlin.

Dinner was a simple vegetarian stew cooked to perfection in the crockpot. "The carrots and kale are from the garden," Sky said, placing a bowl of steaming vegetables and beans in front of Sunny. "My grandniece who lives in town helps me in exchange for most of the harvest. She will stop at the grocery store or Walgreens if I need anything from town. I could drive if I needed to, but I don't think it's safe anymore."

"This is great," Sunny said, admiring the bounty in her bowl. "Thanks."

Sky sat across from her at the kitchen table. "I'm glad you're here. When you called, I think you said you were searching for wisdom from your elders. I certainly am an elder, but I don't know that you'd call me wise. Could you tell me more about what you are searching for?"

"Do you know that JoJo left Desert Haven to me in her will?"

Sky's forkful of stew hovered midair as she looked at Sunny in surprise. "That piece of choice gossip hasn't made it through the lesbian grapevine to me yet. How long have you known about this?"

"Just a few weeks. When I got to Tucson for the memorial, Hawk told me. I'm just as shocked as you are." Sunny shrugged her shoulders and waited for Sky's reply, not knowing what she would say.

"If I think about it, it makes sense. You are the closest thing to the next generation that JoJo had. I know she fought the land trust when it came up years ago, so I would have been surprised if she chose that option." Sky laid down her fork and pushed back from the table, watching Sunny. "So, what advice are you seeking?"

Sunny looked down at her plate and sighed as if speaking were a great effort. Raising her eyes to meet Sky's, she said, "Women are living on the land, and I hold their fate in my hands. As far as I can see, my choices are to turn Desert Haven into a land trust and let them have it, move there and become the new owner with all the problems, or sell it, take the money, and run. Another consideration is that the place is pretty run down and needs a lot of work. I've never owned anything in my life. And to have to make a decision that will affect the lives of dozens of women, a few I've known all my life, is just plain scary."

"That's a lot of responsibility. How are you going to decide?"

"I don't know yet," Sunny sighed. "I've already talked to a few of the Tucson and Desert Haven women and heard lots of strong opinions. What are your plans with this land if you don't mind me asking?"

"We never had much of a community here; it was mostly just Marlin and me. My grandniece and her family have been taking care of me and the land for the last few years so it's going to them when I die."

"Makes sense," Sunny said. "I'd love to hear what you think I should do."

Sky took a few bites of stew and chewed slowly, eyes unfocused, brows furrowed. Sunny was respectfully silent, allowing Sky time to ponder what she wanted to say.

"I don't think you have only the three options that you mentioned," Sky began. "If you really want the benefit of my many years on this planet, the best advice I can give you is to give yourself time to know what your heart wants. Not your fears, not your mind, not what other people want. It's about trusting your inner knowing. Right now, it's all tumbled up in grief and confusion, so give yourself time to let things settle. I think you are courageous and wise to go on a quest to find the correct path."

Sunny squirmed in her seat. "I don't feel brave at all. I feel like a little kid with an adult load of problems."

"You are an adult, and you can face this decision as one. Don't belittle yourself. You were raised to trust the Goddess, and now is the time to put that learning into action. Be kind to yourself." Sky nodded as if to acknowledge what she had just said and resumed eating.

Sunny sat back, placing her fork next to her bowl. Her eyes lingered on Sky's open, beautiful face, and she felt cradled by a lineage of compassionate and loving wise women. "Thank you," she said quietly.

Five days later, after cleaning out the shed and other chores Sky needed help with, Sunny was ready to move on.

"Where are you off to next?" Sky asked as Sunny shouldered her backpack.

"First, I'm going home to Solana for Madrona's memorial service, and then I'm not sure. Maybe I'll head over to California to see Juniper. I think she's living alone on the land since Mel died."

"It's hard to think of Juniper as an elder, but from your perspective, I suppose she is."

"Thank you so much for all these peanut butter and banana sandwiches," Sunny said, swinging the heavy brown paper bag in front of her. "I'm sure they will last me most of the way. Sky, it was great seeing you. I can't tell you how much your generosity and wisdom mean to me."

"Don't know about the wisdom, but I'm happy if what I have to say is helpful. And thanks for your help getting the garden ready for winter. I loved sitting down there with you while you did all the work." Sky opened her arms, and Sunny folded into them for a final goodbye.

Sky watched Sunny's truck drive away until it disappeared around a curve. She maneuvered herself over to her easy chair, pulling her CD player to the edge of a side table. Choosing "Song of the Soul," she cued it up and pressed play. Cris Williamson's clear sweet voice filled the stillness as Sky sat facing the large bay windows salvaged from a razed house in the way of urban renewal. It was the smartest decision they made, those windows, bringing the outside in. Now that she couldn't walk in the woods, Sky could admire them from afar. The first time she saw the view, it reminded her of Michigan, and she knew it would always bring her joy.

So much had changed. Michfest was history. Her mother and Marlin were dead. JoJo was gone. She didn't know how long she could stay at the house alone.

Did she have words of wisdom for Sunny? The best she could come up with was: follow your heart. Well, that's how she and Marlin lived, and it served them well. This next generation of young women will have to figure out what it means to them.

Swaying to the music, she let her mind drift, her memories blending with hope for the future.

Acknowledgments

This book was several years in the making, so I have many people to thank. Big gratitude to my wonderful writing community: creative writing classes with Frankie Rollins, and Cat Beleu who kept my fingers moving across the keyboard; poetry classes with Maggie Golson and Joan Larkin who freed up my inner metaphors to get me out of my literal mind; developmental editing by Sandra Shattuck, who challenged me when I lost the thread; writing groups with Francie McMahon, Jean Emrick, Sandy Butler, and Miriam Ruth Black, who insisted that I go deeper and inspired me by their brilliance; my generous and smart beta readers Beth Lisick, Sheila Wilensky, Lee Fike, Ethel Lee-Miller, Michael Woodward, and Susy Plummer; co-conspirators, Pat Woelke and Lu Withee and our yet-to-be-realized film project about women's land; and of course, my supportive partner, Silvia Kolchens, who knows more about grammar in an English-as-a second language way than I ever learned.

Great thanks to managing publisher of Rattling Good Yarns, Ian Henzel, for giving my run-on sentences pause and trusting that this is an important story to tell. I heard that Mark Twain once filled the last page of a manuscript with all the various symbols of punctuation and instructed his editor to disperse them within the story as he saw fit. This is one of Ian's gifts.

Completion of this book was supported by a Research & Development Grant awarded by the Arizona Commission on the Arts, an agency of the State of Arizona, with funding from the Newton and Betty Rosenzweig Fund for the Arts, an endowment held at Arizona Community Foundation.

About the Author

Penelope Starr is the author of the nonfiction book, *The Radical Act of Community Storytelling: Empowering Voices in Uncensored Events* and the founder of Odyssey Storytelling, in Tucson, AZ. Her sun sign is Cancer, she is a seven on the Enneagram, is an ENFJ Myers-Brings type, and her Human Design type is Manifestor, so she enjoys creative endeavors, facilitating workshops, and giving advice. Born in New York City, she migrated to the West more than fifty years ago and now lives in the foothills of the Tucson Mountains with her partner, Silvia, and their very smart dog, Kosmos. See what she's up to at penelopestarr.com.

Penelope Starr, photograph by Silvia Kolchens